FRANGIPANI CAN BE FATAL

A HIBISCUS ISLAND MYSTERY

LUCY NORMAN

Mulberry Ink

Frangipani Can Be Fatal
Book 4 in the Hibiscus Island Mystery series

Copyright © 2023 by Lucy Norman
ISBN: 978-0-9922664-7-9

Cover by DLR Cover Designs
Editing by Florentia Editing

For Zoe and Camryn, the newest members of our clan.

And for their daddies - Gary and Jarryd - who might one day read this book for themselves.

1

Holly Gold fidgeted, her hazel eyes worried as she stood in the check-in line at the Hibiscus Island airport. "They're going to miss the flight! Where on earth are they?"

"Stop stressing. There's no way Jamie's going to miss this trip." Inspector Rob Tucker held out his hand as the check-in officer beckoned the couple forward. "Where's your passport?"

Holly cast one more despairing look at the airport entrance before rummaging through her bag for the travel document. Where was Jamie? Their flight wouldn't be called for another hour or so, but check-in closed in five minutes. Hibiscus Island was a friendly and informal place in general, but the airport officials were strict.

A screech of brakes outside made heads turn all over the departure area. Disapproving looks turned to resigned headshakes and rueful smiles as Jamie White leapt out of the car, followed closely by Thomas Miller, who grabbed two small carry-ons before thumping the top of the car in thanks. The driver grinned, gave a thumbs up, then roared away.

As the sliding doors of the airport whooshed open, Jamie's anxious voice could be heard. "Hurry up, Miller! Of all days for your car to get a flat tire! We can't miss this flight!"

The fair-haired journalist's response was unconcerned. "Relax, White. There's another plane tomorrow. It's not like Turtle Island's on the other side of the world, you know."

Ignoring him, Jamie made a beeline for Holly and Rob. Despite the harassed expression on her face, Holly's best friend from childhood looked as gorgeous as ever. A short-sleeved black shirt showed off smooth brown skin and toned arms, her long hair was styled in a myriad of tiny braids, gold hoop earrings dangled from her ears, and long lashes framed dark eyes, which right now were bright with annoyance.

"Honestly!" she exclaimed as she reached the check-in counter. "A flat tire. Can you believe it? It's lucky Fred Harrison was up at the Big House doing some work or we'd never have made it in time." She drew in a deep, calming breath, then smiled at the woman behind the counter. "Hi, Aunt Mel."

The check-in officer who had known both Holly and Jamie since childhood, rolled her eyes. "Jamie White, you'll be late for your own funeral." She glanced at her watch, then held out her hand. "Passports? I've got one minute to check you in."

Jamie handed over the documents. "Is the flight on time, Aunt Mel? Oh, and did Mr. Graham already check in?"

"Yes, and yes. Where are your bags?"

"Carry-ons only." Thomas Miller approached the counter. "How are you, Mrs. Patterson?"

"Just fine, Thomas. Just fine. Here're your boarding passes. Quite an exciting trip for you all, isn't it? Where are you staying?"

Jamie leaned against the check-in counter. "At the Ocean Science Research Center. It's pretty cool, actually. Natasha arranged it for us. It's right on the water and, best of all, there's no charge!"

"Yeah, we lucked out there," Holly agreed. "I've never been to Turtle Island before. I can't wait to see it."

Mel Patterson smiled. "It's a pretty island. A little more rugged than our Hibiscus, and a bit bigger, of course, but quite lovely. Mr. Patterson and I went there for our honeymoon." She glanced at her watch again. "You'd all better get going if you want to clear security before your flight goes. Have a great trip."

JAMIE COLLAPSED into a seat at the departure gate with an exaggerated sigh of relief. "Finally."

"Anyone want a coffee or tea?" Thomas dropped his bag on the floor. "I didn't have time this morning, what with the car drama and all."

"Yes. Coffee. Black, strong, two sugars. Thanks." Jamie fished out her phone. "I just want to check that Teddy's okay."

"Holly? Anything?" Rob raised an eyebrow.

"I'm good, thanks," Holly replied.

As the two men strolled away, Holly eyed her friend with amusement. "Teddy's going to be fine. You know Mama will look after him. He'll be in heaven at the Inn with her and Truffle. Good thing you brought him over last night though.

You'd never have made it on time if you'd had to drop him off this morning."

Jamie had delivered her standard poodle, Teddy, to the Hibiscus Inn the previous evening, where he had been greeted with ecstasy by Holly's little cavapoo, Truffle.

Maggie Gold had just laughed and rolled her eyes when Jamie began to give her a list of instructions. "Teddy's stayed here before, Jamie. He'll be fine."

"Well, yeah, but I've always been with him," Jamie had protested. "This is the first time I've left him alone since I got him."

"And he's going to love his little holiday as much as you're going to enjoy yours." Maggie had grinned at the young woman she considered a surrogate daughter. "It's only a few days, Jamie. I'll take good care of him."

Now Jamie's face broke into a smile. She held her phone out to Holly. "Look. He's helping Maggie check in guests."

Holly gazed at the photo of a comatose Teddy sprawled on the rug in the front foyer of the Hibiscus Inn. "I can see that. And he's doing an amazing job."

Her dry tone made Jamie grin.

"Oh, shut up. I'm allowed to worry about my baby." Jamie shoved her phone in her bag, then leaned back in her seat to give Holly a wide beaming smile. "So. Are you excited, Holls? I am! Although I'm sorry you'll be sharing a room with me instead of that handsome policeman over there."

"I don't mind. It was originally supposed to be a girls' trip anyway," Holly reminded her. She followed Jamie's gaze across the lounge to where Rob and Thomas were just turning around from the coffee counter. "They are a handsome pair, aren't they?" She waggled her eyebrows at her friend. "Are you absolutely sure you don't want to—"

Jamie held up a hand. "Stop right there. I know where you're going with this. Enough with the matchmaking, okay?"

"I'm not matchmaking." Holly arched an eyebrow. "What's the matter? Did you two have another fight? I thought you were getting on pretty well lately."

Jamie watched the laughing grey-eyed journalist approach. "Nothing's the matter. Miller is... well, he's just Miller. He doesn't take anything seriously. Including me."

"Oh, I don't think that's true at all. He likes winding you up for sure—you're easy to get a rise out of, you know—but he definitely takes you seriously." A grin hovered around Holly's mouth. "But if you want things to move faster, maybe you should take your own advice. I seem to recall a time when you told me modern women should take charge of relationships."

Jamie frowned. "I don't know if I want things to move."

Holly rolled her eyes. "Uh-huh. And pigs can fly."

"I don't!" Jamie protested. "I'm not sure we're compatible really."

"Oh rubbish. Of course you are. Thomas is easygoing and you're... Hmm, how shall I put this? You're effervescent. A match made in heaven."

"Effervescent?" Jamie snorted. "You make me sound like fizzy water."

"Yep, bubbly. That's you alright." Holly grinned at her mercurial friend as Thomas and Rob approached.

"We saw Jeff Graham over there. He's buried in papers so declined our invitation to join us." Thomas handed Jamie her coffee as he spoke.

"Aww. He's probably panicking about his talk again." Holly was sympathetic.

"Pfftt." Jamie waved an airy hand. "He'll be great. He

knows more about *La Rosa* than anyone, unless it's Peter Mackenzie. And Mackenzie will be on Turtle to help him out anyway. If he needs it, which, personally, I don't think he will. He's always like this before a presentation and then he gives a brilliant lecture."

As the president of the Hibiscus Island Historical Society as well as the official custodian of historic ship-wrecks around the island, Mr. Graham had taken a leading role in the exploration of *La Rosa de España*, a recently discovered eighteenth-century Spanish merchant ship.

The ship had originally been owned by one of Jamie's ancestors and had not only been the catalyst for a murder the previous fall—a crime that had eventually been solved by Holly and her friends—but had also proven to be exciting from a historical perspective.

Under the auspices of Mr. Graham and marine archaeol-ogist Dr. Peter Mackenzie, the shipwreck had been carefully excavated. To Jamie's great disappointment, no gold or jewels had yet surfaced, but the Historical Society had been thrilled with the discovery of carpenters' tools, pottery, and other everyday examples of life in the late seventeenth and early eighteenth centuries.

One of the more interesting finds had been a sealed glass perfume bottle with the original scent still locked inside. When Peter Mackenzie had suggested trying to reproduce the scent, the challenge had been enthusiastically accepted by the Plumeria Perfumery on Turtle Island.

The small perfumery, which still practiced the ancient technique of *enfleurage*, would be sharing its research, find-ings, and, of course, the special *Rosa del Mar* perfume, at a symposium for perfumers during the week.

Jamie had been invited as a special guest and had promptly asked Holly and their other close friend, Becky

Dumont, to accompany her. Becky, seven months pregnant, had declined with regret, but Holly had been thrilled. She'd been even more pleased when Rob Tucker had decided to take a few days' vacation to accompany them.

With Mr. Graham giving a presentation at the conference and Thomas covering the event for The Island Gazette, Jamie had asked her friend Natasha to find them all somewhere to stay on Turtle Island. Nat had come through.

Thomas collapsed into a seat beside Holly, sprawling out with a contented sigh, and took a sip of coffee. "So. Tell us about the place you got us, White. What's it like? Got any photos?"

Jamie sighed. "I already told you it's a cottage. Three bedrooms. On the water at the Ocean Science Research Center. Natasha said it's pretty basic but has everything we'll need for a few days."

"How do we get from there to the perfumery?" Holly asked. "Is it far?"

"No. Nat said it's only about twenty minutes away. She's organizing transport for us but I'm not sure what."

"Did she mention dive gear, by any chance? I was hoping we might get a dive or two in as well. Lots of lionfish around Turtle, you know. Could give you a chance to catch up to me, White." Thomas's eyes laughed at Jamie over the top of his coffee cup.

The two had an ongoing competition to erase the invasive fish from the waters around Hibiscus Island, with Thomas slightly ahead in numbers at the moment.

"Now look," Jamie began, her voice laced with irritation. She paused, drew in a deep breath, then released it slowly. "You know what, Miller? A dive would be great. If we have time, of course."

Holly suppressed a smile as Thomas's eyebrows shot up

in surprise, but before he could respond, he was interrupted by an announcement.

"Ladies and gentlemen, we'll begin boarding in a moment. Could the following people please come to the counter? Alan Cranton, Melissa Smith, Franklin Carter, Thomas Miller, Sierra Fonner, and Paige Halver. Thank you." The intercom clicked off.

Thomas groaned. "Now what's the problem?" Snatching up his passport and boarding pass, he strode over to the gate counter.

As soon as he'd left, Jamie turned a smug look on Holly. "See? I can be easygoing too."

"I'm impressed, Bubbles. Good job."

Rob shook his head in amusement at the byplay. "I don't know what's going on, nor do I think I want to, but I have to admit I'm also looking forward to seeing Turtle Island. I hear they have a small tea plantation there, and I was hoping to find time to visit it. You might be interested in stocking some of their products, Jamie."

Hailing originally from England, Rob had taken over the role of chief police officer on Hibiscus Island a year or so before. While the inspector had embraced the island's cultural traditions, he still appreciated a good cup of tea at Jamie's café, The Bean.

"A tea plantation?" Intrigued, Holly stared at him. "Are you sure? Tea plants need acidic soil. They're camellias, after all."

Jamie, who had looked interested in Rob's statement, grinned. "And why is that a problem, Miss Horticulturist?"

"Well, I thought Turtle Island was like Hibiscus, and we have alkaline soil. How are they growing tea in alkaline soil? Or does Turtle have acidic soil? Hang on, I need to check this out." As Holly pulled out her phone, intent on researching, she ignored both Jamie's eyeroll and Rob's chuckle. This sort of conundrum fascinated her.

"Ladies and gentlemen, we're ready to begin boarding."

"Oh good." Jamie jumped up. "Put that phone away, Holls. You can find out about soils and other boring stuff when we get there. Where's Miller? Did he get everything sorted out?"

Holly nodded. "He's in line already."

Jamie beamed with excitement. "Great! Come on! Turtle Island awaits!"

2

———

The short flight to Turtle Island, one of seven in the Maritime Islands archipelago, passed without incident, although that didn't stop Holly from clutching the armrests when the plane descended.

Rob grinned as he unbuckled his seatbelt. "You can let go now, Holls. We're at the gate. If you move out of the way, I'll grab our bags."

Seated across from them at the back of the small plane, Jamie sniggered. "She's always been like this. You should have seen her when we went on the seventh-grade trip to Washington. I had to peel her off the seat when we landed. She was petrified."

"Such a lie." Holly mock-glared at her friend as she stood up to let Rob into the aisle between the seats. "I'm just not a fan of flying, that's all."

Jamie guffawed. "That's one way of putting it. Oh, thanks, Rob." She took her bright pink carry-on from the inspector. "Where are the others? Nat said she'd meet us outside in the pick-up area and I don't want to lose Mr.

Graham before we even get started. You know what he's like."

Pushing back the red-gold curls which had escaped her ponytail, Holly peered toward the front of the plane where the elderly historian had been seated. Two rows in front of Mr. Graham, Thomas Miller was still in conversation with the man next to him. Holly watched the journalist say a final few words, then jump up to get his and Mr. Graham's carry-ons before ushering the historian out of the plane ahead of him.

"It's alright. Thomas has him in hand. They'll wait for us, I'm sure." Holly grinned at her friend. "Come on, Jamie. I can't wait to see the island!"

Turtle Island was basking under a warm spring sun as Holly and Jamie, followed by the three men, walked out of the airport. Across the road in a small carpark, a tall slim strawberry blonde waved enthusiastically.

"Over here!"

As Jamie hurried ahead toward Natasha and her ancient-looking van, Holly gazed at her surroundings.

Like its sister island, Turtle's airport was beside the water and sported a single runway. Unlike Hibiscus, however, planes to Turtle Island landed on a narrow spit of land that ran between the open ocean on one side and a steep mountain on the other.

From the plane, Holly had already noticed the mountains, much taller than her home island's rolling hills. Now she stopped to stare up at the peak in front of her. Its sides were clothed in green, unbroken by any buildings, while the top was obscured by low-lying clouds.

Thomas nudged her to keep moving. "That's Pico de Fuego. It's a nature reserve."

"Pico de Fuego?"

"Yeah, they've kept a lot of the original Spanish names for places. It's Peak of Fire in English. Old volcano. Great first sight for visitors, isn't it?"

"It sure is." Holly started walking again. "It's so different from Hibiscus."

"Wait till you see the rest of the island. We really should do a tour. You can drive around the whole place in a day, you know. Although I admit it would be a whirlwind and we'd have to start early and finish late."

Holly stared at the journalist with curiosity. "You've been here before? I didn't know that."

"Oh yes, I've been to all the Maritime Islands. When I was little. My dad didn't entirely ignore his heritage." Thomas's smile was reminiscent as he gazed around. "Of course, it's been a few years, so things may have changed."

"Probably not as much as you think," Mr. Graham interjected, coming up on Holly's other side as they approached the van. "Turtle's just starting to embrace eco-tourism in a small way, but for the most part, it's still relatively undeveloped. Nice place with great diving. Dr. Mackenzie's promised to show me a fascinating wreck somewhere off the north shore."

Holly surveyed the older man with a smile. Dressed in one of his signature Hawaiian shirts—this one a cheery teal green covered in cavorting pink flamingos—the historian's blue eyes beamed with anticipation behind round glasses. His grey hair was already disheveled and his carry-on bag looked like it had been through the wars. Holly had known Jeff Graham since she was a small child and had always liked the kindly man.

Natasha looked across from where she was in animated conversation with Jamie.

"Who's that you're talking about? Mackenzie? He got in last week and is making a perfect nuisance of himself as always. You know that wreck I told you about, Mr. Graham? Well, Mackenzie's gone and—"

"Whoa, whoa, whoa," Jamie interrupted the indignant Natasha with a laugh. "You can tell Mr. Graham all about the perfidious Mackenzie later. Come on, you lot, toss your bags in so we can get going."

"Perfidious?" Thomas snickered. "That's a good one, White."

"Why, thank you, Miller," Jamie replied sweetly. "I aim to please."

Thomas blinked, then narrowed his eyes in suspicion.

"You're still on this 'improve your vocabulary' kick?" Natasha rolled her eyes as she tossed Mr. Graham's bag into the back of the van. "Don't know why you have to use big words when little words will do."

"Says the scientist who writes reports about thermoclines and microorganisms," Jamie retorted with a grin.

Rob had been inspecting the van, a dubious look on his face. "Are you sure it's safe to go in this thing, Natasha? It looks a little... uh... battered."

"Who? Henrietta? Oh, don't worry, Inspector. She's passed all the necessary tests." Natasha patted the side of the van as she beamed around at the group. "Welcome to Turtle, all of you!"

~

As the van careened along the narrow, winding coastal road, Holly kept her eyes glued to the passing scenery, ignoring the general conversation around her.

Turtle Island was aptly named, having a central carapace of mountains ranging in height between two thousand and four thousand feet, and four flipper-shaped lowland areas jutting out from the interior.

A few houses dotted the lower slopes of the vegetation-covered mountains, but most people appeared to live in small villages clustered on the coast. Unlike Hibiscus Island, where the majority of homes were white-roofed with pastel-colored walls, Turtle Island houses were almost uniformly white with terracotta-tiled roofs. Here and there, splashes of color appeared where homeowners had painted the exterior walls yellow, pale pink, or peach, or had hung shutters of teal blue or bright green.

Old drystone walls lined parts of the roads, the fields behind them rolling up onto the lower slopes of the mountains, divided by thick hedges and dotted with fat, comfortable black-and-white cows.

Holly eyed the hedges with curiosity. "Are those hydrangeas?"

"What?" Natasha glanced in her rearview mirror. "Hydrangeas? Yeah, they are. Good eye, Holly. You should see them in the summer. It's just a sea of blue everywhere. Gorgeous. But you're not allowed to pick them. They're protected."

Rob grinned at Holly. "Don't tell me. Hydrangeas need acid soil, right?"

She made a face at him. "Yes, they do, actually."

"Oh well, it's volcanic soil here," Natasha explained, waving a hand at the mountains. "The last eruption was ages ago, but yeah, the soil's mostly acidic. And there are some geothermal patches, too, if you're interested. Hot springs and the like. I hear Azure Isle has the same type of geology. I'm dying to go see their crater lake. There's one here but it's a lot smaller. Mist Lake on Azure is supposed to be fabulous."

"It is," Mr. Graham agreed. "Well worth a visit. It's an interesting little archipelago we have here. A mix of pure limestone islands, like our Hibiscus, pure volcanic, like Azure, and some with both. I believe there are limestone areas on the coast here. Fascinating, really. It's all to do with the undersea mountain range that we're part of. I imagine you'll find quite a few different plants here, Holly."

Holly nodded. "Rob said there's a tea plantation here. That's why I was wondering about the soils."

"Ah yes, the Wimsey Plantation. It's quite close to the perfumery, actually. You could definitely take a side trip there, Inspector. I've purchased their tea in the past. It's very nice."

"Wimsey?" Jamie giggled. "Any relation to Peter Wimsey?"

Mr. Graham looked puzzled. "I don't believe I know a Peter Wimsey."

"He's a detective in a mystery series written by Dorothy Sayers," Holly said. "She's a golden age mystery author."

"Oh, I see." The historian's eyes twinkled. "Yes, I've heard of her. From Myrtle. I believe there's a book event of some kind happening later in the year?"

"The Golden Age Murder Mystery Weekend!" Jamie swiveled around from her seat in the front to beam at the older man. "It's on Azure in that fancy resort of theirs, and book clubs from all over the Maritime Islands are going. We have to solve a whodunnit while we're there. There are going to be mystery authors, seminars, all sorts of things. It's going to be great!"

"There're a couple of groups going from Hibiscus," Holly added. "HISS refused to join forces with the Book Ends, and we wanted to have our own team, so there'll be three lots of us. We're still trying to come up with a good name."

"HISS?" Natasha blinked. "What the heck is HISS?"

Thomas guffawed. "Myrtle's book club is called the Sleuths. The Hibiscus Island Sleuths. Get it?"

"Isn't there a letter missing?" Natasha asked, clicking her turn signal to drive the van down a very bumpy, narrow road between tall trees.

Before a grinning Thomas could answer—HISS was actually Jamie's acronym for Hibiscus Island Senior Sleuths, a name which annoyed its septuagenarian president, Myrtle Collier, intensely—Rob interrupted.

"Is that the place, Nat?"

Everyone looked ahead instantly.

As the van turned onto a driveway that circled a large grass lawn, Holly noticed an orchard of fruit trees, recognizing mulberry and guava trees before her attention turned to the long, low white buildings clustered along the water's edge. Mangrove trees hugged the shore on either side of the science center, with a small path leading between the buildings to a large floating dock.

Natasha pulled the van into a parking lot and turned off the engine.

"Here we are! You need to check in at reception and then I'll show you where your cottage is. Everything's really close, and I've arranged for a couple of little electric buggies to be delivered later today. That way you can get around under your own steam, so to speak." She grinned at them. "I figured you could all get settled in, tour the place here—I'll show you where the dive equipment is, Thomas—then I thought we could have dinner tonight, if that's okay. There's a nice little fish place nearby. I can show you the way to Plumeria as well. You don't need to be at the conference until tomorrow, right?"

"We're meeting the liaison person at nine," Jamie agreed. "This looks great, Nat! Thanks so much for organizing it."

"No problem." Natasha flung open the van door. "Come and meet Fee. She's in charge of everything here."

Rob took Holly's hand as they followed the tall marine scientist towards a building marked Reception. "Having fun yet?"

She beamed at him. "Yes. It's all so different and... and exotic, isn't it?"

"Exotic?" Rob laughed. "It's not *that* much different from Hibiscus. Tropical island, blue sea, warm sunshine..."

"We don't have mountains. Or hot springs. Or tea plantations for that matter." Holly gazed up at the nearest peak. "I love the mountains. Maybe we can find out about hiking trails. There must be some."

Overhearing them, Natasha turned her head. "There's a really nice little walk just past the entrance, actually. It'll take you up that hill to an overhang where you can see quite a lot of the coast on this side. About forty minutes or so. You could do it after you settle in if you want. And Fee's got some maps and tourist brochures in here. Come see." She grinned and held the glass-fronted doors open for them.

3

———

Hands on her hips, Jamie surveyed the living room in the cottage with approval. "Well! This is a lot better than I was expecting, I must say."

Natasha grinned. "It's our deluxe accommodation. This is where we put visiting professors and you can thank Mr. Graham for it. Apparently he knows our director."

The elderly historian smiled. "Callum and I go back a long way. Now, which is my room? If you don't mind, I just want to run over my presentation one more time before dinner."

Thomas, who had been prowling into each of the three bedrooms as the others examined the main room and adjoining kitchen area, spoke up first. "You take the master bedroom, Jeff. It's the one at the end of the corridor there. Rob and I will share the room on the left, and the girls can have the one that overlooks the mountains, since Holly is so enthralled with them."

Mr. Graham nodded and trotted down the hallway.

"I'll leave you to get settled, then." Natasha checked her phone as it buzzed. "Oh, that's your little cars arriving. Can someone come and help me drive them down here? I got three for you."

"On it." Thomas tossed his carry-on into one of the bedrooms. "Come on, Inspector. I'll race you."

Natasha laughed as she shepherded both men outside. "They don't go that fast. They're more like souped-up golf buggies with four-wheel drive. They used to rent motor-bikes to visitors but too many people had accidents, so we have these little things now." Her voice faded into the distance.

Holly grinned at Jamie. "Let's check out our space, roomie."

Her friend looked sheepish. "Sorry you have to share with me. I'm sure you'd rather be with Rob. You know, you two could have stayed in town or in a B & B somewhere if you'd wanted."

"Nah." Holly dismissed this with a wave of her hand as she opened the door to the room she and Jamie would share. "We're only here because of *La Rosa* and you. It's more fun to all stay here. Besides, Rob and I don't live together. You know that. Oh, this is nice! And look, there's air condi-tioning! Heaven!"

Two full-sized beds covered in white duvets sat on oppo-site sides of the room, each one beside a large window that looked out over the grounds of the science center and up into the mountains. A small blue rug lay between both beds on top of pine flooring. Overhead, a fan spun lazily from the wooden rafters. It was a simple room, but attractive.

"You stay overnight at his place sometimes." Jamie sat down on one of the beds and bounced experimentally. "Hey, this is quite comfortable."

"Very rarely." Holly answered her friend's first comment as she unzipped her carry-on and started unpacking clothes to place in the small white dresser near the bed. "Rob's a bit old-fashioned that way."

Lying back on the pillow, hands clasped under her head, Jamie snorted as she watched Holly empty her bag. "He's a dinosaur, Holls. I'll bet he's never stayed at the inn with you, has he?"

Holly grinned. "Nope. He feels it would be disrespectful to Mama. She's told him it's fine, but he said he'd be uncomfortable. Anyway, I like that about him. It's kind of sweet. Are you planning to unpack at all?" She opened a closet and stowed her carry-on bag inside it.

"What for? We're only here a couple of days." Jamie rolled over and sat up. "I wonder if Natasha put snacks in the kitchen. Let's go see."

The kitchen was equally simple in design, with a terra-cotta-tiled floor, white wooden cabinets and butcherblock counters. The sunshine-yellow walls brightened it up, as did the framed art prints of tropical fish that hung on the wall.

Holly inspected a print of yellow-and-black sergeant major fish as Jamie pounced on a basket on the large pine table at one end of the room.

"Oh, look. Cookies. I knew Natasha would come through. How about a cup of tea, Holls, while we wait for our transport? Put the kettle on, will you?" She tore open a packet of chocolate chip cookies.

Good-naturedly, Holly rooted around for mugs, then passed Jamie a plate. "Use this. And can you ask Mr. Graham if he wants tea?"

Jamie nodded and left the room. Returning a moment later, she collapsed back in her seat, choosing another cookie. "He said he'll get one later. Oh, thanks, Holls." Jamie took a long gulp of tea, then eyed her friend over the top of her cup. "Did I hear you say you and Rob were going for a walk?"

"Yes, if we can. Do you want to come? Nat says there's an easy trail from here." Holly took a sip of her own tea. "Or are you going to check out the dive stuff? Actually, it looks like there's pretty good snorkeling here too. And did you see the kayaks on that little beach? I wouldn't mind doing that if there's time." She sighed. "It was a great idea to stay here, Jamie, but I wish we had just a little more time."

"We don't leave till next Tuesday. Tomorrow, Saturday afternoon, and Sunday morning are kind of booked at the perfumery, but we still have Sunday afternoon and Monday to see the place. We should have a look at the brochures Nat mentioned. I'd love to swim in a hot spring, wouldn't you?"

A hum of approaching vehicles made both women look towards the window. Jamie gave a snort of laughter at the sight of the little electric cars.

"Good grief! What a color!"

Holly giggled as she gazed at the neon orange-and-green golfcart-sized vehicles. "It must be for safety reasons. They'd be visible a mile away. I must say, I like the pink ones we have on Hibiscus a lot better." She waved through the window. "Nice car, Inspector."

Rob grinned, swinging his long legs out of the little two-seater car. "It's not too bad actually. And Nat tells me there are charging stations everywhere, so we won't get stranded."

The marine scientist laughed as she unfolded herself from her own car. "Make sure you charge her fully before you go to the tea place though. They don't have one. I need to get back to work but I'll see you all for dinner." She waved and trotted back towards the main research buildings.

"Is that tea? Any coffee?" Thomas asked as he entered

the kitchen. "Oh, and cookies too. Pass the plate, White. I'm starving."

Holly flicked the kettle on again, then leaned into Rob as he came up behind, wrapping his arms around her.

"Still feel like a walk? Natasha showed me where the trail starts when we were getting the cars." Rob dropped a light kiss on Holly's head before casting a glance at enquiry at Jamie and Thomas. "Want to come, you two?"

Thomas shook his head. "I've got a couple of things I want to check up on before we go to the conference tomorrow. Nat gave us the network password for this place, didn't she? I'm going to take a rain check on dinner tonight as well. I told a guy I'd meet him for drinks."

Holly gazed at him in surprise. "What guy? I didn't know you knew anyone here."

"I don't. I met him on the plane. A fellow journalist."

"A journalist? What was he doing on Hibiscus?" Holly wriggled loose from Rob to pour boiling water into cups, then handed a steaming mug to Thomas, who took it with a nod of thanks.

"He missed the flight from Grand Island to Turtle yesterday so got the one to Hibiscus instead. Said he had a meeting he had to make today which meant he had to re-route a bit. The Grand Island flight would have got in too late."

"He's covering the conference for a paper on Grand Island?" Rob sounded interested. "It seems like it's quite a big deal. Are there reporters from all the islands coming?"

"Hmm, I'm not sure. Azure might send someone, I suppose. Maybe Castle Island. They both have a small paper. Dickenson didn't tell me much about his paper. It sounded like it might be more of a personal interest of his, rather than professional. He said he had family in the perfume business. Anyway, since he's a fellow journalist and all, I thought it would be nice to have a drink and swap secrets." Thomas grabbed another cookie, then stood up. "I want to brush up a bit on what's involved with this *enfleurage* method they use here so I can ask intelligent questions tomorrow." He grinned at Rob. "Must be nice to be on holiday, Inspector."

"It is." Unfazed, Rob lifted his teacup in salute. "Enjoy your research. We'll take photos for you."

HOLLY WAS WHEEZING as she reached the top of the trail, making Rob laugh. The inspector, looking ultra-casual in lightweight hiking pants and a red t-shirt, extended a hand to pull her up the last part.

She batted it away. "I can do it myself!"

"'Said the little red hen.'" Rob's grin broadened. "Come on, then. You're almost there."

Holly glared at him, her face beet red as she pulled herself onto the tiny plateau, only to collapse on the ground. "I'm sure it's the altitude. I can't possibly be this unfit!"

The inspector's lips twitched. He handed Holly her water bottle, dark eyes dancing in his brown face. "We're about eight hundred feet above sea level. I don't think altitude is the problem."

"Hibiscus's highest point is two hundred," Holly pointed out, wiping her mouth after guzzling thankfully from her water bottle. "And how do you know we're eight hundred feet anyway?"

Rob waved a brochure at her. "It says so right here. 'We are now standing on Gorch Plateau, eight hundred feet above the Reach, part of the southern coast of Turtle Island.

If you look to the east, you may be able to catch a glimpse of the airport; to the west you can see the rooftops of Azalea Village.'"

"Azalea? That sounds pretty. I wonder if they actually grow azaleas. They'll be in bloom right now too. Like the rhododendrons."

Rob grinned. "Ah, so you did see those on the way up here. I thought perhaps you were too busy gasping for air to notice flowers." He laughed when Holly swiped at him, then pulled her to her feet and towards him.

In Holly's opinion, going down the trail was worse than going up. She slithered and squeaked the whole way, grabbing at branches to slow her descent.

"An easy trail! Ha!" she snorted. "How long did Nat say it would take? Forty minutes? Again, I say, ha! What's the time, Rob? We're going to be late, aren't we? I knew we should have started sooner. And I told you we shouldn't have gone all the way to the top."

The inspector glanced back. "And miss that view? It was worth every wheeze and gasp. Don't worry, we're nearly at the bottom. You'll have time to shower and change."

Rob's lips twitched as he gazed at Holly's t-shirt and khaki pants, now covered in mud from where she'd slipped on the way down. She'd also lost her hairband, setting her long red-gold curls free to frizz and riot in abandon.

Oblivious to his amusement, Holly dragged her hand across her forehead, leaving another smear of mud on her face, then heaved a sigh of relief as she saw the small post that marked both the beginning and end of the trail.

"Thank goodness. I mean, the view was fantastic, but

that is not an easy walk. And I'll be telling Natasha that when I see her!"

～

JAMIE'S MOUTH dropped open when Holly staggered into the cottage.

"Don't say anything!" Holly warned, then did a double-take. "Is that what you're wearing to dinner? Is this a fancy restaurant? I didn't bring anything dressy!"

Jamie glanced down at her red silk shirt and black leggings. "This isn't dressy." Just like Rob's had done, her mouth twitched as she looked back at Holly. "Um, you are going to shower, right? You know you have mud on your face."

"What?"

"Mud. Right here. And here." Jamie touched her own forehead and cheeks. "Good thing there's plenty of hot water. You're going to need it. What'd you do? Fall down the mountain or something?" Giving Holly another once-over, she added, "I'm glad I skipped that walk. It was lovely out on the water in a kayak. And clean too." She sniggered as Holly glared at her.

Rob eased past Holly, trying not to laugh. "I'll just go get ready myself. How are we getting to the restaurant?"

"Natasha's taking us. She'll be here in,"—Jamie glanced at the clock on the wall—"twenty minutes, so you'd better get a move on, you two."

"Twenty minutes?" Holly gave a wail of despair and fled towards the shower, leaving Jamie convulsing with laughter behind her.

4

The Wharf Tavern was a small, cozy restaurant about a twenty-minute drive away and obviously popular with locals, judging by the number of cars in the parking area.

The proprietor hailed Natasha with pleasure, kissing her on both cheeks before smiling at the rest of the group.

"Your other guest has already arrived, Nat. I've put you all on a table on the patio, okay?"

"What other guest?" Natasha peered through the restaurant towards the patio. "Oh, it's Thomas. I thought he was meeting someone else tonight." She glanced at Jamie, who just shrugged. "Well, it's good you could add a chair, Bruno."

"No problem." The owner beckoned a waiter over. "Enjoy your dinner. The snapper's fresh, by the way. Caught it myself this morning." He turned to greet the people behind them.

"That's Bruno. He owns the place," Natasha explained as they threaded their way through tables. "Hi, Thomas. I thought you weren't joining us. What happened?"

"My guy was a no-show. I waited for thirty minutes,

wandered around a bit, then thought I may as well try and find this place." The journalist grinned at them, holding up a glass. "They've beer on tap here, Inspector. Pretty good. You want one, Jeff?"

Mr. Graham shook his head with a smile as he pulled out a chair. "I'll pass, thanks."

Holly sat down beside Thomas. "Your reporter guy didn't show up? I thought you were going to be swapping state secrets."

"Oh well, he mentioned family here so perhaps he got caught up with them. It's no biggie. I'll find him tomorrow." Thomas shrugged before adding, "I hear the snapper's fabulous, by the way. Anyone else decided what they're getting?"

HOLLY WAS UP bright and early Friday morning. She beat Jamie to the shower by seconds, threw on jeans and a teal blue t-shirt, and had the kettle boiling by the time the rest of the group made it to the kitchen.

Mr. Graham looked flustered as he accepted a cup of tea. His gray hair already standing on end, he gazed around the kitchen. "Has anyone seen my glasses? I thought I left them in my room, but they aren't there. I need them for my presenta— Oh, thank you, Inspector. Where were they?"

"On the coffee table by the sofa. Beside your laptop." Rob smiled at the historian. "I'm looking forward to hearing your presentation, Jeff. You're up first, according to the program." He glanced down at the paper he held.

"Where'd you get a program? Can I see it?" Holly asked.

"From the inestimable Fee. I went out for an early walk this morning and stopped by reception." Rob handed the folded brochure to Holly. "It looks like we'll have an interesting day."

Holly leaned against the kitchen counter, studying the schedule. "After Mr. Graham's presentation, we can get a tour of the gardens. Oh, that will be fun! And then we can also go behind the scenes in the perfumery where someone will explain the *enfleurage* method. Sounds interesting. Didn't you say you researched this, Thomas?"

"Uh-huh." From where he was slumped over a cup of coffee, Thomas groaned. "I think I had a little too much home brew last night."

Jamie rolled her eyes as she sauntered into the kitchen, looking elegant in slim white jeans and a rose-pink shirt. "You think? You were singing sea shanties on the way home, Miller."

Holly giggled. "'He sang sea shanties by the seashore.' Say that fast, Thomas."

"Ugh." The journalist groaned again, then picked up his coffee. "I've got to brush my teeth. Back in a few."

"We're taking the little cars, right?" Holly asked. "I want to drive."

"I'm driving," Rob responded instantly. "I can't fold myself into the back of that thing. I'd never get out."

"Well, you take Thomas, then. He certainly can't drive in his condition." Holly grinned at the inspector. "And either Jamie or I will take Mr. Graham. If that's okay with you, of course," she added, looking at the historian.

He smiled. "I'd rather be a passenger."

"I'll take all our stuff," Jamie offered. "That way people won't be so squashed. The cars are a little on the small side." She glanced at her watch. "We should leave in a few minutes if we're going to get there on time. Where's Miller?"

"Here. I'm ready." Thomas leaned against the doorframe, still clutching his coffee. He cast a piteous look at Rob. "Try to avoid any bumps in the road, Inspector."

As HOLLY TURNED onto the road leading to Plumeria Perfumery, following the neon-orange cars driven by Jamie and Rob, Mr. Graham tapped her on the shoulder from his seat behind her.

"Frangipani trees," he said, directing her attention to the trees lining the sides of the road. "Very appropriate, aren't they?"

Holly nodded. *Plumeria* was the botanical name for the frangipani, so it was certainly a good idea for the Plumeria Perfumery to have examples of its namesake. These particular trees were laden with waxy white and yellow flowers, almost smothering the long oblong leaves.

"They're stunning," she agreed. "Looks like *Plumeria rubra* to me."

"Yes. There must be a bit of a microclimate here as well. I don't think our trees are so far along on Hibiscus."

"Ours are at the inn." Holly grinned. "But Gramps has a few different varieties. He likes frangipani. You were right about Turtle having limestone areas, by the way. I looked it up. The perfumery soils aren't as acidic as other parts of the island." She took her eyes briefly off the road to look up at the canopy above her. "These trees look very healthy."

"Yes, I'd say the soil here must have a pH between six and seven point five." Mr. Graham, an avid member of the Hibiscus Island Garden Club, pointed to rows of fencing on one side of the road. "Look at those passionflower vines, Holly! I must get some photos if I can. And— Oh my! Look at that allamanda."

Holly grinned at the enthusiasm in Mr. Graham's voice as she pulled into the graveled parking area in front of Plumeria Perfumery. The allamanda was gorgeous. Golden yellow flowers bloomed profusely, spilling over the welcoming arms steps that led up to the entrance.

The perfumery was a sprawling two-story building painted white with black shutters at each window and the ubiquitous terracotta tiled roof. An enormous *Cassia* tree, not yet in flower, towered over one corner. As she pulled herself out of the car, Holly eyed the clumps of *Agapanthus* crowding circular flower beds with approval. The spiky blue Lilies of the Nile, which would bloom at the same time as the golden *Cassia*, would look stunning against the white walls of the old building. In front of the dark green spikes was a mix of white alyssum and blue salvia, newly planted judging by the disturbed earth around them.

Stretching out on either side of the perfumery were gardens. More like fields, Holly amended to herself, peering over the drystone wall that encircled the parking lot. Beside her, Mr. Graham pointed out more rows of passionflowers, these ones surrounded by oleander hedges, all nestled in a valley enclosed in green-cloaked mountains.

"These must be working gardens," the historian said, indicating two gardeners in the fields. "Plumeria has been making perfumes since 1928, you know. Look! Are those jasmine bushes too?"

Holly peered at a field full of green clumps. "Possibly," she agreed. "It would make sense. Nice fragrant flower. I can't wait for our tour. I wonder if they'd let us take some cuttings of things."

"Come on, you two. Stop gawking at the flowers." Jamie's voice held a laugh.

Holly turned to see the rest of the group waiting at the

bottom of the steps. Beside them, a smartly dressed woman with brown hair done up in a smooth chignon wore an amused expression as she watched the two gardening enthusiasts approach.

"Lily O'Connor," she said, holding out her hand to Mr. Graham. "You must be Jeff Graham. I can't tell you how excited we are to hear your presentation about *La Rosa de España*. We were just so thrilled when we heard about the perfume and to be able to have a part in its restoration... Well, it's just been a wonderful experience for all of us at Plumeria."

Mr. Graham beamed. "The perfume was certainly a remarkable find."

"It was." Lily smiled. "If you'd like to come in, I'll introduce you to our other special guests. We'd like to get the symposium started as soon as possible, but if you'd like coffee, tea, or a pastry, we have a little time for that. After you." She gestured towards the open doors.

GAZING around the mix of people in the room from her seat by the window, Holly nibbled a croissant. Nearby, Rob listened to a professorial-looking man, nodding from time to time as the man expounded at length about something.

Jamie appeared beside Holly, holding another cup of tea balanced on a saucer. "So much for starting as soon as possible," she remarked. "Why's Rob talking about cows?"

"Cows?" Holly blinked. "At a perfume symposium? Is he really? Poor thing. Maybe I should go rescue him."

"Nah, he's fine." Jamie sat down on the seat across from Holly, placing the delicate porcelain teacup on the piecrust table between them. "I can barely get my finger in this handle," she complained. "It's very posh here, isn't it?"

"I kind of like it." Holly picked up her own teacup with care. "Someone told me this is part of the original house, built around 1900. It used to be a farm before they started growing flowers and making perfumes. The woman said these are the original floorboards and beams."

Jamie surveyed the foot-wide wooden planks beneath her feet. "It's nice but my nose is so stuffed with perfume I can barely taste this." She gestured at her teacup.

Holly grinned. "You probably shouldn't have tried every single tester."

Jamie followed her gaze across the long lounge to a smaller room beyond double door, where tiny glass bottles rested in velvet-lined, wooden cases along the counters. "Yeah, probably. Have you tried any yet?"

"No. What are they like? Nice?"

"They have a lot named after flowers. Oleander, jasmine, lily, that kind of thing. There's a frangipani too. *Frangipani Allure* it's called. Apparently, it was released only a few months ago. I liked it. We should buy some to take back for Becky and Myrtle."

"Buy what?" Thomas asked, materializing beside them with a half-eaten croissant in his hand.

"Perfume. We should get some for Angie and Denise too," Holly said, reminding her friend of the employees who were manning The Bean in Jamie's absence.

"Yeah, good idea." Jamie took another sip of tea, glancing around the room at the chattering guests. "Who are all these people, do you think? They can't all be perfumers, surely."

Thomas hooked a nearby chair with his foot, sitting down beside Jamie. "There are a couple of local bigwigs. For instance, the guy talking to Rob is the mayor of Silver Landing, the main town here. Although, it's really more like a village, size-wise. But everyone else is related to perfume somehow. Only four actual perfumers though."

He jerked his chin towards a very chic, elderly lady with silver-white hair worn in a bun. "That's one there. Madame Sylvie Lestrade, originally from France but now residing on Azure Isle. The blonde beside her is Cressida Billings, Lily O'Connor's personal assistant."

Both women stared at the journalist.

"And just how do you know all this?" Jamie inquired.

Thomas grinned. "I met some of them yesterday. I did a little reconnaissance after I went to meet Dickenson—my no-show friend, you remember. We were supposed to meet at the Fire Drake, that little inn just down the road. Anyway, when he didn't show, I ambled up to check out the place and Cressida was here with the perfume people."

"Who are the others? Perfumers, I mean." Holly asked.

"Susan Hill, daughter of Olivia Hill, now deceased but supposedly a big name in the industry. Amelie Lestrade, head perfumer here at Plumeria, and yes, she's Sylvie's daughter. And Gabriel Manout. He's the main speaker for the symposium. He and Susan Hill don't get on. They were having a bit of an argument when I saw them yesterday."

"About what?" Holly was curious.

"No idea. They shut up when they saw me." The journalist shrugged, then grinned. "I've heard there's some serious rivalry between the two Grand Island perfumeries. The rest of these people are business representatives who have dealings with Plumeria. It's not a bad crowd for such a tiny place. Looks like, what? Forty, fifty people?"

Jamie nodded, pursing her lips as she gazed around the

room. "I've got to say, I wonder why they even have a symposium at all. I mean, there are only four of them."

"Big fish, small pond syndrome." Thomas grinned. "But it makes sense to keep in touch with your competition." Something caught his eye and he paused. "I see Nat and Mackenzie made it finally. And hey, look who's with them!"

Following his gaze, Holly stared in surprise at the woman in the doorway beside Natasha. "Is that Sage Craft? From Juniper Island? I didn't know she was coming."

"Sage? Where? Oh, so it is." Jamie waved furiously across the room, drawing the threesome's attention.

Natasha nodded, tapping the shoulder of the man next to her to direct his attention to them.

The ringing of a small bell quieted the room, everyone looking towards the sound to a petite blonde who stood in the center of open double doors.

"Ladies and gentlemen, I'd like to just go over today's schedule briefly before we get started. In a moment, we will all proceed to the lecture room where Mr. Jeff Graham will be sharing a presentation about the exploration and salvage of *La Rosa de España*. Following his talk, we will begin tours of the perfumery and grounds, reassembling here for lunch, which will be served on our outdoor patio since the weather is so favorable today. After lunch, we will reconvene in the lecture hall to listen to our esteemed guest speaker, Mr. Gabriel Manout from Manout Perfumes on Grand Island. Afternoon tea will be served in the conservatory after Mr. Manout's presentation."

Cressida Billings smiled again, then turned and waltzed through the open double doors behind her. The buzz of conversation resumed as the crowd of guests began to follow her.

5

Holly grinned with appreciation. "Afternoon tea in the conservatory. Sounds lovely, doesn't it? And I'm dying to see the gardens. I wonder who's in charge of them. Any idea, Thomas, since you seem to know all there is to know about this place?"

"Nope. Sorry. I'm more interested in seeing the actual perfumery," the journalist replied.

Jamie drained her tea before replacing the cup in its saucer, then stood up. "Come on. I can see Rob waving at us from over there. He's obviously escaped the cow-loving mayor."

Laughing, Holly followed her friend across the room to the entrance to the lecture hall. Rob had disappeared inside, presumably to save them seats, but Natasha arrived at the same time as the trio.

"Look who's here! She pulled in at the exact same time as us!" Natasha beamed as she pushed Sage slightly forward.

Holly greeted the Juniper Island woman with pleasure. She had met Sage Craft earlier in the year when she and her sister, Tansy, had attended the Maritime Quilting Expo held on Hibiscus Island in January. Both women, with their younger sister Marigold, owned a small shop that sold teas, lotions, essential oils, and soaps, some of which Holly's mother ordered for the Hibiscus Inn.

The tall burly man beside Sage grinned at them, his teeth flashing in the middle of a black bushy beard. "Sorry we're late. I underestimated the amount of time it would take to get back from the dive this morning. How's Jeff Graham? Nervous? I said I'd provide moral support if he wanted it."

"He needs it," Jamie agreed. "He's a great lecturer, but he works himself into a frenzy every time he has to deal with a computer."

Peter Mackenzie nodded. "Right. I'll just pop up there and assist, then. You're okay to sit with these guys, right, Nat? Yeah? Good."

Without waiting for an answer, the marine archaeologist strode through the other guests, heading towards the flustered-looking Mr. Graham at the front of the room.

Natasha rolled her eyes with vigor. "Honestly. The man drives me crazy. He didn't underestimate the time at all. He stopped at another wreck site on the way back in! Got totally distracted and lost all sense of time. I was just about to give up and leave when he came flying in. No apology either, mind you. It's lucky he's so good at his job, that's all I can say."

"At least you didn't get a flat tire," Jamie said. "Or have a plane to catch."

"Oh, here we go. I knew that would come back to bite me at some point." Thomas's grin was unrepentant. "I'm going to find a spot to take notes. Nice to see you, Sage. You going to join us for dinner tonight?"

"Yes, do," Holly urged. "Nat's promised us a barbecue."

"I'd love to." Sage smiled. "Thanks."

With a wave, Thomas strode ahead, pulling out his phone as he moved to the front of the room. Holly scanned the rows of seats for Rob, then herded the others in his direction.

"How come Tansy's not with you?" Jamie asked Sage, pausing to let an older man enter the row in front of her.

"Our youngest sister's on holiday right now so someone needed to stay and mind the store. I'm killing three birds with one stone on this trip—stocking up on some Plumeria scents and essential oils, finding out about all the new trends in the Maritime Island perfume business, and, hopefully, getting some bottles of the new *Rosa del Mar* perfume for the shop. Lily said they'd have small sample sizes available. It's a whirlwind trip. I leave on Sunday. Oh, thank you, Inspector."

Rob grinned as he stood to let the women file into the row of seats. "I'm on holiday, Miss Craft. It's Rob."

Sage smiled again. "Rob, then. On holiday? Well, that's nice. How long will you be here? I hope you're going to get a chance to tour the island. It's a lovely place, that's for sure. Eco-holidays are becoming pretty popular here."

"We're only here till Tuesday," Holly replied, sitting down beside Rob. "And yes, Mr. Graham mentioned the eco-tourism here as well. You go in for that on Juniper too, don't you?"

Sage's face clouded. "Yes, but we're having a bit of a problem right now. Some big hotel guy has applied to build on a part of the island that's always been zoned reserve land. People are protesting all over the place. It's a mess, actually."

Before Holly could respond, Cressida Billings tapped the microphone at the front, calling for quiet.

"Ladies and gentlemen, Mr. Jeff Graham."

~

A HUGE ROUND of applause erupted as Mr. Graham finished speaking. The historian beamed behind his spectacles. "Thank you kindly, but as I've already said, the exploration and salvage of *La Rosa de España* was a joint effort. Dr. Peter Mackenzie provided tremendous support and advice to our admittedly somewhat amateur team. I'm sure he'd be more than happy to join me up here to answer any questions you might have. Dr. Mackenzie?"

The black-bearded archaeologist grinned amiably. "Sure. Why don't we start with you, sir." He pointed to a dignified-looking gentleman.

Questions flew thick and fast for about twenty minutes before a smiling Cressida Billings made her way to the front of the room.

"Mr. Graham, Dr. Mackenzie, I think I speak for all of us when I say we thoroughly enjoyed your talk and your willingness to answer so many questions. Could we have one more round of applause for our speaker and his assistant, folks? Thank you. I'm sure if you have further questions, Mr. Graham and Dr. Mackenzie would be willing to chat at lunchtime as well."

Receiving a nod from both men, Cressida beamed. "That's lovely. Thank you so much. Now, ladies and gentlemen, we have a mixed schedule for you today. Members of the Maritime Perfumer Association, we'll be starting our annual general meeting in fifteen minutes in the board room. And I promise you, we will be finished by lunchtime."

Her eyes twinkled at the ripple of laughter that sounded around the room before she continued. "If you're a sales representative, your time is your own right now, but we've set aside the Frangipani Room if you'd like to talk shop."

Sage smiled and nodded to some other people in the room.

"What's the Frangipani Room?" Jamie whispered.

"Where all the samples are," Sage replied. "It's one of the original rooms in the house."

"And finally, for our honored guests," Cressida continued, "we've arranged special tours of the perfumery for you. If you'd like to see how we make our products at Plumeria, please make your way downstairs. Our guides can take five or six through at a time, so please feel free to grab a tea or coffee or snack while you wait. If you'd like to visit the gardens first, you can wander anywhere you like. Our head gardener, Mr. Santorini, will be happy to answer any questions you might have. Lunch will be served at one thirty. Enjoy your tours."

A buzz of conversation filled the room as Cressida stopped speaking.

"I suppose you want to see the gardens, right?" Jamie grinned at Holly, who nodded.

"Yes, but I'm going to grab Mr. Graham first. I think he needs rescuing, and he said he wanted to see the flowers." Holly nodded towards the historian who had been button-holed by an earnest-looking woman.

Rob grinned. "I'll collect Jeff and meet you outside, Holly. I'd quite like some fresh air anyway, so I'll join you on the garden tour. What are the rest of you going to do?"

"I need to call Tansy to check in," Sage said. "And I want a quick word with Lily O'Connor and then there are a couple of other people I'd like to catch up with. The gardens are gorgeous, Holly, but you must make sure you see the perfumery as well. It's fabulous. Like stepping back in time."

Natasha and Jamie exchanged glances.

"Let's do that first, shall we?" Natasha suggested. "Where are these stairs she was talking about?"

"I'll show you."

As Sage led the others away, Holly smiled at Rob. "Come on, Inspector. Let's kidnap Mr. Graham and go check out the passionflowers."

HOLLY PEERED at the flower Mr. Graham was indicating. "Oh, that is a pretty one."

"*Passiflora coccinea.*" The older man nodded. "Very showy and produces lovely fruit."

Beside him, the head gardener of the Plumeria Perfumery smiled in appreciation. "You two do know your flowers, I'll give you that."

"Oh, I'm only an amateur," Mr. Graham disclaimed. "Holly here is the professional. She has her own garden design business now, you know."

Mr. Santorini eyed Holly with approval. "Good to know the younger generation is still interested in gardening."

"Well, she's Stuart Mackintosh's granddaughter. It's in her genes." Mr. Graham patted the now-blushing Holly on the arm.

"Are you now? I know Stuart very well. You tell him Mick Santorini said hello when you next see him." Mr. Santorini beamed at Holly. "In fact, I've been promising Stuart a cutting for ages. Perhaps you could take it with you when you go."

"A passionflower?" Holly looked at him in interest.

"No, no. A frangipani. *Plumeria pudica.* Unless he's got one already?"

"Not that I know of," Holly said. "Isn't that an evergreen variety?"

Mr. Santorini nodded. "Grows about fifteen feet. Pure white flowers with a yellow center. Pretty thing. I'll get you the cutting, then."

"How big is it?" Holly asked warily, knowing that some gardeners cut quite large branches of frangipani to root. She'd done it herself after a hurricane on Hibiscus took down an old tree.

Mr. Santorini laughed. "Oh, I haven't taken it yet. But we can go look now if you'd like. Maybe collect a few for better success. If we cut through the fields here, you can see the tree and then I'll take you back to the perfumery by another route."

Holly glanced at Rob. "Would that be okay? I know Gramps would love it."

The inspector grinned. "Not a problem with me." As they started to walk across the field between the rows of passionflowers sprawling over wire fences, Rob glanced at Mr. Santorini. "I'm curious about these passionflowers. They don't all appear to be scented. Aren't they grown for perfume?"

The head gardener nodded. "We grow a lot for the perfumes, yes. *Passiflora caerulea* is very fragrant." He stopped to indicate a small blue-white flower with a corona of blue filaments before moving on to another flower. "And this beauty here is *Passiflora stipulata*, or at least we think it is. It's been grown on the island a long time and is somewhat unique as far as we can tell."

"It's lovely." Holly eyed the rose-purple three-inch-wide flower with appreciation.

"We have a similar one on Hibiscus," Mr. Graham added.

Mr. Santorini smiled as he gestured to them to keep walking. "When old Mr. O'Connor started the perfumery, the first perfume he produced was from the Easter lily, then the frangipani and then the passionflower. He became fascinated with the vines and started collecting them, so now we grow as many different varieties as we can. If they aren't scented, they still attract bees and butterflies, which our visitors seem to enjoy as well. Fritillary butterflies lay their eggs on the vines, so we have lots of those in the summer months. It's quite pretty to see them fluttering above the fields."

"How many people do you have helping?" Holly asked curiously.

The head gardener grimaced. "Not enough. I have a staff of three, although Carleton really only works in the slat house at this point. I could use more hands, for sure, but that's all we can afford right now. Plumeria is a small company, but *enfleurage* is a time-consuming and exacting process, and it needs a lot of flowers. It's my job to make sure the flowers are available. Right now, we're harvesting frangipani every day. Its peak blooming time starts in late spring, early summer on the island, with different varieties blooming in succession. Passionflowers bloom around the same time, so we're often making both scents simultaneously."

"Fascinating," Rob murmured. "I had no idea perfume was still made this way."

"It's not common, but *enfleurage* is making a bit of a come-back with do-it-yourself enthusiasts. I've heard you can buy all the equipment you need to set up a little home perfumery, if you're really interested. But you still need the flowers. You can see how it all works if you do the tour of the perfumery."

"It's on our list," Holly assured him.

"Good." Mr. Santorini gestured ahead. "Look, here are the frangipani trees I mentioned. Some of them are just coming into bloom, but it's still a good time to take the cuttings. What do you think of our underplanting, Holly? It's hard to grow things under frangipani, as I'm sure you know. They're huge water suckers."

Holly gazed at the clumps of greenery massed under the trees. "Are those *Agapanthus*? I saw you have a lot outside the perfumery building as well."

"Right you are." The head gardener beamed in approval. "A mix of standard blue and dwarf white. Nice, aren't they? Or they will be when they flower. I was planting alyssum and salvia in those beds all yesterday afternoon, as I'm sure you noticed as well. We stick to a white, blue, and yellow theme around the main building. Now, the tree I'm talking about is just over there."

Rob eyed the multi-branched small woody trees with curiosity. "How do you know which is which when they aren't flowering? They all look the same to me."

"The leaves of *Plumeria pudica* are different," Mr. Graham pointed out. "They're longer and thinner than those of *Plumeria rubra*."

Rob looked blank. "Uh-huh. Well, I'm sorry, Jeff, but that doesn't help me much."

Mr. Santorini laughed as he moved purposefully into the small copse ahead of him. "Most of the trees have at least a few flowers now, and there are a couple of varieties in full bloom, but I know every tree, plant, and vine on this property like the back of my— Oh!"

The exclamation jolted out of the head gardener as he came to an abrupt halt, staring ahead at something on the ground.

Holly, Rob, and Mr. Graham hurried forward.

"What's the matter?" Holly asked, reaching the older man's side. "Oh no. Rob, look!"

"I see it." The inspector's voice was grim. "Stay still, all of you." Mr. Santorini's face had drained of color, making Rob urgently beckon Mr. Graham forward. "In fact, better yet, go stand over there at the edge of the field. Jeff, will you look after Mr. Santorini?"

Mr. Graham nodded, his face sober. He escorted the unprotesting head gardener back to where the passion-flower hedges ended, making him sit down before offering a bottle of water.

Rob crouched down beside the body of a man dressed in a blue checked shirt and dark blue jeans. The man lay face down beside the bumpy grey-brown trunk of a frangipani tree, partially obscured by the spiky clumps of lilies. Above them, clusters of white frangipani flowers peeked through the dark green leaves, one gently wafting to the ground as Holly watched Rob.

"Is he okay?" Holly kept her voice low.

"No."

Rob removed his finger from the man's neck, pulled out his phone, and punched in some numbers. "Police, please... Plumeria Perfumery... Man dead... Yes. Inspector Rob Tucker... Hibiscus Island... No, I'm on holiday... Yes, I'll wait with him... Right you are, Sergeant. See you in a bit."

"Uh, Rob, do you think he had a stroke or some—?" Holly hesitated, unwilling to ask anything else.

"No. He has a head injury. Whether accidental or deliberate, I don't know, but it looks like someone tried to hide the body." Rob's brow creased in thought. "Holly, a Sergeant Frampton is on his way. I don't think Mr. Santorini will be fit to guide him. Can you remember how to get back here from the perfumery?"

Holly nodded.

"Do that then. Jeff can take Mr. Santorini back more slowly." Rob turned back to the body.

6

———

Jamie's eyes bugged out. "But who is he? And how did he end up among the passionflowers?"

"Under the frangipani tree," Holly corrected in a distracted way. "*Plumeria pudica* to be exact. And I have no idea who he is." She peered down the driveway. "How long does it take the police to respond here? Rob's going to think I got lost."

"And he thinks it might be murder?" Jamie pressed.

"He didn't say that," Holly began only to be interrupted by a moan.

"Murder?" Lily O'Connor wrung her hands. "Surely not! Oh, this is just dreadful! A dead man on the grounds of Plumeria! How could this happen? And at this time too! When we're unveiling a new perfume." She gave a heartfelt groan, glancing back at the guests clustered on the second story veranda, all eagerly peering out over the fields.

Cressida Billings cleared her throat. "I don't expect it has anything to do with the perfumery, Lily. It's a large property, only enclosed in low walls that anyone could climb over, and it's certainly not guarded or patrolled at night. I doubt we can be held liable in any way."

"Liable!" Lily was horrified. "I hadn't even thought of that! Could we be sued, do you think? Oh, good heavens!" She twisted her hands together again. "Where are the police?"

"It's only Sergeant Frampton on the island at the moment. And he's based in Azalea Village, so it will take him a little time to get here. I think I hear sirens now."

As a yellow and white police car came into view, Lily O'Connor gaped at her assistant. "What do you mean it's only Sergeant Frampton? Where's Inspector Moore?"

"On holiday in the Alps," Cressida replied in laconic tones.

"But... but that means... Oh no."

"What does it mean?" Natasha, hovering beside Jamie, had listened to the conversation with interest. "What's wrong with Sergeant Frampton? Can't he do the job?"

"No, Harry Frampton is perfectly capable," Cressida replied, "but that's beside the point. If murder is suspected, then the investigation will require a police inspector. And with our own inspector on holiday, that means the commissioner will send someone from Azure to help."

"It might *not* be murder. Rob said it could have been an accident." Holly's interjection was completely ignored.

"Does it have to be Azure?" Natasha asked. "I mean, Rob's a police inspector, isn't he? Why can't he help this Sergeant Frampton?"

"Oh, I forgot you haven't been here that long. No, it doesn't work like that," Jamie explained. "The Maritime Islands all fall under one Commissioner of Police, who's based on Grand Island. Each island has at least an Inspector in charge of its police force. I think Azure has a Chief Inspector as well because, let's face it, they're snobby."

A tiny smile flickered across Cressida's face at that comment.

"Rob can get seconded to Coral Island," Jamie continued, "and vice versa, since they're closest to us. Their inspector will be on call for any Hibiscus emergencies right now since Rob's here."

Cressida nodded. "Azure and Juniper are the closest islands to us, but unfortunately, since Azure, as Jamie said, has a Chief, they can spare their inspector more easily than Juniper can. It doesn't happen often, thank goodness."

"I take it there's a problem with the Azure inspector?" Natasha raised an eyebrow as the police car drew to a halt in front of them.

Cressida shrugged. "You could say that."

As a big, burly policeman got out of the car, Lily uttered another moan and rushed forwards. "Sergeant Frampton! Have you heard? A man might have been murdered! Here!"

"Rob didn't *say* it was murder!" Holly exclaimed in exasperation.

Overhearing her, the sergeant grinned even as he patted Lily's arm in a reassuring way. "Miss Holly Gold? The inspector says you'll take me to the body."

HOLLY LED the genial Sergeant Frampton and two constables through the mountain-surrounded fields towards the grove of frangipani trees where the body lay.

"So, you're Solid's girl, eh? I met your dad, you know, while I was on Grand Island. I was doing my sergeant exams at the time. He was doing his inspector ones, of course. Nice guy. He's a real miss to the force. I expect lots of people tell you that, eh?"

"Yes." Holly smiled at the burly man beside her. "But it's always lovely to hear."

Her dad, Inspector Peter 'Solid' Gold, had died a few years earlier, finally losing his fight with acute leukemia. Holly loved it when people remembered him.

"And I hear you're dating the new guy on Hibiscus. The Englishman. Good detective, too, I hear."

"How on earth do you know that?" Holly asked, surprised. "Is there some kind of island police spy network?"

Sergeant Frampton's dark brown face creased with merriment. "Spy network. Ha. Don't know about that, but people talk. And there's been a fair amount lately about Tucker and some others solving murders down Hibiscus way. Others, by the way, who would be wise to keep their little noses out of this case. Our Azure inspector isn't as... hmmm... forgiving, shall we say, as Inspector Tucker appears to be."

Holly frowned. "What's wrong with the Azure Isle inspector? Lily and Cressida didn't seem too thrilled about him either."

Sergeant Frampton didn't answer. Instead, he looked ahead to the frangipani trees at the end of the field. "That your Inspector Tucker there?"

"Well, he's not *my* Inspector Tucker, but yes, that's him. Shall I wait here, Sergeant? I don't want to contaminate the scene."

Sergeant Frampton's eyes twinkled. "Good idea. I'll just go have a word with the inspector and see what's what." He gestured to the two young constables to precede him.

The two police officers shook hands, Rob smiling at the older man, before saying a few words to the constables, who promptly disappeared under the trees. Dressed casually in jeans and a polo shirt, Rob still exuded authority, his muscled six-foot frame slightly taller than the stocky sergeant's.

"Where's the body?"

Holly turned in surprise to see a man wearing white overalls and a peeved expression.

"The body?" he repeated. "Where is it?"

"Under the trees." Holly pointed towards Rob and the sergeant, blinking again when the man pushed past her without another word.

The young woman behind him grinned at Holly. "That's Doctor Shaw. Supposedly retired police surgeon. He's annoyed because we were on the golf course when he got the call, and he was one under par at the time." She held out her hand. "I'm Dr. Miranda Shaw. Supposedly new police surgeon on Turtle Island, if the previously mentioned old, retired doctor ever stops trying to do my job."

A laugh escaped Holly as she shook the woman's hand. "Nice to meet you. I'm Holly. Holly Gold. Is Doctor Shaw your dad?"

"Yep." Miranda rolled her eyes. "And nope, there's absolutely no need for him to be here. He could have continued playing golf. Really, he's just nosy." She eyed Holly with interest. "So, you found a body, did you? I hear you do this quite often, Miss Holly Gold."

"Who told you that?"

Miranda's grey eyes sparkled with laughter in her brown face. Her long dark hair was tied back in a ponytail that was tucked firmly inside the white overalls she wore. Over her shoulder she held a blue canvas bag. "That would be a Miss Jamie White, who would very much have liked to show me the way. I assured her I could manage to walk across a field by myself. Now, back to the body."

"It's over there." Holly pointed again. "Under a frangipani tree."

Miranda tutted lightly. "I'll go and have a quick look. Fortunately, Sergeant Frampton is a sweetie and I'm assured your Inspector Tucker is very capable. Nice to meet you, Holly, even under the circumstances."

Holly couldn't help grinning as the police surgeon trotted away to be greeted with pleasure by the sergeant. Knowing there wasn't much more she could do in the fields, she walked back to the perfumery, intent on finding out just what Jamie had managed to say in the thirty seconds of time she'd had with Miranda.

VIRTUALLY FROTHING at the mouth with anticipation, Jamie pounced on Holly as soon as she arrived back at the perfumery.

"Well? What's going on? Did you find out anything?"

Holly ignored her, instead looking around in surprise. "Where's everyone gone?"

"The AGM's still going on, so Cressida and Lily went back in for that." Jamie huffed with impatience. "The police said people who are here can still tour the perfumery, but they've got constables stopping cars from coming or going."

"Interesting. I wonder why. They can't think anyone here has anything to do with the death, surely. Rob said the body had been there at least overnight."

"Been where? And what happened? Were you there when the doctor arrived? What did she say?" Jamie pelted Holly with questions as they walked toward the building.

"The body is under a frangipani tree. A man. Hit on the head with something. Or he fell and hit it," Holly added hastily. "Dead a while. Yes, I saw Dr. Shaw. I don't know what she said because I wasn't allowed near the body again." Holly paused. "And, by the way, Sergeant Frampton says the Azure Isle inspector won't appreciate any interference. So, you should put any ideas about investigating right out of your little head."

"Head injury? So, murder is still a possibility then."

"Bit ghoulish, aren't you?"

Jamie ignored her. "Well, Rob should be able to give us more details."

Holly stopped walking. "Did you hear anything I just said? This isn't our island, Jamie. We absolutely cannot get involved in an investigation here. Even Rob can't, really. The Azure inspector and the Turtle Island police will handle it. It's nothing to do with us."

"Yeah, yeah, I know. Come on, Holls. I told the others to save us a seat."

Holly raised an eyebrow. "A seat?"

"Yeah. Lunch is all set up. It's a buffet. Looks pretty good."

Holly looked at her watch in surprise. It was almost one thirty. They'd been walking around the gardens for some time before finding the body.

"Miller's a bit peeved he wasn't around when the police arrived. He's got lots of questions. We all do."

"Well, I don't have any answers for you." Holly paused. "Where *was* Thomas anyway? I'm surprised he didn't hear the sirens. Everyone else seemed to."

"He was touring the perfumery. Asking a million questions about the way they make the perfumes." Jamie glanced sideways at Holly as they finally reached the patio. "Actually, the perfumery's pretty cool, Holls. You definitely need to go see how it all works. Apparently, some people do it on an amateur basis as well. I was thinking it might be fun to try when we're back home."

"Mr. Santorini told us it was becoming popular with DIY people. Are you serious? You'd like to make perfume?"

"It might be fun to try. Look, there's Miller, Nat, and Co." Jamie waved to their friends.

Thomas, Natasha, Peter Mackenzie, and Sage had plates of food and were already eating. They all paused, forks halfway raised as Holly and Jamie reached them.

"About time!" Thomas exclaimed. "What's going on, Holls? What have you learned?"

"Not much unfortunately." Jamie made a face as she pulled out a chair, collapsing into it. "The police wouldn't let her go back to the body. Where's Mr. Graham?"

"Still with Mr. Santorini," Natasha replied. "He was pretty upset. Mr. Santorini, not Mr. Graham. He took it in stride."

"Probably used to dead bodies." Peter Mackenzie took a sip of his drink. "I've heard Hibiscus Island's a pretty lethal place."

"It is not!" Holly was indignant, then saw the grin on the archaeologist's face as Thomas snorted. "It's not funny, you two. Dead bodies aren't a joke!"

Thomas sobered. "Sorry, Holls. You're quite right. So, you really have no idea who the body was? No ID on him?"

Holly frowned, still annoyed at the apparent callousness, then shrugged. "There might have been, but I didn't see it. And when I took the sergeant back, I was basically told to keep away." She glared around the table. "We all were. Sergeant Frampton was nice about it, but he was clear that we weren't to interfere. He said the inspector wouldn't like it."

"Interesting. Anyone know anything about this Azure Isle inspector?" Thomas raised an inquiring brow. "No? I'll go sound out Cressida, then. Looks like the AGM is just finishing. You did say she and Lily were upset at the thought of him, right?"

Jamie nodded as she swiveled to watch the perfumers coming on to the patio. "Yes, but Lily looks a little calmer now. Maybe you can talk to her as well. Go charm her with those winning journalist ways and see what you can find out."

"Winning ways? *Moi*?" Thomas clutched at his chest. "Words fail me, Miss White. I didn't know you considered me charming."

Jamie rolled her eyes. "And ask her if she saw anything suspicious yesterday as well," she added.

Still grinning, Thomas paused, one eyebrow raised. "Suspicious? Like what?"

"Well, *I* don't know, Miller! But it's her perfumery, she was here yesterday, and Holly said Rob said the body's been there some time. Maybe Lily saw something." Jamie flapped her hand at him. "Just ask her, okay?"

Thomas opened his mouth, then thought better of whatever he was about to say and closed it again.

"Well, go on," Jamie said, impatience edging her voice. "Go charm. We'll figure out the next steps while you're gone and fill you in when you get back."

Holly sighed and slumped back in her chair.

7

——————

Natasha swallowed a mouthful of food, then leaned across the table to pat Holly's hand. "Stop looking so worried, Holly. Go get your lunch. I'll keep an eye on Jamie for you."

"What do you mean, 'keep an eye on me'? What do you think I'm going to do?" Jamie sounded affronted.

"Well, that's the sixty-million-dollar question, isn't it?" Natasha drawled. "No one ever knows what you're going to do." She grinned at Jamie before picking up her fork again. "Go on, Holly. The potato salad's really good, by the way."

With a small sigh, Holly followed the marine scientist's orders. She scanned the cloth-covered tables laden with food. Salads, cold cuts, cocktail shrimp, and... Was that sushi? She picked up a plate, suddenly starving. As she helped herself to a generous serving of potato salad, there was a touch on her shoulder.

"Are you Holly Gold? The one who was with Mick Santorini when he found the body?"

Holly eyed the woman beside her in surprise. "Yes, but

I'm sorry. I can't really talk about it," she began, only to be interrupted.

"Did you see the body? Was it a man?"

The woman appeared to be in her early forties. With her brown hair swept back in a smooth bun, her elegant red suit, and the gold earrings that glinted in her ears, she looked professional and wealthy. In a slightly harassed tone, she continued, "I think it might be my cousin."

Holly's mouth dropped open. For a moment, she stood gaping at the woman, then found her voice. "Your *cousin*? But... But..." She took a deep breath. "I'm sorry, but why on *earth* would you think that, Mrs... Uh... Ms... ?"

"Hill. Susan Hill." The woman made a clicking sound with her teeth. "I quite realize how odd this sounds, Miss Gold. And believe me, I don't make a habit of wanting to identify bodies, but my cousin was supposed to meet me here yesterday and didn't show up, and now he's *still* not here and there's a dead body on the premises. It's a logical conclusion, I think."

Balancing her full plate in her hands, Holly gawked at Susan Hill. A logical conclusion? Hardly. And how could she be so matter-of-fact about the possibility that her cousin was dead?

Glancing around, Holly caught Natasha's eye. Her face must have shown something because the strawberry blonde scientist immediately nudged Jamie, directing her attention to Holly.

"Well, uh... Perhaps he's just been delayed? Have you tried calling him?" Holly shifted the plate in her hands.

"Of course I have. Jonathan arrived on the flight from Hibiscus Island yesterday. I've confirmed that he checked into his bed and breakfast, but he hasn't answered a single call. It was an important meeting to do with my mother. He would never have missed it. In fact, he's the one who arranged it! I waited for two hours for him to show up. Luckily, I was able to talk to my office on a video call during that time, or it would have been a wasted afternoon. Although, honestly, the number of people who walk in and out of that office like they own it is astonishing!" Susan Hill's eyes narrowed at Holly's blank stare. "You *have* heard of my mother, haven't you? Olivia Hill was a very well-known perfumer on Grand Island."

"Olivia Hill? I think I've heard her name, but I really don't know much about the perfume business." Out of the corner of her eye, Holly saw Jamie approach. "Grand Island, you say? Did she work with Gabriel Manout?"

Susan stiffened. "Certainly not. It's the other way around entirely. Gabriel worked with my mother. She taught him everything he knows. And what did he do? Turned his back on her and went to work for that Lestrade woman! Then had the nerve to come back to Grand Island and set up in opposition to us." Susan's voice squeaked with indignation. Realizing it, she took a deep breath. "But it's water under the bridge now. Ancient history." She frowned at Holly. "So, you have no idea who the dead man is? No one said anything to you?"

Holly shook her head.

"I suppose you think I'm overreacting. Can you at least confirm the body was male? I presume you saw that much, at least."

Holly's brow furrowed in annoyance. "I can't confirm anything. I think the best thing for you to do is speak to Sergeant Frampton and tell him what you told me."

"Everything okay here?" Jamie came up alongside Holly, eyebrows raised in inquiry.

Holly indicated the older woman. "Ms. Hill was

wondering if the body Mr. Santorini found could be her cousin."

Jamie's eyebrows arched higher. "Your *cousin*? Why on earth would you think that? Who's your cousin?"

"Jonathan Dickenson. He arrived on Turtle Island yesterday and was supposed to attend a meeting. He didn't show up then and he's not here today." Susan Hill's voice was impatient. "I've already told Miss Gold this."

"Jonathan Dickenson?" Jamie pondered. "Dickenson... Why does that name sound familiar? Oh, I know!" Her eyes widened. "That was the guy Miller said he was meeting with yesterday. The one who stood him up, remember? The fellow journalist. He was on our flight."

"On your flight? Well then, you should certainly be able to tell me if—"

"We didn't meet him." Holly interrupted Susan Hill's indignant speech. "He sat next to a friend of ours on the plane. So we have no idea if the dead body is your cousin." Movement on the far side of the patio caught her eye. "But *there's* someone who can address your concerns, Ms. Hill. Sergeant Frampton's just arrived."

Jamie and Holly exchanged glances as Susan Hill immediately left, making a beeline for the burly sergeant.

"Well, she's a bit odd, isn't she?"

"That's putting it mildly." Holly rolled her eyes at the understatement.

"Do you think it really could be her cousin?" Jamie asked.

Holly shrugged. "I've no idea. Like I said, I wasn't allowed near the body. Thomas might know—if he was able to see it. Which he's not. Oh look, there's Rob." She waved, catching the eye of the Hibiscus Island inspector who was scanning the room.

Rob said a few words to the sergeant, then crossed the room towards Holly, neatly avoiding Susan Hill on the way.

"Well, is it murder or what?" Jamie blurted the question as soon as Rob came into earshot.

The inspector paused, his eyebrows arching upwards. "I'm sure the police surgeon will inform the inspector in charge of the case about the cause of death. I, however, am not that person." His repressive tone just made Jamie grin.

"You're not denying it. Hmm. That means it's a possibility. Do you know who he is?"

Rob sighed, then shook his head. "There was no ID, but one of the constables found what looks like a room key for his bed and breakfast in his pocket, so the good sergeant will follow up with that, I'm sure." He held up a hand as Jamie opened her mouth again. "Before you go any further, let me repeat: it's not my case, Jamie. Inspector Plummet from Azure Isle is on his way. He should arrive shortly."

Holly eyed his deadpan expression. "Have you met this inspector before? What's he like?"

"He's a qualified police officer," Rob responded, his tone bland.

"Hmm. That doesn't sound like a ringing endorsement." Jamie narrowed her eyes. "Lily and Cressida weren't very happy about him either."

Rob smiled. "I can't discuss a fellow officer. Now, I'd quite like a cup of tea if there's one going. And then I thought we could tour the perfumery, Holly. We should just have time to go round before Mr. Manout's talk."

Jamie scowled. "Fine. Be like that. I'm going to go talk to Miller."

As she stalked off, Rob sighed. "I hope she's not going to start poking around in this." His look at Holly was serious. "I've only met Inspector Plummet once, but as I recall, he's an officer who goes by the book. He's not going to tolerate civilian interference."

"I've already told her that. We're not going to investigate." Holly eyed Rob as they crossed the room towards the large tea urns, wondering if she should say anything else. It didn't take her long to make up her mind. "Rob, do you see that woman over there? The one with the sergeant?"

Rob glanced over and nodded.

"Well, her name's Susan Hill. She's a perfumer and she thinks the body might be her cousin."

Rob stopped short, a look of exasperation crossing his face. "I thought you just said—"

"I'm not investigating!" Holly was indignant. "*She* came up to *me* and *I* told her to go to the sergeant. And I've also told Jamie and Thomas we can't get involved! So—"

"Okay, okay. I'm sorry." Rob placed a hand on Holly's arm in apology. "Let me get a cup of tea first, okay?"

A few minutes later Rob eyed Holly over his cup. "So, this Susan Hill thinks the body might be that of her cousin. Did she give you a reason?"

"Well, she said her cousin is Jonathan Dickenson. He's the journalist Thomas met on the plane. Remember? The one he was supposed to meet for drinks but didn't show up? He was also supposed to be at a meeting yesterday with this Susan and didn't show up for that either."

"Hmmm. Big leap to assume he might be dead." Rob pondered for a moment. "Where was Miller supposed to meet him, do you know? I have this vague memory that he mentioned a place. Do you remember?"

Holly shook her head. "No. You could ask him though. He's over there."

Rob looked where Holly was pointing. Thomas and Jamie were in the middle of what looked like a heated debate, with Natasha, Sage, and Peter Mackenzie as interested onlookers. The inspector groaned. "Tell you what, I'll just make sure Frampton knows so he can pass the information on to Inspector Plummet. Then you and I are going to go take our tour. I'm on holiday, remember?"

THE PLUMERIA PERFUMERY was a large sprawling building, with the actual working part of the business housed on the lower level. Holly paused at the bottom of the stairs.

A long, wide, well-lit room stretched out in front of her. A glass partition divided it, leaving a narrow walkway for visitors on one side. On the other side of the glass, long counters ran down both sides and the center of the room, almost like kitchen counters. The center counters were covered in wood and glass frames. A few women in white coats were working, chatting to each other as they checked the white frangipani flowers on the trays, occasionally removing a few to toss into large bins.

A young guide greeted Rob and Holly with a smile. "Welcome to Plumeria. I'm Kat and I'll be explaining the *enfleurage* method we use here at the perfumery. If you've any questions, feel free to interrupt at any time."

Rob gestured to Holly to precede him into the room, smiling at the guide who eyed him with appreciative interest before continuing.

"Do you know anything about making perfume?" Kat asked. "I always ask because quite a lot of our visitors are very interested in natural perfumery and have tried it themselves. I don't want to bore you with stuff you already know."

Holly shook her head. "All we know is it takes a lot of

flowers. Oh, and that you're making frangipani perfume right now."

"Well, technically, in this room we're making frangipani pomade," Kat corrected. "*Enfleurage* is the process of making pomade. It's been used for hundreds of years to extract the scents of delicate flowers like oleander, jasmine, frangipani, and gardenias, just to name a few. We use cold plant-based fat, the *corps*, which we spread over the glass frames—or *chassis*. You'll see there are ridges in the *corps*, which helps to maximize the surface area for the flowers to exhale their scents."

"Exhale?" Rob repeated, peering through the glass wall at the trays with their layers of white fat covered in waxy frangipani blossoms.

Kat smiled. "Yes. Plants breathe, but flowers exhale. They exhale fragrance. And *enfleurage* is the way we collect those exhalations. *Enfleurage*, in the old French, means 'to impregnate with the scent of flowers.'

Holly watched the women on the other side of the glass wall carefully using tweezers to remove yellow-and-white frangipani flowers from some trays.

"How long do the flowers stay on the... the *corps*?"

"It depends on the flower. We make sure every flower is perfect before it's placed in the *chassis*. They must be freshly picked and moisture-free. We spread them by hand on the *corps* every morning and check them periodically throughout the day. If any begin to turn brown or mold, they're removed. In general, they remain for one day, perhaps two, depending on the flower."

"It's incredibly labor intensive," Rob noted. "How long does it take until the pomade, I think you called it, is ready?"

"Again, that depends on the flower. It takes longer for the really delicate scents. Jasmine, for instance, can take a month to properly infuse the *corps*. Passionflower has a stronger scent so it takes less time."

"It's fascinating. And this has been going on here since 1928?" Holly asked.

"Well, not quite. The perfumery went through some hard times when the solvent extraction process for perfumes became popular. *Enfleurage* is time-consuming and expensive, and the economy couldn't support the perfumery as it was. For a while, we used synthetic fragrances, like the rest of the big perfumers around the world. But several years ago, we made the decision to return to the natural, time-tested methods. The world is shifting back to wanting natural organic products, and that includes perfumes. So far, it's proving to be a good decision. We have many small businesses that will only purchase oils and scents from us."

"Yes, we know one of them. The Black Cat," Holly said. "Sage Craft's shop on Juniper Island. They supply our Inn on Hibiscus Island. I love her soaps."

Kat beamed. "Oh, you know Sage? She's great, isn't she?"

Holly smiled in agreement, then changed the subject. "So, do you get a lot of tour groups visiting here? I imagine it would fit in with the eco-tourism the island is trying to promote."

"A fair number," Kat agreed. "People seem to enjoy seeing how it works."

"What do you do when you're not giving tours?" Rob asked.

"Oh, well, I'm actually on a gap year before college right now." Kat smiled. "But this is a family operation so most of us shift in and out of the different jobs. I'm being a guide today, but I also help in the workroom and the packaging room, and I work in the gardens when I'm needed. It keeps life interesting."

"A family operation? Are you related to Ms. O'Connor, then?" Holly asked.

"She's my aunt." The young woman grinned. "My Uncle Jake works in the grounds, and my granddad runs the whole property." Kat's face clouded. "He had rather an unpleasant experience earlier. Did you hear about it? The dead body, I mean? I thought for sure we'd have to close the perfumery, but Aunt Lily said the police said we could carry on as long as everyone stays out of the gardens." She frowned. "I heard the body was found under some of the frangipani trees. I hope we can still get to them tomorrow, otherwise we're going to have a problem with this pomade. Sorry, I know that sounds callous, but we're using a specific flower right now and the *corps* hasn't been completely saturated yet."

Rob jumped at the chance to change the subject. "Do you mean you use different frangipani flowers at different times?"

"Yes." Kat smiled. "For instance, our signature scent, *Frangipani Allure*, was created earlier this year using one particular variety of frangipani."

"Which one?"

Holly's question made their guide laugh.

"I have no idea. Our head perfumer, Amelie Lestrade, keeps that a deep dark secret. It could be the ones in there, or it could be any of the other varieties that we grow here. Mind you, some are more fragrant than others, so they get used more often." She smiled. "Let's move on, shall we? Next stop is the separation room."

8

After learning how the infused pomade was removed from the *chassis* and washed with high proof alcohol to obtain an *extrait* or extract known as an absolute, Holly and Rob were escorted down a twisting corridor past several closed doors.

"It's like a rabbit warren, isn't it?" Holly murmured.

Overhearing her, Kat smiled. "These used to be cellars under the old house. It's where my great, great—I forget how many greats—grandfather first experimented. When the family got serious about perfume, they renovated and modernized and added on. We call this part the 'catacombs.'"

Rob laughed. "I can see why."

Kat paused beside another glass-fronted wall, behind which they saw counters littered with paraphernalia, although no one was working in the room. Another door on the far side of the room was closed.

"This is part of the lab where Amelie works. She was at the meeting this morning but she's not been very well lately so she may have gone home early again. We need her in good health for the unveiling tomorrow, you know. When she's here, visitors can watch through the glass. It's kind of interesting. You can't see everything, of course. There's another small *enfleurage* room back there where Amelie experiments with her own pomades and things."

"She's related to Madame Sylvie Lestrade, isn't she?" Holly asked, remembering that Thomas had mentioned a French perfumer by that name.

"Yes. The Lestrades used to own a very small and exclusive operation on Azure Isle," Kat replied. "It's closed down now but Amelie was brought up in the perfume industry and has worked here for a number of years. She and Gabriel Manout worked on the *Rosa del Mar* perfume. She's made a few other scents, but *Frangipani Allure* is the best. It's been getting rave reviews everywhere. We're very proud." Kat grinned. "And Amelie may become part of the family soon. That is, if Uncle Jake ever gets his act together."

In the packaging room, Holly leaned against the wooden railing that separated visitors from the staff, watching in fascination as two older women quickly and expertly folded small boxes before sliding tiny vials into them.

"I can't believe you do this manually!" she exclaimed.

Kat smiled. "We're a small business and we believe in quality over quantity. It helps that we rotate jobs but honestly, I find this part quite soothing. Today we're packaging an oleander scent that's been aging for the past several months and is now ready for sale."

"Perfume ages? You mean, like wine? I didn't know that." Holly raised an eyebrow in surprise.

"Yes. Those frangipani in the *enfleurage* room won't become perfume for quite some time," Kat said. "Once the essential oils are extracted, Amelie will blend them with other ingredients according to a specific formula and then the scent will be left to mature."

"It's quite a process, isn't it?" Rob sounded impressed.

"Yes, but we believe there's a place for the old techniques in today's world. People seem to be interested in nature-inspired fragrances again. Florals are making a come-back and essential oils are popular. We're hoping the trend will continue." Kat smiled and glanced at her watch. "The next stop is the sampling counter, and I think you'll just have time for—."

She stopped talking, raising her eyebrow as a constable appeared in the doorway. Seeing Rob, the young police officer cleared his throat. "Could I have a word, sir?"

As Rob excused himself, accompanying the police officer up the stairs, Kat turned to Holly, curiosity written all over her face.

"Who's your boyfriend, then?"

Holly hesitated, then shrugged. It wasn't a secret. "Rob's Hibiscus Island's police inspector. We were with your grandfather when he found the body. Rob's the one who called the police."

Kat's mouth dropped open. "Oh wow. And here's me telling you all about it as if you didn't know. Mind you, I expect everyone knows, really. Aunt Lily wasn't exactly quiet out in the parking. area. Everyone's saying the guy was murdered, you know." Holly sighed as Kat made a wry face. "I suppose the Plum's arrived now and that's why the constable came for your dreamy inspector. Too bad he can't investigate the case instead."

Holly choked. "My dreamy inspector? Rob would die if he heard you say that." She raised an eyebrow at Kat. "I take it the Plum is Inspector Plummet? From Azure Isle? I've heard he's very... uh... official."

Kat snorted. "He's a pompous prat. And useless to boot. He couldn't catch a murderer if the guy stood in front of him and held out his hands to be handcuffed." A bell rang upstairs, making Kat jump. "Oh, that's the bell for Gabriel's talk. You'd better hurry if you're going to hear him. Come on, I'll show you the way."

∿

HOLLY WAS JUST ABOUT to slip into the lecture room where Gabriel Manout had begun his talk when she felt a tap on the shoulder.

"Excuse me, Miss. The inspector would like to ask you a few questions."

"Me?" Holly looked at the constable in surprise. "Why me?"

"You were present when the body was discovered, Miss. It's just a formality." The constable smiled, gesturing for Holly to precede him.

The police had commandeered Lily O'Connor's office, Holly noticed, reading the sign on the closed door. She glanced at the constable.

"Inspector Plummet will be ready in a minute, Miss."

As he spoke, the door opened and Rob emerged, his face at its most impassive. He was followed by a short, stout man wearing a brown suit.

"Well, Tucker, thanks for your time. I think we'll have this wrapped up very quickly." The short man gave a tight smile. "Enjoy your holiday."

Rob nodded, then caught sight of Holly. A small frown crossed his face and he half-turned towards the other officer, who produced a supercilious smile.

"Ah, you must be Miss Holly Gold, the fourth member of the group that discovered the body."

Holly nodded. "Yes, but I don't think I can tell you any—"

"If you don't mind, I'll be the judge of that. Come with me, please." Inspector Plummet gestured towards the doorway.

Holly glanced at Rob. He nodded. "Go on, Holly. I'll wait in the conservatory for you."

"Miss Gold." Inspector Plummet sounded impatient now.

Holly followed the inspector into the large office where a constable waited.

"Sit down." Inspector Plummet waved Holly into a chair, then sank into the seat behind the desk. "Before we begin, let me just say that your relationship with Inspector Tucker is entirely irrelevant and will gain you no special treatment."

Holly blinked. "I never thought it wou—"

"Now. Tell me about the body. How did you come to find it? Why did you go to that particular part of the garden?"

"We were with Mr. Santorini, and during the conversation it came up that he knows my grandfather. He wanted to give me some cuttings from a frangipani tree to take back to him, so he took us to the trees."

Inspector Plummet folded his hands over his stomach, leaning back in his chair. "He wanted to give you frangipani cuttings?"

"Yes. You see, my grandfather is a horticulturist. He maintains the—"

"Have you ever been to that part of the garden before?"

"No. This is my first visit to Turtle Island and to the perfumery. Mr. Santorini was showing us the—"

"Did you know there is a trail that leads from the perfumery to the trees? Why trek across the entire field?"

Holly stared at him in annoyance. She was getting tired of being interrupted. And what did these questions have to do with the body? "No. I didn't know that. As I said, this is my first visit to the island. We were touring the gardens when the subject of the trees came up and Mr. Santorini took us there."

"I see. Let's move on to the body. You were with Inspector Tucker, Santorini, and... and..."

"Mr. Jeff Graham," the constable in the room murmured.

"Yes. Graham. And you were all together when you found the body?" Inspector Plummet asked.

Holly nodded. The inspector knew all this. He'd already questioned the others. Why ask her again?

"Did Santorini seem surprised?" Inspector Plummet leaned forward.

"Surprised? Well, he was sick, so I'd say he was shocked and horrified."

"And you?"

Holly suppressed the urge to roll her eyes at the line of questioning. "Was I sick? No. Was I surprised? Yes, Inspector, I was very surprised to find a dead man under a frangipani tree."

A small choking sound, hastily covered with a cough, came from the constable in the corner.

The inspector glared at her. "Had you seen this person before?"

"Not that I know of. But he was face-down on the ground. Once Inspector Tucker realized the man was dead, he told us all to move away. I never saw a face."

There was a knock on the door. Sergeant Frampton stuck his head in the room. "We've got an ID, Inspector."

Inspector Plummet frowned. "From whom?"

"Ms. Susan Hill."

Holly's eyes rounded in surprise. "Oh wow. Was it really her cousin like she thought?" she blurted without thinking.

"I beg your pardon?" Inspector Plummet turned his glare on Holly. "What do you know of this, Miss Gold? You've just told me you didn't know the man. How do you know he was Ms. Hill's cousin?"

"I *didn't* know him," Holly said. "But Susan Hill came up to me earlier to ask me if—"

"Now, look here, Miss Gold. I'm well aware that in prior cases on Hibiscus Island you've been allowed to poke around in things that are none of your concern, but I do not allow civilian interference in my cases."

"No, but you just asked me—"

The inspector held up a hand. "Don't argue, Miss Gold. Sergeant Frampton, who is the victim?"

The sergeant cleared his throat, flicking a glance towards Holly. "Uh, sir, perhaps it would be better—"

"Don't waffle, Sergeant. Who is the victim?" Inspector Plummet repeated in testy tones.

"Yes sir. A Mr. Jonathan Dickenson, sir. Arrived on the flight from Hibiscus Island yesterday morning and checked into the Fire Drake Inn. We've confirmed that with the receptionist, sir. She said he left the inn yesterday some time in the afternoon and, as far as she knows, didn't return."

"Flight from Hibiscus Island?" The inspector's head swung back to Holly. "When did you arrive here, Miss Gold?"

Holly leaned back in her chair. "On the morning flight from Hibiscus Island. Yesterday."

The inspector's eyes narrowed. "The same flight as the victim, huh?"

"There's only one flight a day, Inspector, so yes."

"And yet, you still claim you never met him?"

Holly drew in a deep breath. "It was a full flight, Inspector. Loaded with tourists and holidaymakers. There were tons of people on that plane I didn't know."

"Huh." Inspector Plummet scowled first at Holly then at the sergeant. "Well? Is there something else, Sergeant? Spit it out, man. Spit it out."

This time, the sergeant didn't hesitate. "Yes sir, we have the medical examiner's preliminary report. She says death occurred within the last twenty-four hours. Anywhere between two o'clock in the afternoon and eight o'clock at night. Injury caused by a smooth, hard object. The victim could have been struck on the head or he could have fallen and hit something, although Doctor Shaw thinks the position of the injury would make that difficult. She'll have more information after she's done a more thorough examination. Inspector Tucker and I had a quick look at the scene earlier, of course, but didn't see anything resembling such an object, so I've got constables searching the area again now."

The inspector's face reddened. "Sergeant Frampton! That was confidential information!"

"Sorry, sir. You did tell me to spit it out, sir." Sergeant Frampton spoke in deferential tones, his face wooden.

Biting her lip in an effort not to laugh as the inspector sputtered, Holly cleared her throat, redirecting his attention to her. "Am I free to go, Inspector? Or do you have any more questions for me?"

Inspector Plummet glowered. "No. You can go. Leave your name and address with the constable. And don't leave the island. Jones, see her out. Sergeant, you stay here."

9

Holly was still grinning when she arrived in the conservatory. Scanning the room, she located Rob at a small table and hurried across to him.

"So!" She sank into the chair opposite him. "Truthfully, what's your opinion of Inspector Plummet?"

Rob gave an imperceptible sigh, holding up his teacup. "Want some? Mr. Manout's lecture should be finishing any minute, but you can beat the crowd if you're quick."

"You're avoiding the topic." Holly smirked at him. "Want to know what I think?"

"Not really." Rob took a sip of his tea. "There's a certain etiquette involved here. I can't discuss the way a fellow police officer handles his case. Especially not with a civilian."

Holly's smirk widened. "Well, I can tell you this. He's *much* more forthcoming than you were in our first case."

"What do you mean?" Rob's eyes narrowed. He put his teacup back on the table with a decisive clink. "Forthcoming in what way, exactly?"

"Well, for one thing, I know who the dead body is."

Holly held up her hand as Rob opened his mouth. "I also know what time he died and how he died. Between two and eight and head injury caused by a smooth object that might or might not have been deliberate."

Rob stilled. "Inspector Plummet did *not* tell you all that."

"No. But Sergeant Frampton said it all in front of me." At Rob's expression, she added, "Oh, he tried to suggest he should wait until I wasn't there, but Inspector Plummet interrupted and ordered him to 'spit it out.'" Holly giggled when Rob closed his eyes briefly. "Personally, I think he wanted me to know so I could tell you. Seriously, Rob, what do you think of the Plum? Nobody here seems to have a very good opinion of him."

"I'm not discussing Inspector Plummet's capability with you, Holly," Rob warned.

"Or lack thereof?" Holly giggled again. "Oh, okay, Rob. Don't get all riled up. I won't say anymore."

"And *you're* not to investigate this either. No matter what you might have heard. The sergeant really shouldn't have given all that information in front of you, so you have to keep it confidential. Understood?" Rob leveled a stern look at Holly. "Especially from Jamie. I don't want the Hibiscus Island Detective Club running amok on Turtle Island."

"Well, half the club's not even here, so— Okay, okay, Rob. I'm just joking. I don't want to investigate either. We're on holiday, I know."

A burst of applause, followed by the sound of chairs moving and chattering voices, prevented Rob from answering.

"That's the lecture finished," Holly said, jumping up. "I'm going to grab some tea quickly before the hordes descend."

～

JAMIE EYED HOLLY with curiosity as she approached the table. "And just where were *you*? You missed the entire keynote speech."

"Touring the perfumery. And then being interviewed by the police." Holly grinned when Jamie's mouth dropped open. "And you were right. The tour was fascinating. Although I can't quite picture you making perfume in your kitchen."

Jamie ignored the final comment. "Interviewed by the police? How come?"

"Because I was there when the body was found. Oh, it's been identified, by the way. It is Jonathan Dickenson."

"Holly. You agreed—" Rob gave a heartfelt groan as Jamie leaned forward in excitement.

"No! Really? That woman's cousin? The guy Miller sat next to on the plane? Does he know yet?" She looked around. "Where is Miller, anyway? He was right behind us."

"That nice sergeant buttonholed him as soon as he left the lecture room. Said he had some questions for him. They went that way." Natasha, who had accompanied Jamie into the conservatory, pointed across the room.

"Why would they want to talk to Miller? He didn't find the body!" Jamie was indignant.

Holly pursed her lips. "Hmm. What do you want to bet Susan Hill told the police Thomas was supposed to meet with Dickenson yesterday? You told her that, Jamie, remember?" She grinned. "I wonder how much information Thomas will get out of the Plum?"

"What do you mean?" Natasha asked. "Did he tell you stuff?"

"Not on purpose." Catching Rob's eye, she added, "But

I'm not supposed to talk about it. It's none of our business anyway because we're on holiday. Right?"

Jamie eyed Rob with incredulity. "Are you serious? You told her not to talk about it? Oh, come on, Rob. You guys found the body! You must be curious." She rounded on Holly. "Spill. What did you find out?"

Rob interrupted. "I'd much rather you 'spilled' what you learned in Mr. Manout's lecture, if you don't mind."

Jamie rolled her eyes, mouthed a "Tell me later" to Holly, then stood up. "I want some tea first. It looks like there's little sandwiches and things over there. Nat should tell you about the lecture anyway, because, frankly, I felt like I was back in chemistry class for most of it. Anyone want anything? No. Okay, I'll be right back."

As she trotted away, Holly grinned. "Chemistry class?"

Natasha laughed. "It wasn't that bad, but yeah, Manout talked a lot about aroma compounds and formulae. Jamie's eyes kind of glazed over when he started showing diagrams."

Holly giggled. "I wonder if she'll still want to try the DIY perfume thing."

"Aroma compounds, you say?" Rob asked. "I think our young guide mentioned those when she was telling us how perfumes are created. They're part of a flower's fragrance, aren't they?"

Natasha looked impressed. "Very good, Inspector. Yes. Every flower scent is made up of a mix of compounds, and perfumers take those into account when they write their recipes. Basically, every perfume is a mix of aroma compounds, oils, fixatives, and solvents. So, when they were analyzing the perfume from *La Rosa*, they had to isolate all the different parts and then try to reproduce them."

Jamie reappeared just then with two plates of food,

which she deposited on the table. "I got food for all of us just in case you changed your minds. What were you saying about *La Rosa*, Nat?"

"Just that there are quite a lot of different things in the perfume you found on it." Natasha grinned.

"Oh. Yeah, Manout said they found neroli and rose and some other things in it. I can't wait to smell it."

"I'm very glad to hear that, Jamie." Lily O'Connor had approached unnoticed and now smiled at them all. "We're also excited for the unveiling tomorrow. I'm sorry to inter-rupt your tea, but I don't believe you've been formally intro-duced to Gabriel Manout, have you?" Lily gestured to the man beside her. "Gabriel, this young lady is the direct ancestor of the original owner of *La Rosa de España*, Don Miguel Perez Rosales. She's also the one who found the perfume at the wreck, along with Holly here. Natasha worked with the salvage expedition. And this is Inspector Rob Tucker, also from Hibiscus Island."

In his early forties, the perfumer was slimly built, with dark hair beginning to grey at the temples. His neutral grey suit and white shirt was accessorized with an eye—popping bright orange floral-patterned silk tie that made Holly smile at the sight of it.

Gabriel Manout beamed around the table. "It's a plea-sure to meet you all." He shook Jamie's hand, then the others'. "May I join you?" He indicated an empty chair at the table.

"Yes, of course," Jamie said.

As the perfumer settled himself at the table, Lily O'Connor glanced at Rob. "I hate to bother you, Inspector, but Sergeant Frampton would like a word, if it's convenient?"

Rob directed an apologetic smile at the perfumer as he stood up. "Please excuse me."

Holly watched him go with a frown, then returned her attention to the table.

Natasha had leaned forward as the perfumer sat down. "I found your talk very interesting, Mr. Manout."

"Oh please, call me Gabriel. And what part did you find most interesting? I have to say it was prepared for perfumers, not laypeople. I worried that it might be too technical."

Jamie grinned. "Well, to be honest, you lost me with all the chemistry."

"I hadn't realized perfume making was such a science," Natasha added.

"It's not. Well, not exactly," Gabriel responded. "Perfume making is an art, but it's grounded in science. It's important to understand how fragrance compounds react with one another, change molecular shape, how they're affected by heat or pressure, but in the end, the most important thing is the nose." He tapped his own as he spoke. "Creating a fragrance is a complex operation, of course, but it is the nose that makes the final decision as to when it is complete."

Natasha wore a look of interest. "But you have a degree in science, right?"

"I do. I have a degree in chemistry and a graduate degree in scent design and creation. But some perfumers learn on the job, so to speak. There are many paths."

"Natasha's a marine scientist," Jamie informed the perfumer. "That's how she got involved with *La Rosa de España*."

"Indeed? Marine odor is considered one of the green, modern fragrances nowadays."

Holly stared at him in surprise. "You mean like seaweed? You can use that in perfume? Isn't it kind of strong?"

"Oh, there are plenty of strong notes in the perfume business. Musk, civet—I'm sure you've heard of those before, although they're now banned substances, of course. But ambergris is a marine product with quite a distinctive odor. And natural oils can also be found in some algae, or in coastal plants like sea fennel, for instance. I've even attended symposiums where people have reported using seagrass or mangrove. We also use synthetic molecules that reflect the marine environment." Gabriel smiled. "I won't bore you with all the chemistry, but yes, there's considerable interest in using marine natural resources in the perfume business. I'm investigating one myself, as a matter of fact."

Jamie zeroed in on one part of Gabriel's comments. "Ambergris? Doesn't that come from whales? Are you still allowed to use it?"

The perfumer leaned back in his chair. "Well, it depends. Animal raw materials, of course, are banned in the perfume business nowadays, but ambergris is the exception in some jurisdictions. It's expelled naturally by sperm whales, so they aren't harmed at all, then floats around in the oceans and eventually washes up on shore. Usually in New Zealand or Madagascar, interestingly. It's incredibly rare and very expensive."

Holly pursed her lips in thought. "So, apart from the ethical considerations, the perfume industry actually has a vested interest in protecting the whales. More whales, more potential supply of ambergris if you can find it."

"Correct. But it does depend on how ambergris is defined in various countries. In Europe, it's allowed because it's considered a benign byproduct of the whale, but in the USA, where the sperm whale is. an endangered species, it's illegal to trade or possess ambergris." Gabriel shrugged. "Although we're not bound by US law here, we err on the side of caution and don't use ambergris at our perfumery."

Natasha nodded in approval before changing the subject. "One thing I wondered about, Gabriel, is you mentioned that perfumes today are considered male or female. How does that work?"

Gabriel laughed. "Modern fragrances have often differentiated scents into female or male notes, yes. Female fragrances are usually floral or fruity, while male fragrances are often woodsy."

"And which is *Rosa del Mar*?" Holly asked. "Male or female?"

"Ah, well back when *La Rosa de España* sailed the seas, perfumers didn't make a distinction between genders. The bottle you found contained many different notes of both the male and female variety. We used analysis and a 'nose' to determine the key ingredients in the perfume. Then we went through many iterations before we settled on a combination that we think is close to that of the original bottle of scent."

"But you think it's better for women, right?" Jamie pressed.

The perfumer's eyes twinkled. "In these modern times, it will be more suited for women, I believe. You must tell me what you think when it is unveiled tomorrow. It was a fascinating project. Should you find any more fragrances under the sea, please do let me know."

Jamie laughed. "I will."

"Do you use the *enfleurage* technique in your perfumery, Gabriel?" Holly asked.

Gabriel shook his head. "No. As you've no doubt realized, it's both expensive and time-consuming. We use as many natural ingredients as we can—extracting scented oils in a variety of ways—but we also use some synthetics."

"Do you have signature scents at Manout Perfumes?"

"We do, of course, but naturally our recipes are closely guarded. I may sell the rights to a fragrance, but the formula is always mine." The perfumer's eyebrows rose sharply as something caught his attention across the room. "My, my, what's going on over there? Do you think it's to do with the body found in the garden earlier? I heard the man might have been murdered and now it looks like the police have discovered a 'person of interest.' Isn't that what they call it?"

Holly and Jamie's heads swiveled as one.

"What on earth?" Jamie exclaimed, leaping to her feet, Holly right behind her.

Dumbfounded, the two watched as Thomas Miller was escorted out the conservatory doors by a young constable, followed closely by an impassive Sergeant Frampton and a supercilious-looking Inspector Plummet.

10

As speculative conversation broke out around the conservatory, Jamie left the table, heading full speed to the door. With a nod of apology to the perfumer, Holly rushed after her onto the porch, where a frowning Inspector Rob Tucker watched the Turtle Island police and Thomas go down the steps to the parking lot.

"Rob!" Jamie exclaimed, hurrying over to the railing. "Where're they taking Thomas? What happened? Have they arrested him? Why?"

The inspector stepped back a pace, holding up a hand in warning. "Take it down a notch, Jamie. No, he hasn't been arrested. The police just want to ask him a few more questions."

"Like what?" Jamie's voice rose louder, making heads in the conservatory turn their way with interest.

Holly glanced around, catching the worried gaze of Lily O'Connor, who was hovering nearby with her assistant, Cressida. She nudged Jamie.

"Calm down. You're making a scene, and it's not Rob's fault. Come over here. And stop shouting!"

Jamie's glare could have seared concrete, but she allowed herself to be herded into a quiet corner away from curious eyes, where she turned on Rob again.

"What's going on?" she hissed. "What questions could they possibly have for Thomas?"

Rob Tucker sighed, running a hand through his hair. "Jamie—"

"Don't you dare say you can't talk about it!" Jamie snapped, peering over the balcony again to watch Thomas get into the back of the police car.

The inspector kept his voice mild. "I wasn't going to say that. Miller sat next to the victim on the plane and was supposed to meet with him yesterday. Inspector Plummet would like more information and feels this isn't the place to get it."

"More information? Like what?" Holly asked.

Rob shrugged. "I don't know. The inspector hasn't taken me into his confidence."

"Then why did Sergeant Frampton want to talk to you?" Jamie demanded.

Rob hesitated. "He was... uh... clarifying where we all were yesterday."

Jamie's face was like thunder. "I can't believe it! They really think he's a suspect? So have they actually confirmed it was murder?"

"Not yet. And Thomas isn't an official suspect." Rob looked uncomfortable. "Inspector Plummet just wants to—"

"They haven't confirmed anything yet? Then Inspector Plummet is a complete fool!" Jamie was irate and didn't bother to keep her voice down. "And anyway, why on earth would Thomas want to murder a total stranger? He has no motive whatsoever!"

A whistle behind them made Holly turn. Peter

Mackenzie and a worried-looking Natasha stood on the porch.

"So, it really is murder? And Miller's been arrested?" The marine archeologist's eyebrows arched skyward as he watched the police car drive away. "Seriously? Why?"

"He hasn't been arrested." Rob's voice was exasperated. "He's just been taken in for further questioning."

"Yeah, but doesn't that mean they think he's a suspect?" Peter Mackenzie asked.

Jamie's mouth opened, but before she could speak, Natasha turned a look of annoyance upon the man.

"Don't be ridiculous, Mackenzie! Thomas can't possibly be a suspect."

"That's what I said." Jamie found her voice. "But apparently this Plummet feels differently!"

"Would you all stop!" Rob snapped. He heaved an enormous sigh. "This is totally against my better judgement, and highly unprofessional to boot, but I will go to the police station and find out what's going on." He held up a warning hand as Jamie opened her mouth. "And while I do that, you will all take yourselves back to the cottage, start the barbecue, have a glass of wine, and relax! Just. Relax. Okay?"

Holly nodded, taking hold of one of Jamie's arms. Natasha linked her arm through the other, winking at Rob.

"We've got it, Inspector. You do your thing; we'll look after her." She glanced at Peter Mackenzie. "You go find Sage Craft, Mackenzie, and make sure she gets to the Center. She's invited for dinner too. Come on, Jamie, let's go find that wine. And don't worry about Miller. If anyone can look after themselves, it's him."

"I'm not worried," Jamie muttered.

Holly wondered if Jamie even realized how many times she'd said "Thomas" instead of her usual "Miller." Of course she was worried. And that spoke volumes about her feelings for Thomas.

Holly glanced at Natasha. "Nat, perhaps you could round up Mr. Graham and take him in one of the buggies? Rob will be taking his to the police station and I'll take Jamie in mine." She gave Jamie a gentle tug. "Come on, you. Let's get going."

BACK AT THE COTTAGE, Jamie vanished into the bedroom, pleading the need for a shower and change of clothes, leaving Holly and Mr. Graham in the kitchen. The historian gazed after her, the worried expression on his face at odds with his cheerful blue Hawaiian shirt covered in yellow frangipani flowers. He turned to Holly.

"The police don't truly suspect Thomas of murder, do they, Holly? My understanding was that they haven't even had a full medical report yet. How can this inspector have made an arrest already? And what reason would Thomas have to murder this man anyway?"

Holly moved towards the kettle. They would be meeting Natasha near the dock on the grounds of the Ocean Science Research Center in about forty-five minutes, so there was time for a cup of tea.

"We've all been asking the same questions." She held up a mug. "Want a cup, Mr. Graham?"

"Yes, please. That would be lovely." His brow still furrowed, the historian sat down at the table. "When I spoke to the police, they only wanted to know what I'd seen when we found the body. Which was very little, actually. Rob shooed us all away pretty quickly. What made them focus on Thomas, I wonder?"

Holly placed teabags in two mugs, then rooted around in the small fridge for snacks. Finding some chocolate chip cookies left, she piled them on a plate and slid it onto the table.

"I think Susan Hill told the police that Thomas had met her cousin. The victim," she clarified when Mr. Graham frowned in confusion.

While the kettle boiled, she filled the older man in on everything Sergeant Frampton had said. He nodded in comprehension.

"So, Susan Hill is the cousin of this poor dead man, Jonathan Dickenson. And she says they were supposed to have a meeting yesterday and he didn't show up. And from this the police suspect murder? It seems to be a very thin reason to me. Surely Rob doesn't think this."

"Rob's not involved in this investigation." Holly's voice was dry. "But you're right. He wouldn't have jumped to conclusions like this. Inspector Plummet is... different."

Mr. Graham nodded. "Did this Susan Hill tell you what time the meeting was?"

Holly shook her head, sliding into a seat across from Mr. Graham with two full mugs. She pushed his cup of tea towards him and took a cookie from the plate. "No. But it must have been earlier than four thirty, because that's when Thomas was supposed to meet him, I think. Remember he said he wouldn't be going to dinner with us and then he turned up after all?"

"Presumably, then, the man was dead by that time, since he didn't attend his meeting with Thomas." Mr. Graham nodded in thought as he chewed a cookie. He swallowed his mouthful. "We got to the restaurant at six thirty. How long did Thomas wait for Mr. Dickenson? And where did he wait? Do you know?"

Holly paused. "Hmm. Well, Thomas mentioned an inn. He said he waited for about thirty minutes and then wandered around a while. He told Jamie and me that he explored the perfumery a bit, saw Lily O'Connor and some others, and then made his way to the restaurant. He was there when we arrived."

Mr. Graham frowned. "And you said the sergeant told Inspector Plummet that the time of death was likely between two and eight?"

"Yes. Oh." Holly froze with her cup halfway to her mouth. "Oh, I see what you're saying. That could put Thomas on the scene at the time of death! But still! That doesn't prove the man was murdered! I think Plummet is jumping the gun for sure."

Mr. Graham nodded soberly. "Agreed. But should it turn out to be murder, then Thomas could be a suspect. It might be better not to mention this to Jamie just now though. Perhaps wait to see what our good inspector can find out first."

The sound of a bedroom door opening made Holly nod in quick and fervent agreement before changing the subject. By the time Jamie entered the kitchen, Holly and Mr. Graham were earnestly discussing whether they could squeeze in a visit to Azalea Village to view the supposedly stunning collection of plants that grew there.

SAGE CRAFT WAS RELAXING in a chair watching Natasha and Peter Mackenzie argue over how to grill the burgers when Holly, Mr. Graham, and Jamie arrived at the barbecue area.

It was a grassy space with mangrove trees lining the edge of the water and easy access to a floating dock. A stone barbecue sat on one end of a paved patio outfitted with a teak table and chairs, as well as a selection of outdoor seats arranged around a firepit. Adjoining the area was one of the cottages which were rented to interns or visiting scientists, the small verandah of which held a cooler full of sodas.

"Help yourselves," Peter Mackenzie said, gesturing towards the cooler before he batted Natasha's hand out of the way. "Leave the burgers alone, Nat! If you want to help, go get the rolls from the kitchen. Jeff, come over here and make yourself useful."

"I'm not much good with a barbecue," Mr. Graham warned, wandering closer.

Peter Mackenzie grinned. "Just keep me company, then. Male solidarity and all that, you know."

Natasha made a face at them. "Fine. I'll go get the rolls. But I'll have you know that I'm an expert at grilling!"

Sage smirked. "Oh, let the men do it, Nat. Why work if you don't have to?" She twirled her glass of wine before taking a sip, then stretched out her legs with a sigh of contentment. "This is lovely."

"Want to give me a hand, Holly?" Natasha asked. "There're just a couple of things to bring out." She glanced around. "Where's Jamie gone?"

Holly pointed to the dock. Jamie was standing on the edge, peering into the water. As they watched, she sat down, dangling her legs over the edge.

Natasha frowned. "Is she okay? She's not still worrying about Thomas, is she? Have you heard from Rob, by the way?"

Holly shook her head as she followed Natasha inside. "He hasn't messaged me, so I'm going to assume there's nothing to be concerned about. The best thing for us to do is act normally. It'll drive Jamie crazy if we tiptoe around her."

"Gotcha." Natasha nodded, opening the fridge to pull out a huge bowl of potato salad. "It's kind of handy no one's staying in this place right now. We've all been using it to store stuff for barbecues. There're plates and cutlery on the counter as well, if you don't mind grabbing them. Oh, and the potato chips. Don't forget those. I'll bring the wine in a minute."

Outside, the sky was turning dark orange and red as the sun set over the ocean. The science center was located on a tiny peninsula on the north shore of Turtle Island, affording a fabulous view not only of the sun slowly disappearing into a dark purple ocean, but also of the towering, almost primeval mountains that ranged down the middle of the island.

After depositing the plates on the table, Holly poured herself a soda, then settled into a chair beside Sage with a sigh of pleasure. The Juniper islander smiled at her.

"It's gorgeous here, isn't it?"

Holly nodded. The gentle splash of waves against the shore and the cheeping of the whistling frogs that began to emerge as the sky gradually darkened created an ambience of serenity.

"Beautiful sunset tonight. Is Jamie still down on the dock?"

"Yes." Sage hesitated. "I hadn't realized she and Thomas were an item."

"They're not." Holly grimaced when Sage raised a skeptical eyebrow. "Well, not officially. They've been dancing around each other for months, but neither seems ready to make the first move toward being a... a real couple, I guess. Becky and I have given up on them."

Sage smiled. "How is Becky? Is she still feeling ill?"

"Oh, she's had a rotten pregnancy," Holly said with feeling. "Poor thing. She's been sick the whole time. That's why she's not here. She said she couldn't bear the thought of a flight, and perfume would just turn her stomach. She only has a couple of months to go now though."

"And Myrtle? How is she?"

Holly grinned. Myrtle Collier, an energetic and rather bossy septuagenarian, was the undisputed leader of Hibiscus Island society and highly involved in every event on the island. Sage had met her at the annual quilt expo in January.

"She's fine. We have our Annual Exhibition coming up on Hibiscus. Sort of like a county fair, you know, and naturally Myrtle's in charge. Jamie did invite her to come along, but she said she didn't trust her committee to get the job done without her." Holly rolled her eyes. "There's always a theme for the exhibition, you see, and this year's is a bit of a problem."

When Sage looked puzzled, Holly's grin widened. "This year, all the entries in the exhibition—food, jams, quilts, handcrafts, whatever—have to be related to passionflowers."

Sage blinked. "Um... Isn't that a little challenging?"

"Yep. People have been complaining non-stop. As I said, Myrtle has a real problem on her hands." Holly leaned back with another sigh of contentment. "It really is lovely here. So peaceful."

She spoke too soon. The quiet of the evening was suddenly shattered by loud frenzied barking.

Holly jumped wildly at the noise, spilling her soda as she jerked around to see what was happening. Around the corner of the cottage raced two large brown-and-white boxer dogs.

Barking loudly, they galloped on to the patio, one leaping at Natasha, who squealed as she grabbed its paws, trying to keep it away from her face. The other skidded to a stop, looked around as if deciding who to grace with its attention, then gave a loud woof and charged toward Holly.

Before she could react, she found herself buried beneath sixty pounds of determined boxer.

11

_____

"Ewww! Get off me!" Holly tried to defend her face from the slobbering tongue as Sage jumped up to help.

"Charlie! Bailey! Down, girls! Down, I say!" An emphatic bellow stopped both dogs in their tracks. For about five seconds. Then they resumed their onslaught on the humans they had chosen.

An elderly man, about Mr. Graham's age, rushed over to Holly, grabbing the boxer by her collar. "Charlie! Stop that! Down! Sit! Stay! Oh, for goodness' sake, stop it, I say!"

Huffing and puffing, he pulled the excited, wriggling boxer away from Holly. "I'm so sorry! They're still young and woefully ill-mannered. I should have had them on their leashes, but I didn't think anyone was down by the dock."

Peter Mackenzie had corralled the other dog by now and was holding it firmly by its collar. "They'll settle down in a minute, Callum." He directed a compelling look at the boxer, saying firmly, "Sit, Bailey!"

The dog plopped her hindquarters on the ground imme-diately, her tongue lolling out of her mouth. Her dark-brown eyes looked like they were laughing as her body continued to wiggle even in a sitting position.

Holly glanced down at her pink t-shirt, grimacing at the dog slobber and paw marks that covered it, then looked up to see Sage trying desperately not to laugh. She gave a rueful smile.

"Oh well, I never liked this shirt that much anyway." She eyed the boxer, who was still panting and grinning. "Well, you're a fine excuse for a dog, aren't you?"

The man holding the dog rushed into speech again. "I am so sorry, my dear. I had no idea you were down here or I'd never have let them go. They have absolutely no boundaries whatsoever."

In his late sixties or early seventies, with white hair and a bushy beard, he resembled a slim athletic Santa Claus in his red plaid shirt and khaki trousers. Anxious brown eyes peered at Holly through round glasses.

"Are you okay?"

"I'm fine." Holly grinned as she brushed ineffectively at her shirt. "My Gramps has a boxer, so I know exactly what they're like. Mind you, Roxie is old now, so she's slowed down a lot, but when she was young, she was just like these two. You said their names are Charlie and Bailey? They're gorgeous."

"Well, that's very generous of you." The man looked down at Charlie. "You hear that, you reprobate? You're forgiven." He smiled at Holly. "I'm Callum Stewart. It's a pleasure to meet you, Miss...?"

"Holly Gold." Holly shook hands with him. "And this is Sage Craft."

"Delighted." Callum kept a firm grip on the eager boxer as he shook Sage's hand as well.

"Callum is the director here at the Ocean Science

Research Center," Peter Mackenzie said before glancing down at Bailey. "Are you going to behave now? You are? Okay."

He let go of the collar but kept his hand near, ready to grab it again if need be. Bailey looked up at him in an assessing way, then sighed and stayed sitting. She knew who the boss was.

"Holly's here for the unveiling of the new perfume at Plumeria, Callum," Peter continued. "And you already know this fellow, don't you?"

The director turned around, catching sight of Mr. Graham. A smile lit his face. "I certainly do. Jeff Graham, how are you? How's the accommodation? I went by the cottage earlier to try and find you, but you must have been at the perfumery still. How'd your talk go?"

"I'm afraid it was eclipsed by later events." Mr. Graham gave a rueful smile.

Callum Stewart looked puzzled. "Later events?"

"Yes. Haven't you heard? Holly and I found a dead body today."

"A dead—!" The director's mouth dropped open. "Good heavens. What happened?"

"That's what we'd like to know too." Having heard the commotion, Jamie had come running from the dock. Now she sank into a chair beside Holly's and held out her hand to one of the dogs. Charlie immediately trotted over, resting her head on Jamie's lap to be stroked.

"This is Jamie White." Peter continued with the introductions, even as he turned back to the grill to flip the hamburgers. "*La Rosa de España* was her ancestor's ship, Callum."

Callum Stewart eyed Jamie with interest. "Ah yes. Now that's a lovely dive site, isn't it? I've seen photos of some of the artifacts from the ship. A fascinating project." He hesitated. "Wasn't there a murder or some such thing connected with that ship? I seem to remember reading something recently."

Natasha placed two bottles of wine on the table. "You'll stay for dinner, won't you, Callum? We've got plenty." As the director nodded, a pleased look on his face, she continued, "Yes, there were two murders on Hibiscus because of the ship. Holly and Jamie helped solve them, actually. You know, you really should see if you can find out what happ—"

"No." Holly held up a hand. "Absolutely not. Inspector Plummet doesn't want anyone poking around. He made that quite clear."

"Plummet? What's he got to do with..." Callum Stewart's voice trailed away. "Oh. Oh dear. That's right. I forgot. Inspector Moore's on holiday, isn't he? Hmm. Well, that's unfortunate."

"Tell me about it." Jamie's voice was curt. "He's already arrested a friend of ours."

As Callum's mouth dropped open in astonishment at this statement, Holly sighed.

"Thomas hasn't been arrested, Jamie."

"Have you heard from Rob yet?" Natasha asked, inserting a corkscrew into the top of a wine bottle. "Blast it. I hate these things. I can never get the cork out. Oh, thanks, Sage." As Sage removed the bottle from her hand, competently popping it, Natasha continued. "I would have thought they'd be back by now. They know we're down here, right?"

Holly nodded just as both boxers stiffened, then launched into a volley of barks again. Rob and Thomas rounded the cottage, pausing when they saw the dogs.

"It's okay. They're just loud," Peter Mackenzie called. "Bailey. Charlie. Settle down."

Grumbling, the dogs settled back into place. Charlie nudged Jamie's hand insistently, asking to be petted.

Jamie's face had lit up with relief when she saw Thomas, but now she smoothed out her expression. "Well, finally. About time you two got here."

Thomas grinned. "Nice to see you too, White. Is that wine, Natasha? I could seriously do with a glass. Or a beer, if you have it."

"No beer, sorry." Natasha poured a full glass and handed it to the journalist who took it with a nod of thanks before collapsing into a chair at the table. "So, what happened? We're all dying to know. You've obviously not been arrested, which is good."

The journalist rolled his eyes. "Well, if that disaster of a Plummet had his way, I'd be languishing in a prison cell right now. What an idiot." Thomas took a sip of wine before gesturing towards Rob. "You can thank our inspector here—and the good Sergeant Frampton, of course—for my release. Whatever they said convinced the perfidious Plummet that he didn't have enough evidence to charge me with anything." He grinned at Jamie. "Like how I used that word, White? Perfidious?"

A small smile quirked at the edge of Jamie's mouth. "'Pernicious' or 'pigheaded' might be a better choice."

"Or pompous," Holly added as Thomas laughed outright at Jamie's comment. "He's certainly that."

Rob sighed. "Can I have a glass of that as well, Nat? I have a feeling I'll be needing it."

"So, what's the deal?" Natasha asked, pouring Rob's wine. "What'd they ask you?"

Peter Mackenzie turned around from the barbecue. "Hold the conversation for a bit, will you? Burgers are ready. Everyone, grab a plate and load up."

～

THOMAS SWALLOWED the last piece of his burger, shaking his head when Nat offered more potato salad. "I'm stuffed."

"Me too." Holly wiped her mouth with a napkin, leaning back with a small groan. "I ate way too much. That was delicious, Nat."

"Yes, well now that everyone's pleasantly full—and before I bring out dessert, which is just fruit salad, by the way—how about you fill us in on what happened, Thomas?"

By common consent, they had avoided the topic of Thomas's incarceration during the meal, but now Nat directed an enquiring look across the table. "I'm dying of curiosity."

"Oh, Plummet just wanted to know how I met Dickenson, what we talked about on the plane, and why I was supposed to meet him yesterday." Thomas looked mildly disgusted. "The man's a nincompoop." He glanced at Rob. "Sorry, Inspector, but your colleague is the quintessential bumbling policeman in a book. How on earth he got promoted to inspector is a minor mystery all its own."

Rob sighed. "You antagonized him deliberately, Miller."

Thomas grinned. "Now, the good sergeant, on the other hand, is a smart cookie. I could see him wincing in the corner every time the Plum said something idiotic. Poor guy."

"Sergeant Frampton is an exemplary officer. I'm quite sure he didn't wince." Rob's voice held mild reproval.

"Uh-huh. I get it. You have to be discreet, Inspector. But, come on, even you have to admit Plummet's incapable of solving this."

"No comment."

Thomas's smile widened. "As I said, not a hope of solving it. So, guess what that means?"

"I think it means the Hibiscus Island Detective Club has a new case," Jamie said, grinning when Thomas gave her a thumbs-up of approval.

"It certainly does not!" Rob straightened abruptly in his seat, his expression severe. "Now, you listen to me, all of you." He glared around the table before zeroing in on Thomas. "Don't mess about in things that don't concern you!"

The two dogs sprawled near the firepit raised their heads, ears pricking at Rob's tone.

Thomas smirked. "Don't agitate the dogs, Inspector." He sobered abruptly. "Seriously though, it *does* concern me. The man's incapable. He hasn't even received confirmation that Dickenson was murdered—he could have just fallen and whacked his head, you know—and yet he's already focused that pitiful stunted organ he calls a brain on me. I mean, why bother investigating at all when you could just arrest someone? If I don't 'mess about' as you call it, I'll find myself back in that police station in a heartbeat, likely in a cell. The man's that dumb! Come on, Tucker, you know it as well as I do!"

Callum Stewart, who had been listening to the conversation in confusion, interrupted. "I understood you were a journalist, Mr. Miller. Are you a private investigator as well?"

"Investigative reporter." Thomas grinned at the director before jerking his chin toward Jamie. "The detective club is run by Jamie and Holly, with a little help from some friends."

As Callum's head swiveled in their direction, Holly sighed. "It was a childhood thing."

"But we've helped solve a couple of cases on Hibiscus

Island." Jamie sounded smug. "Even our inspector here has to admit that. Right, Rob?"

"You've been interfering pains in the neck is what you've been." Rob rubbed the back of his neck.

"You know, you could help." Jamie raised a pointed eyebrow. "Sergeant Frampton likes you. He'd probably tell you anything you wanted to know."

"It's not my case." Rob kept his voice mild with an effort. "It would be unprofessional in the extreme for me to get involved."

"Exactly. It's not your case, so you can't actually tell us what we can and can't do." Jamie pursed her lips as a thought occurred to her. "In fact, this isn't even your jurisdiction, so basically, right now, Rob, you're a civilian like us." She shrugged. "But if you don't want to help, that's fine."

"Oh, come on, Jamie," Holly protested. "That's unfair. Rob can't just—"

"It's okay, Holly. I can speak for myself." Rob's eyes narrowed. "You're quite correct, Jamie. With regards to this case, I am a civilian. And, moreover, one who's on holiday. So, unless my assistance is requested by the officer in charge of the case, I will not be making a nuisance of myself. And I would strongly suggest you do the same."

There was a moment of silence. Thomas and Jamie exchanged speculative glances, then grinned in unison.

Rob rolled his eyes. "So help me, I don't know why I even waste my breath trying to talk sense into you lot."

"Yeah, best just to go with the flow, Inspector," Thomas agreed. "Besides, it would be unprofessional of me not to get involved. That's what we newspaper people do. We find news." His eyes sought Jamie's. "And I have a sneaking suspicion that this death is going to be big news."

Jamie's smile matched his in anticipation.

"Uh-huh." Rob sighed. "I'll just say this, then. Don't put yourself in dangerous situations. And don't provoke Plummet." He leveled a stern look at Holly. "That means you too, Holly. I didn't bring a lot of money with me. I don't want to have to bail anyone out of jail."

Holly scowled, affronted. The nerve. After she'd tried to support him too!

Peter Mackenzie gave a snort of amusement. "Seems you know them pretty well, Inspector."

"To my sorrow, I do. Give me a refill, Mackenzie." Rob held his wine glass out to the archaeologist.

12

_____

"Oh good, you're up." Jamie beamed as Holly staggered into the kitchen. She picked up her pen, tapping it on the paper in front of her as she sipped her morning tea. "Right. Let's recap, shall we?"

"Not now," Holly groaned. "I want a cup of tea. And then I want a shower, so I look less like the walking dead. I don't know how you can be so bouncy in the morning. It's disgusting."

Jamie grinned. "You do look a little... uh... bedraggled. Have you even brushed your hair yet? Just as a matter of interest."

Holly eyed her friend with something approaching dislike. Jamie's outfit of a teal green t-shirt and slim jeans somehow managed to look chic instead of just casual. She wore her long hair in a simple braid and her brown eyes were bright with anticipation.

"It's not fair. You went to bed at the same time as me, and I feel like something the cat dragged in this morning, while you're all bright and chipper." Holly scowled down at her plaid pajama bottoms and grey sleep shirt as she flicked the kettle on.

"I'll make your tea and put it in the bedroom for you. Go get your shower before the guys get back. They've gone to get the cars from the charging stations." Jamie paused. "There may not be any more hot water though. I think Mr. Graham said his shower was a little cool."

Holly groaned again. "Great. Just great." She trailed out of the kitchen ignoring Jamie's laughter.

The cold water, while it made Holly squeal, had the salutary effect of waking her completely. By the time she dressed, combed her red-gold curls into a semblance of tidiness, flung on jeans and t-shirt, and finally gulped down her tea, she felt more human.

She found everyone in the kitchen. Leaning against the counter, casually handsome in khaki trousers and a. blue polo shirt, Rob watched Mr. Graham pack a bag with fins and a dive mask.

"Where are you going?" Holly asked the historian, surprise etching her voice. "I thought you were coming with us."

Mr. Graham smiled. "No. Peter Mackenzie has kindly invited me—and Callum Stewart—to visit a wreck site, so I've taken him up on his offer." The historian's eyes gleamed. "It's an 1881 iron-hulled steamer that's become encrusted with fire coral, he says, but you can still follow the propeller shaft the entire way. The rudder and boilers are still intact as well, apparently."

"Oh. Well, that sounds nice."

Holly had no idea what a propeller shaft was—or why it would be exciting—but clearly Mr. Graham thought it was wonderful.

"Yes, Natasha is picking me up any minute, so if you'll excuse me, Holly, I have to collect a few things still."

As the elderly man bustled out of the room, Rob smiled at Holly. "Good morning."

Holly looked down her nose at him in disdain. "Huh."

Rob winced. "Ouch. Are you still mad? I did say I was sorry."

"It'll take more than an 'I'm sorry,' Inspector." Holly kept her face absolutely straight, but her eyes twinkled.

Rob grinned. "'Inspector,' is it? I must really be in the bad books. Would it help it I said it again?"

"It might."

Rob took hold of Holly's hands. "I'm sorry I implied you might put yourself in a dangerous situation. I'm sorry I implied you might provoke a police inspector. I'm sorry I said I didn't want to bail you out of jail."

Holly pressed her lips together, trying not to smile. "Are you sorry you laughed when you saw what that dog did to my shirt?"

"I am. Deeply sorry." Rob paused. "And may I just say, you look lovely today, Miss Gold."

"Humph. Well then, Inspector, I suppose you're forgiven." Holly finally allowed herself to smile as he bent down to kiss her.

"Aww. So sweet."

Thomas and Jamie were smirking from ear to ear.

"You guys are just so cute!" Jamie laughed when Holly made a face at her. "If you're ready, Holls, we can leave for the Wimsey plantation any time."

"What about Nat?" Holly asked. "I thought she was coming too."

"No, she said something about a crisis with an intern.

Said she'll catch up with us later. She's going to try and get to the perfumery for the unveiling this afternoon but can't guarantee it. Mackenzie's promised to have Mr. Graham there though." Jamie picked up her phone and shoved it into her light backpack. "So, are you ready? Let's go check out the tea."

~

THE WIMSEY TEA plantation was about a thirty-minute drive away. As the road wound up into the mountains, Holly's head turned from side to side in mounting appreciation of the breathtaking scenery. Every now and then she begged Rob to slow down, hanging out of the window to take photos on her phone. Ahead of her, she could see Thomas doing likewise, although Jamie didn't appear to slow her driving in the slightest, judging by the way the journalist was bouncing around.

The lower slopes of the mountains were divided into pastures, each one bordered in six-foot tall hydrangea hedges that, in the summer, would turn vibrant blue. Curious black-and-white cows peered over the hedges as the little neon-orange cars zoomed by.

As they turned a corner, a white house with a red roof appeared, almost buried in pink and magenta azaleas, interspersed with tall spikes of gladioli in a variety of colors. Behind it, fields sloped down to the dark blue sea, where a tiny village nestled on a headland.

Jamie stopped in a pull out marked Scenic Viewpoint, Rob following close behind.

"Wow!" Holly breathed, getting out of the car to approach the fence at the edge of the cliff.

The others joined her, all of them staring out at the panoramic view below them. Sheer cliffs dropped down to a patchwork of fields surrounded by dark green forest. A bright blue lake glistened like a jewel in the valley, while more hills rose up around it. Behind the hills, the sea stretched out to the horizon, sparkling in the sunlight.

Rob consulted a guidebook. "That must be Twilight Lake. There's supposed to be a fantastic hiking trail around it. And, according to this, there's a hot spring waterfall nearby."

"Really?" Jamie looked intrigued. "That would be fun to visit if we have time."

Holly took the book to read through the description. "It looks gorgeous. Maybe we could go back that way. Oh, and there are Australian tree ferns growing there! That's kind of unusual. I'd love to see those. And ginger lilies too. Oh, we definitely have to stop there."

Thomas glanced at his watch. "We won't have time today. Not unless we skip the tea plantation. We have to be at the perfumery by two o'clock, right?"

"Yeah." Jamie nodded. "They're unveiling *Rosa del Mar* at three, but their perfumer is giving a little talk before that happens."

"I'd like to have lunch before that," Thomas said.

"Well, maybe we can go to the lake tomorrow," Holly suggested.

"Maybe," Jamie agreed. "Come on. Let's go see the tea."

Climbing back into the little electric car, Holly flipped through Rob's guidebook.

"Wimsey tea plantation... Hmm. It's been in operation since— Wow. 1883. Pretty cool. Hmm. Family owned. It says here the humid and mild climate plus acidic and volcanic soil has allowed for the production of green and black tea. They harvest tea between April and October. Well, that's good. We've come at the right time. Oh, and it's all organic.

Interesting." Holly looked up just in time to see a large sign on the road. "And it looks like we've found it."

As Rob turned onto the narrow, unpaved road that led further up into the hills, Holly's eyes widened at the scene. "Gosh, it almost feels like we're in Peru or somewhere, doesn't it?"

Rows and rows of neatly trimmed tea shrubs stretched across the hills in terraced layers, with some fields laid out in straight lines, while others appeared to be planted in a complex maze pattern.

The road to the factory wound its way up the mountain between the fields, finally opening into a large parking area. Two small cottages sat off to the side behind drystone walls, their verandas draped in magenta bougainvillea that clambered up over the red tiled roofs. Pink, white, and orange azaleas clustered around the white walls, intertwined with clumps of hydrangea not yet in flower.

A sign at the far end of the parking lot, directed visitors to the Wimsey Tea Plantation and Factory, a long, low white building surrounded by hydrangea bushes.

"It must look gorgeous in the summer," Holly remarked, climbing out of the little electric car. "I wonder who lives in the little cottages?"

As she spoke, the door to one of the houses opened. Two small dogs, one black and one golden, raced along the path, barking madly. Holly laughed in surprise.

"Look! They're cavapoos. And that one could be Truffle's twin." She crossed over to the gate. "Hello there. Who are you guys?" Crouching down, she offered a hand for them to sniff. "I have a little dog exactly like you at home," she said to the black curly one.

A laugh from the verandah made Holly look up. She blinked in surprise at the sight of Dr. Miranda Shaw walking toward the gate, looking casual and very unmedical in jeans and a white t-shirt. Her brown hair was pulled into a ponytail and tucked under a red baseball cap.

"That's Earl and Lady Grey." The doctor grinned. "Earl is the golden; Lady is the black curly one. It's Holly, right? I met you at Plumeria yesterday. Did I hear you say you have a cavapoo too?"

Holly smiled as she stood up. "Yes. Her name's Truffle and she's the spitting image of your Lady. They're lovely little dogs, aren't they? Do you live here?"

Miranda opened the gate to let the dogs out. "I do. The plantation belongs to my mom's family." She smiled past Holly. "Hello, Inspector. Nice to see you again. I thought you might be helping with the case."

Rob shook his head as he bent down to stroke one of the dogs cavorting around him.

Miranda made a face. "Ugh. That's a shame. Poor Sergeant Frampton, having to deal with Plummet all by himself. And in a possible murder case at that." Her grey eyes sparkled with mirth at the disapproving look Rob gave her, even as Jamie gave a loud exclamation. "Oops. That was very unprofessional of me to let that slip, wasn't it? Don't frown, Inspector." Miranda grinned at Jamie. "And hello there. We meet again. Jamie, isn't it?"

"That's right. Good memory. And this is Thomas Miller. I don't think you've met, have you? Did you say it's a murder case?"

"Possibly." Miranda grinned as she extended her hand to Thomas. "And no, we haven't met. Although your name's familiar for some reason. Miranda Shaw. Nice to meet you."

"You're the police surgeon, aren't you?" Thomas asked. "Holly said you were the one who examined the body at the perfumery."

"That's me." Miranda snapped her fingers. "I know where I've heard your name. Weren't you in custody yesterday? I'm sure I heard the Plum squawking about cross-examining someone called Miller. Although how he could take a suspect into custody before he'd even read my report is beyond me."

"Cross-examine?" Thomas snorted. "That man couldn't cross-examine a rabbit."

Rob cast his eyes heavenward as Holly giggled.

Miranda gaped at the journalist, then her lips twitched. She burst into laughter. "Oh, I have to tell my dad that. He complains about the Plum all the time! Cross-examine a rabbit!"

Jamie grinned. "You're not impressed with Inspector Plummet, I take it."

"Oh, he's useless. Everyone knows that. It's such a shame Moore's away." Miranda heaved a sigh before continuing, "You know, I've heard of you before. Didn't you guys find a dead body last year? In your garden or something? I'm sure I read about it somewhere. Something to do with a ship?"

"*La Rosa de España*. It was my ancestor's ship." Jamie nodded. "And yes. Someone stuck a sword in the back of a pirate and left him in my garden. You probably saw the story Miller wrote. It kind of went viral in the islands."

Miranda regarded her with greater interest. "A sword in his back? I don't think I've ever come across something like that before." She looked at Rob. "It was your case?"

"Nominally, yes."

Miranda's eyebrows rose in inquiry.

"I have a slight problem with overly enthusiastic citizens on Hibiscus Island," Rob explained. "They have this tendency to... interfere, shall we say."

"Oh, I see." Miranda grinned as Thomas snorted and

Jamie rolled her eyes expressively. "You'd get on well with Inspector Moore. He has similar problems, I believe. Too bad he's hiking somewhere in the Alps." She made a face, then smiled. "But you're here to see the tea, aren't you? Want me to take you around?"

"Oh, we couldn't ask you—" Rob was interrupted.

"That would be great," Jamie said immediately. "If you don't mind."

"Not at all. Let me just put the dogs back inside." She returned the two little animals to the cottage, then trotted back down the path. "Come on, then."

"Did you say this tea plantation belongs to your family, Dr. Shaw?" Thomas asked, falling in alongside the doctor as she started walking toward the factory building.

Miranda grinned. "So formal, Thomas. I'm 'Miranda' to my friends. And yes, my family owns the plantation. My mom's maiden name was Wimsey. And before you ask, no, she isn't related to Lord Peter." Her smile widened when they all laughed. "Ah, you know him. Some people don't get the joke."

"Dorothy Sayers's detective. I love her books," Holly said.

"Me too," Jamie agreed. With a sly grin, she added, "You know she wrote a book called *Busman's Honeymoon*, right? Where Lord Peter has to solve a murder *on holiday*." She emphasized the last two words.

Miranda eyed Rob sideways. "Sounds like your civilians are trying to make a point, Inspector."

"Perhaps we should start our tour," Rob suggested with a smile.

The doctor laughed. "No comment, huh? Okay, then. This way to the tea tour!"

13

The tour of the factory took just under an hour.

"It's like stepping back in time, isn't it?" Holly whispered to Rob at one point, absolutely enthralled. "Look, they're still using nineteenth century machines!"

"I'm impressed they can still repair them," Rob said, eyeing the rolling machines with fascination.

Miranda, obviously very proud of her family's heritage, explained the whole process of making tea, from picking the fresh leaves of the tea shrubs, to rolling, drying, second rolling, polishing, and then on to sorting and packaging.

Pausing at the wooden drying racks, where trays and trays of black tea was laid out to dry, she told them the tea leaves were left to wilt naturally before being rolled and exposed to air to begin the slow process of oxidation, fermentation, and drying.

"The trays let the air pass over and under the leaves, you see."

"It's very hands-on, isn't it?" Thomas marveled, taking photos with his phone. "This will make a great story for the Maritime Moments section. When you think about it, Turtle

Island is doing an amazing job of preserving old techniques. You're doing it with tea, and the Plumeria Perfumery is doing it with fragrances."

Miranda nodded. "We're proud of our business. It's time-consuming, but we take great pride in producing a high-quality product. And there's something kind of meditative about sorting through the dried tea when you're inspecting it." She grinned. "My best friend and I had similar summer jobs growing up here. I spread tea leaves on trays and Lily spread flowers on white fat."

Holly gazed at her in surprise. "Is that Lily O'Connor you mean? The owner of Plumeria?"

"Yeah. Lily did a business degree in college and came back to run her family business. She looks after the perfumery side. Her uncle is in charge of the grounds."

"That's Mr. Santorini, right?" Holly smiled. "He's lovely. And Kat Santorini took us round the perfumery. She said the whole family works there."

"Well, three generations, anyway," Miranda agreed. "One of Lily's cousin's—Jake—works in the grounds as well. Nice to have a family business."

"Is the tea plantation still family run?"

Miranda grinned. "Not by me, but yes. My brother is in charge now. He's probably out in the fields today. It's harvesting season at the moment. Which reminds me, if you come this way, we have tea for sale. You should definitely take some home with you."

In the little shop, Holly eyed the packaged tea with delight. With labels of different colors, the foil packets were emblazoned with the name Wimsey Tea Plantation and then the type of tea. She picked up a bright red package of Wimsey Orange Pekoe.

"I'll get this for Mama. She's a fan of it."

"You know orange pekoe's a grade of tea, not an actual flavor, right?" Miranda asked. "It's a grading system for British black tea, depending on what percentage of the tea has whole leaves compared to broken. It's considered a medium to high quality tea."

"Oh. Well, Mama likes it and that's all that matters. I'll get some for Becky and Myrtle as well." Holly chose another two packets, then fingered a small bowl on another shelf with curiosity. "What do you use this for?"

"That's a mortar and pestle set," Miranda replied. "They're used by some tea aficionados to grind whole tea leaves into a powder. Some people like them for herbal teas. Personally, I'm okay with a teabag."

Having overheard, Thomas hefted one of the bowls experimentally, his eyebrows raising. "It's heavy."

"It's made of granite. We have some marble and wood sets too."

Thomas picked up the pestle, turning it in the bowl with a grating sound. "And people use this for tea, you say? Interesting. I'll add it to my newspaper piece on the plantation."

"There's something called pestle tea," Miranda offered. "People grind nuts, seeds, and tea leaves into a paste, then add freshly brewed tea, usually green or oolong, stir it up, and pour it into a cup. You get a nutritional boost with your morning cuppa. It can take twenty minutes of grinding to make the paste, though."

Thomas had whipped out his phone and was taking notes. "Do you make that here? I saw there was a tasting station over there."

"My mother does it for special tours." Miranda smiled. "She's a real tea enthusiast. I just drink the stuff."

"Yeah, me too." Holly nodded. "Is it okay if we walk through the tea fields, Miranda?"

"Oh sure. Wander to your heart's content. We have thirty-two acres of tea shrubs. It's great for the dogs." Miranda grinned. "Although, my two like running in the passionflowers at Plumeria too. Lily has a whippet, so we have doggy playdates sometimes."

"Oh, Thomas has a whippet too." Holly smiled. "And a pug. And Jamie has a standard poodle."

"What's that? Are you talking about Teddy?" Jamie came up with some packets of tea and pulled out her phone. "Want to see him? Look, this is him helping Maggie at the Hibiscus Inn. He's having a holiday there."

"He's a cutie." Miranda smiled as she handed the phone back. She hesitated a moment, then said, "So, I'm curious about something. Do you guys investigate lots of cases? What I mean is, do you really help the inspector over there?" She nodded towards Rob, who was looking at a variety of different teas.

"Well, I think we've been very helpful," Jamie said at once. "And no matter what Rob says or how much he complains, he actually made us consultants on his first case, you know. It's only lately that he's got stroppy about it. He waffles. One minute he's okay with us helping, the next he's being all stiff and formal. He needs to make up his mind."

"He doesn't *waffle*." Holly was indignant on Rob's behalf. "You put him in a difficult position sometimes. He has to balance being a friend with being a policeman. It's tricky."

"He's the one who said he wanted consultants. He can't take it back whenever he feels like it." Jamie sniffed, ignoring Holly's glare.

Miranda grinned as she watched them. "Well," she drawled, "if you're police consultants, then I guess it's okay if I tell you something."

Jamie's head whipped around. "What?"

"Jonathan Dickenson. The guy found under the frangipani? He was moved there after he was dead."

"Really?"

"He was moved?"

Thomas pursed his lips in speculation. "Well, that changes the situation, doesn't it?"

Rob looked around at the loud exclamations, his eyes narrowing in sudden suspicion.

"Moved from where?" Jamie asked. "And how do you know?"

"Uh, police surgeon, remember?" Miranda pointed to herself. "And another thing—"

"Dr. Shaw, please tell me you're not sharing confidential information about a possible murder case!" Rob interrupted in a pained voice.

"Well, only with qualified consultants." Miranda laughed at his expression. "You can pass this on to Plummet if you want. He refused to listen to me when I tried to tell him. And I can practically guarantee he hasn't read my report."

Rob frowned but didn't say anything.

"But you're the police surgeon." Holly gazed at her in astonishment.

Miranda shrugged. "That's the Plum for you. He never listens to anyone. He knows all."

Thomas snorted.

"You said another thing," Jamie prompted. "Did you find out something else?"

"Yeah." Miranda sobered abruptly, looking at Rob. "And I'm telling *you*, Inspector, because you can make sure it gets passed on properly. Dickenson's body was moved to those frangipani trees. There's no trace of blood on the ground and that head injury would have bled. And I found a couple of interesting things."

Rob's eyes narrowed. "Like what?"

"Well, for one, Dickenson had an abnormally thin cranium." Miranda shrugged. "Mind you, where his head was struck is about the worst place you can get hit on a head, so he would have died anyway from the artery bleed, but he does have a very thin skull."

"Anything else?"

"Someone socked him one right before he died. He had a huge bruise on his jaw."

The inspector frowned. "He couldn't have got that from hitting the ground?"

Miranda shook her head. "No. It's from being punched. Guaranteed. New wound too."

"Well, it would have had to be. He didn't have a bruise on his face on the plane that morning," Thomas confirmed. "I can vouch for that."

"Anything else?" Rob asked.

"I found a frangipani flower inside his shirt collar." Miranda grinned. "And a petal in his hair."

"He was under a frangipani tree," Holly pointed out. "It could have just dropped on him when he was dumped there."

"Yes, probably," Miranda agreed, "but I'm letting you know anyway, Inspector."

Rob nodded absently, thinking.

Thomas's eyes narrowed. "Do you think he could have been killed at the perfumery?"

Miranda sighed. "Maybe. It's the only place near to where he was found." She looked at a now-frowning Rob. "I just want you to know if our own Inspector Moore was here, I'd be keeping my lips tightly buttoned, Inspector. But the fact of the matter is, the Plum is incapable of solving this case. I'm sorry to say it, but he couldn't find a murderer if one stood right in front of him and said, 'Here I am!' Inspector, Lily O'Connor is one of my best friends. She's worried sick about this. If there's to be any hope of finding who killed Jonathan Dickenson, well, someone capable has to investigate."

Everyone looked at Rob.

He sighed. "I'll see what I can do. *If*," he added, "Inspector Plummet is agreeable to having some assistance."

~

HOLLY GAVE a happy sigh as the last of the tea fields disappeared around the corner.

"That was great. I'm really glad we went there."

Rob took his eyes off the road for a second to smile at her. "Me too. Fascinating place. Did you hear Miranda say it's been in her family for twelve generations? Amazing when you stop to think about it."

"Yeah." Holly's phone began buzzing wildly before she could say anything else. As she pulled it out, a dozen texts appeared, all bearing Becky's name—and all bristling with exclamation points.

Holly skimmed through them. Becky Dumont, who was Rob's sister as well as the head librarian of the Bridgeport Library on Hibiscus Island, had found out about the body at the perfumery and was making her opinion known in no uncertain terms.

"What is wrong with all of you?" the first one read.

It was followed in quick succession by:

"How is it possible for any one person to find so many dead bodies?!"

"Is it true Thomas was arrested?!"

"Is Rob helping with the case? Who's keeping an eye on Jamie?!"

"What's this Plummet like? Everyone's talking about him! Apparently, he's useless?"

"Holly! Call me! ASAP! I need to know what's going on!"

"Also, Myrtle is foaming at the mouth because she's not there! She wants you to call her tonight too!"

Holly was giggling by the time she finished reading them. "Your sister's on the warpath," she said to Rob, who had raised an eyebrow. "Word of the murder is out on Hibiscus."

The inspector rolled his eyes. "Of course it is. The grapevine in these islands is the most prolific I've ever seen. How'd Becky find out?"

Holly sent a quick text back, telling her friend she'd call her when they weren't driving down a mountain. Then she added a few tidbits: Thomas was free at the moment but not out of danger yet; Jamie was in ecstasy at having a new case; and how had Becky found out?

Within seconds she had a reply. Holly read it, then grinned. "A quilting Turtle told Myrtle, and Myrtle has informed the whole island. I'll bet that's Caroline Cunningham. Do you remember her from the Quilt Expo? She was very gossipy."

Rob eyed her sideways. "As opposed to just slightly gossipy?"

"Ha ha." Holly typed a few more words to Becky, then leaned forward as the little car in front veered onto a side road. "Where are those two going?"

"Miller found a restaurant he wanted to try," Rob replied, clicking his turn signal to follow. "We can have a bite to eat before going to Plumeria. It'll give you time to call

Becky. Put her mind at ease. She shouldn't be getting stressed right now."

Holly suppressed a smile as Rob's brow furrowed in concern. With his first niece or nephew due in just a few months, the inspector was very protective of his younger sister. Although it drove Becky nuts to have him hovering, Holly thought it was kind of sweet.

As soon as Rob parked the car, Holly hopped out and grabbed Jamie. "Becky wants us to call her. ASAP, she said."

"Ha! I'll bet word of the murder's reached her, right?" Jamie turned to the men. "Go ahead, you guys. Get a table and order drinks. We'll be right behind you."

"Don't get Becky agitated," Rob warned, giving them a stern look.

"Yeah, yeah. Go." Jamie waved them away.

Holly had barely pushed the video call button when Becky's face filled the tiny screen of her phone.

"What on earth is going on over there?" she exclaimed, her brown eyes wide in her tanned face. "Have you really found another dead body? How is that even possible? What happened? Is Rob helping to investigate? Please tell me you're not involved!" She looked at Jamie's face, then gave a heartfelt groan. "Oh no. You are. Myrtle's going to be furious!"

As Jamie and Holly started to laugh at the final remark, Becky glared at them. "It's not funny! You don't have to listen to her. I do! And she's already in a ferment about this blasted Exhibition. It's a good thing you two will be back for it because you *have* to chip in and help. I'm at my wit's end dealing with Myrtle. I'm telling you—"

"Whoa, whoa, whoa," Jamie cut in, still laughing. "Relax, Becks. If you get stressed, Rob's going to have our guts for garters."

"That's a revolting saying!" Becky shuddered, then took a deep breath. "Okay. I'm calm. Fill me in."

The librarian leaned back in her chair in her office on Hibiscus Island, resting her hands on top of her very cute baby bump, now covered in a yellow and pink flowered top. Holly always thought Becky looked a bit like a pixie, with her brown curls and delicate build.

Becky listened to Jamie's summary of what had happened, a frown on her face. "So let me see if I have this straight so far. This Jonathan Dickenson was on your flight and sat next to Thomas. He and Thomas were supposed to meet for drinks, but he didn't show up. Thomas waited a while, wandered around the Plumeria perfumery then met you for dinner. The next day, Holly and Rob found the man dead under a frangipani. This Plummet policeman thinks Thomas did it, but let him go because he has no evidence. And you're afraid he isn't going to look for the real murderer because Thomas is an easy suspect."

At Becky's raised eyebrow, both Holly and Jamie nodded.

"Hmm. Why was Thomas meeting this man?"

Jamie blinked, then looked annoyed. "I don't know. He hasn't actually told us."

"Well, you need to find that out. What did they talk about on the plane? And did Thomas see anything when he was wandering around Plumeria? He was on the scene around the time the murder took place. Maybe he noticed something."

"Huh. Well, he hasn't volunteered anything." Jamie frowned. "Mind you, I haven't asked. Have you, Holls?"

Holly shook her head. "I didn't even think about it. It feels like we've been rushing around like chickens since we got here. And besides, we only got confirmation that it was probably murder today."

"Well, get on with it," Becky said. "I think you need to know more about this Dickenson person. Who was he? Why was he there?"

"Oh, I know that," Holly said. "He was meeting his cousin to talk about her mother's legacy." As Becky raised an inquiring eyebrow, she added, "Susan Hill is the cousin. Olivia Hill is her mother. Apparently, she was pretty famous."

"You could check all that out for us, Becks," Jamie suggested. "Oh, and maybe find out about the other perfumers while you're at it. Gabriel Manout and Sylvie Lestrade. Maybe there's a motive in there somewhere."

"You think they might have something to do with it?" Becky jotted the names down on a piece of paper.

"Well, we spoke to the police surgeon today," Jamie said. "Nice woman. She told us the body was moved after death. It's possible Dickenson may have been killed at the perfumery, and the only people there that day were people who worked there and some guests from the symposium. Miller did say he saw them when he wandered around."

"Huh. What about the owner of the perfumery? What's her name? Anyone else I should check on?" Becky nodded as Holly added Cressida's name and the head gardener's, then directed a severe look at them. "You're both to be careful, do you hear me? Don't do anything silly! No confronting murderers or creeping around in places you shouldn't be. Okay. I'll call or email tonight."

As Becky hung up, Jamie's lips tightened. "It's time to have a little chat with Miller, Holly. Come on."

14

The restaurant Thomas had found was small, cozy, and specialized in seafood. Situated at the edge of a little village on the coast, it boasted a tiny outdoor eating patio that overlooked the sea. A bright pink bougainvillea sprawled over the pergola, shading the teak tables and dappling the grey concrete pavers with shadows. Jamie and Holly found the two men sipping tall drinks while peering at handwritten menus.

"They have octopus. Ever tried it?" Thomas laughed when Holly grimaced.

"No. And I don't want to either. They're intelligent creatures. I definitely don't want to eat one!" Holly pulled out the chair next to Rob, who pushed a menu toward her. "Don't they have sandwiches?"

The inspector indicated a section of the list. "Plenty to choose from. I'm getting fish and chips. It's supposed to be a specialty."

Jamie plopped herself down in her chair, directing a severe look at Thomas.

The journalist blinked. "Now what've I done?"

"It's what you haven't done!" Jamie said. "Somehow, you've neglected to tell us exactly why you were meeting Jonathan Dickenson. What did you guys talk about on the plane? Why was he even going to the perfumery in the first place? Do you know?"

"I was wondering when someone would ask." Thomas shot a sideways look at Rob. "Plummet certainly didn't. I was actually going to say something yesterday at afternoon tea, but if you recall, you told me to go question Lily O'Connor." He held up his hands as Jamie drew in her breath. "Oh, relax, White. I'll talk, I'll talk. As soon as we've ordered, that is." He gestured to the approaching waiter.

Once the waiter left, Jamie raised an eyebrow at Thomas. "Well?"

"Jonathan Dickenson was a journalist on Grand Island. He said he was attending the event because his aunt, Olivia Hill, was a well-known perfumer at one time."

Holly nodded. "Susan Hill told me Gabriel Manout used to work with her, before he set up his own business."

"I think a lot of people did," Thomas said. "From what Dickenson told me, his aunt created some amazing perfumes and people wanted to learn from her." He took a sip of his drink. "To be honest, I don't know much. All he said was he'd found out something that would be a big story. He said he'd be willing to fill me in on the details after he'd confirmed some things. And told me when and where to meet him. I went as a matter of professional courtesy, really."

The journalist shrugged. "People blow up things all the time. You know, make a story sound bigger than it really is. When he didn't show up, I thought perhaps it had turned out to be a dud and he was too embarrassed to admit it."

"But really he was lying dead under a frangipani tree," Jamie said.

Rob shook his head. "Probably not at that point."

The waiter returned carrying their meals and conversation ceased while everyone inspected their plates.

"What's that you got?" Thomas asked Holly.

"Portobello mushroom and goat cheese sandwich." She beamed as she surveyed it. "On homemade gluten-free focaccia too!"

As Rob started to add salt and vinegar to his fish and chips, Jamie returned to his previous comment.

"When you say, 'probably not,' do you mean you think the body was moved much later? Like at night?"

The inspector paused with a french fry halfway to his mouth. A look of resignation, coupled with acceptance of the inevitable, passed across his face before he sighed. "Possibly." He popped the fry into his mouth.

"Why?"

Rob swallowed. "Because there were people around all afternoon. Someone transporting a body would be noticed. Time of death is estimated between two and eight. It's dark just after seven, so I presume that was when the body was moved."

"Exactly what time were you there?" Jamie demanded of Thomas.

"You know, I did tell you all this before. Yesterday morning, before Jeff's talk. But let me recap. I think I left the Fire Drake just before five, then ambled up the road to Plumeria. The Inn's at the end of the main driveway, you know. It took maybe ten, fifteen minutes to walk up. There's a small trail on the side of the road, so you don't have to stay on the main street."

Holly eyed him with curiosity. "How'd you get to the Fire

Drake, anyway? You didn't have one of the buggies, did you?"

"No. I wasn't sure how convivial we would be so didn't want to risk driving." He grinned at Jamie's snort. "Actually, Nat ran me over and then I called a taxi from Plumeria to get to the restaurant."

"Oh, so you actually went inside the perfumery?" Holly asked in surprise. "I didn't know it was open. What time do they close?"

"Normally, at four, but as I also told you yesterday, the perfumers were there. And Lily and Cressida as well, of course."

"Were any of the tour guides there?" Rob asked. "Or gardeners?"

Thomas frowned, thinking. "That young guide—Kat— was setting tables in the conservatory. I saw a gardener with a tub of flowers—I presume for the *enfleurage* room— Oh, and I did see a motorbike going down the road as I was walking up. Someone heading home, I imagine."

"But other than that, you didn't see anyone in the grounds?" Holly asked.

"What? Lurking under the frangipani trees? Not that I remember." Thomas grinned. "They have a lot of those trees. But maybe Rob should check if that trail goes anywhere near where you found the body."

"If Inspector Plummet is okay with that, then yes, I think that's a good idea." Rob glanced at his watch. "We'll need to leave soon if we're going to make it to the presentation. I'd like dessert. Anyone else?"

"Me. But are you really going to talk to Plummet, Rob?" Jamie asked.

The inspector nodded. "I'll at least suggest he search the

perfumery buildings for any traces that might indicate Dickenson was killed there."

"He should have already done that," Thomas pointed out. "That is, if he'd actually listened to his police surgeon. I'm telling you, the man's a—"

"Yes, we already know your opinion of Inspector Plummet." Rob cut him off with a sigh. "I'll talk to him. Discreetly."

"And then?" Jamie prodded. "What if he doesn't listen?"

"Well, let's just see what happens first."

A SHORT WHILE LATER, as the two little orange cars zipped up the main driveway to the Plumeria Perfumery, Thomas pulled over to the side, flagging Rob's car down. He gestured at the frangipani trees lining the road.

"That's the trail I was telling you about. See it through the trees there? It runs alongside the whole driveway."

Holly peered over the hydrangea bushes that grew right next to the road. Sure enough, a tiny worn path meandered along the other side, winding in and out of the frangipanis.

"I can't quite get my bearings," she said to Rob. "Where was the body in relation to here?"

"I'm not sure either," Rob admitted. "All these trees look the same to me. I can try and find out though."

As they started driving again, Holly watched the trees fly by on either side. She glanced sideways at Rob, a worried expression on her face. "If Thomas was walking along here, do you think someone saw him and told Plummet? Maybe that's why he suspects him."

"Don't worry about Miller," Rob replied. "There's no evidence to connect him to this murder."

"I hope Inspector Plummet realizes that too," Holly muttered.

~

AS THEY DROVE into the perfumery parking lot, Holly noticed two police cars and a constable stationed outside the building. Glancing at the fields, she saw a few more constables coming through the rows of passionflowers, accompanied by Sergeant Frampton. She nudged Rob to draw his attention to them. The sergeant raised an arm in greeting, then picked up his pace.

"Inspector," he called. "A word, if you don't mind?"

"Save me a seat," Rob murmured to Holly.

"Holly! Come on!" Jamie, already out of her car and heading to the entrance, glanced back. "The presentation starts in five minutes!"

Inside the crowded lecture room, Natasha had saved four seats in the row she shared with Mr. Graham and Sage Craft.

"I thought you weren't going to make it! Where's Rob?" she whispered, as Holly sat down beside her, Jamie and Thomas slipping in behind.

"Talking to Sergeant Frampton," Holly whispered back.

On the other side of Natasha, Sage grimaced. "Plummet's here too. Being obnoxious. Lily's really upset."

"Are they searching the place?" Jamie asked in a low voice, leaning across Holly.

Sage shrugged. "I don't know. I don't think so. But Plummet's been interviewing people who were here on Thursday afternoon."

"Were you here?" Holly asked.

Sage shook her head. "No. I came in from Juniper on the afternoon flight and met up with a friend here for dinner."

"Who's Plummet talked to so far?" Jamie asked in a low voice.

The Juniper islander glanced around. "Lily and Cressida. And I saw Mr. Santorini come out of the office, and two other men who I guess work here too. Gabriel has been questioned, and Sylvie Lestrade. She was furious. We could hear her from in here!"

"What about visitors to the perfumery that day?"

"There weren't any on Thursday. Apparently, they were closed to the general public to get ready for the symposium. *Rosa del Mar's* a pretty big deal."

"Hmm. Narrows the suspects, doesn't it?" Jamie pursed her lips. "Especially since we know the body was moved."

Natasha's eyes shot up. "Moved?"

"Shh." Holly hushed her as the scientist's voice rose involuntarily. She gestured to the front of the room where Lily O'Connor and another woman were approaching the podium. "We're about to start. We'll fill you in later, Nat."

The murmur of conversation in the room faded away as Lily tapped the microphone.

"Ladies and gentlemen," she began. "Before we begin, I just want to thank you all once again for your cooperation and understanding today. It's been a trying time for all of us, and certainly not how we envisaged this occasion." She took a deep breath, then gave a determined smile. "However, now is the moment we've all been waiting for: the unveiling of Plumeria's latest fragrance, the historic re-creation of the perfume found on the wreck of *La Rosa de España*. Please welcome Ms. Amelie Lestrade, head perfumer here at Plumeria. Ms. Lestrade."

Holly eyed the perfumer with curiosity.

A slim, pale woman with short dark hair, wearing a white lab coat over black trousers and pink blouse, Amelie Lestrade looked to be in her early thirties.

With no preamble, she launched into speech, her voice surprisingly deep.

"Scent is tied to memory. The slightest whiff of a perfume or any scent can recall vivid memories of events, of loved ones, of special occasions. I'm sure you've all experienced this at some time."

Although it wasn't a question, heads nodded around the room.

"For instance," Amelie continued, "the scent of freesias, the wild white ones that grow in the spring on Azure Isle, immediately recall childhood memories of playing on an old swing that hung on a poinciana tree. The freesias grew beneath it and every time the swing passed over them, their scent rose into the air."

Holly stared at her with interest. It was obviously a real memory, but the perfumer's delivery was almost dispassionate. The same wild freesias grew on Hibiscus Island, and judging by the smiles around the room, many people could relate to the anecdote. Amelie Lestrade didn't smile.

"And the scent of *Rosa del Mar*," the perfumer continued, "this fragrance from the past, is the scent of history. Imagine the Spanish merchant ship crossing the Atlantic from Spain to the Americas, sailing along the sea trade route. Imagine her putting into the islands for supplies, the sounds of the busy ports, the bright sunshine, and the slapping waves against the docks. Imagine her sailing through storms, chased by pirate vessels, and finally slipping beneath the waves to lie fathoms deep on the ocean's bed."

Again, Holly's curiosity was piqued. The words were emotional, but the speaker's voice was flat. Holly wondered if someone had written the speech for her. It sounded more like something Gabriel Manout would say. She searched the room for the Grand Island perfumer, blinking in surprise when she spotted him in the front row beside Susan Hill.

She nudged Jamie, nodding towards Susan.

"I saw her. Kind of weird she's here, but maybe she and her cousin weren't close," Jamie murmured.

Amelie Lestrade continued talking. "We analyzed the perfume found on the ship and have re-created the floral notes of rose and neroli, sharp tones of citrus, and base notes of rosewood and amber. But it is the feel of history that we strove to capture in our essence, a glimpse into the past, into the story of *La Rosa de España* herself."

She paused before opening a small cedar box that stood beside her on the podium. Inside, nestled in blue velvet, was a square glass bottle with a ship engraved on the front.

"Ladies and gentlemen, I give you... *Rosa del Mar*."

15

_____

"I loved how she said the perfume is meant to make us feel the history of the ship," Sage remarked as they waited their turn to sample the new fragrance.

"Yes. And how freesias brought back a childhood memory," Holly added.

Natasha grinned. "For me, it's seaweed." She laughed at their expressions. "My granddad used to take me to the seaside in England in the winter when the seaweed gets left on the beaches for environmental reasons. We would poke through it, watch the birds, watch the wildlife. It's one of the reasons I became a marine scientist. But to this day, when I smell that seaweed, I remember our expeditions. How about you? Any smells that bring back memories?"

"Peanut butter cookies."

"Narcissus."

Holly and Jamie spoke together, then laughed.

"Why peanut butter cookies, Jamie?" Sage was curious.

"Oh, my great-aunt used to bake them for me when I was little and visited her at Rose Cottage. The smell reminds me of that."

"And narcissus?" Sage transferred her gaze to Holly.

"It grows wild in one part of our garden. My dad used to sit out there a lot. Whenever I smell narcissus, I remember seeing him stretched out in his chair in the sun, eyes closed, just relaxing."

Jamie glanced at Holly, then changed the subject. "Amelie said there was neroli in this perfume. What's that?"

"It's made from the flower petals of the bitter orange plant. Countries of origin—Spain, Italy, Morocco, and Tunisia." Sage grinned at their surprised expressions. "I do know a little bit about perfume, you know. We sell a lot of essential oils at The Black Cat. Supposedly, neroli was the favorite scent of Marie-Anne de la Trémouille."

Jamie looked blank. "And who's she? Should I know her?"

"She was a seventeenth century aristocrat. Born in France but lived in Italy for a while, and eventually headed the household of Marie Louise, wife of King Philip V of Spain. She'd have been alive when *La Rosa de España* was sailing the sea between Spain and the Americas." Sage's eyes twinkled. "There're a lot of very interesting stories attached to perfumes, you know. I'm kind of fascinated by them so we attach them to the scents in our shop. Lots of people like to know the history behind fragrances."

"Like what?" Holly was curious.

Sage pondered a moment as they moved closer to the front of the room. "Well, there's the story of frangipani. Have you heard that?"

Holly shook her head. "I didn't know there was one. All I know is it's the common name for *Plumeria*, and named in honor of Charles Plumier, a French botanist."

"Actually, there are a couple of stories connected to the flower. Lily told me them once when I was here on business." Sage smiled. "One story says that the word 'frangipani' came from the name of an actual perfume created from orris root and some other ingredients, by an Italian family called Frangipani. The Marquis de Frangipani is said to have used the perfume to scent gloves, known as 'frangipani gloves.' When the frangipani flower was first discovered, its fragrance reminded people of these gloves."

Jamie grinned. "So, the flower was called after the perfume. Usually it's the other way around, isn't it?"

"Yep. But it gets better. The other story—and you'll often find this one on websites—is completely false. In the nineteenth century, a luxury perfume company called Piesse and Lubin wanted to make perfume more desirable, so they created a story to go with a scent they had manufactured.

"They invented Mercutio Frangipani, a botanist who supposedly sailed with Christopher Columbus to the New World. He gained fictional fame because he used his nose to discover shorelines."

Holly giggled. "His nose? You mean he sniffed out land?"

"Well, that's the story." Sage grinned. "Mercutio is credited with sniffing out the Bahamas or Antigua—the story varies—because of the smell of white frangipani flowers, which attracted him to shore. He passed his discovery to his grandson, who used the flower to make perfume. His grandson was this Marquis de Frangipani who made the gloves." She laughed.

Natasha raised an eyebrow. "And it was all fake?"

"Yeah. Piesse had actually made a synthetic scent which he called 'Frangipani.' He played on the two stories to advertise the product."

Holly laughed. "It was a good marketing ploy, I guess. What do you think of the frangipani perfume they make here, Sage? The *Frangipani Allure*?"

"Oh, I love it," Sage said instantly. "We keep a supply in our shop all the time. That perfume is how Amelie Lestrade finally got a name for herself in the business."

Holly looked toward the front of the room, where the perfumer stood near the new perfume, nodding but unsmiling as people chatted to her about it.

"She's very... uh... serious, isn't she?"

"I heard she's not been very well this past week." Sage glanced around, then lowered her voice. "Plus, she's kind of lived in the shadow of her mother. Sylvie Lestrade, along with Olivia Hill, was considered a Creative Perfumer, maybe even a Master. Amelie isn't as creative—or as passionate about it—even though she trained with both of them. At least, I don't think she is. And I heard that's why Gabriel Manout was helping on the project. He's a better 'nose.'"

"Wait a minute. Amelie Lestrade trained with Olivia Hill?" Jamie's eyebrows rose in surprise. "I didn't know that."

"Oh yes. But she was only a teenager at the time." Sage stopped talking as they finally reached the row of samples of *Rosa del Mar*.

On the long counter, an array of tiny square glass vials lay in velvet-lined cedar boxes. Larger bottles, also square but etched with the sailing ship design and with round gold stoppers, stood behind them. Delighted exclamations arose from the guests who were already sniffing the scent and applying it to wrists.

Gabriel Manout, dressed again today in a dark suit and white shirt, but this time sporting an emerald-green tie, smiled at Jamie as she picked up one of the vials. "You can test it first if you'd like. It will smell differently on your skin, of course, but there's no point in putting it on if you don't like it."

He handed her a length of yarn, then gave one to Holly, Natasha, and Sage. Holly stared at it in surprise.

"What's this?"

"Cashmere yarn. It holds the scent much better than those paper strips and you'll be able to smell the base notes better. If you try the perfume on your skin, you'll notice the top notes first, then the heart notes."

Jamie glanced sideways at Holly, making Gabriel laugh. "No chemistry, no lecture, Jamie, I promise. Start by sniffing the yarn and tell me what you notice."

There was silence for a moment as they all sniffed.

"It's kind of woodsy and sweet," Natasha said after a moment.

"Yeah. I like it," Holly said.

Jamie nodded. "Me too."

Gabriel smiled again. "Good. Now, try a drop on your wrist or the back of your hand, if you prefer. Don't rub it in. Just let it dry for thirty seconds. Bear in mind, the scent will evolve as you wear it. First, you'll notice the top notes which in *Rosa del Mar* are citrus. They're the most volatile. The heart notes of rose and neroli will last longer. Probably ten to twenty minutes. And finally, the base notes of rosewood and amber. Ah, these, these are the soul of the perfume and will last the longest. Hours, a day, even longer. It depends."

All four women stared at him until he flapped a hand at them.

"Experience history, ladies. Try *Rosa del Mar* for yourselves."

Holly dabbed a little perfume on the inside of her wrist, bringing it to her face. "It's pretty. Kind of like grapefruit or orange."

"Those are the top notes," Jamie said knowledgeably,

waving her hand in the air to dry it. "Can anyone smell the rose?"

"A tiny bit. And the neroli as well, which I love." Sage bent her head to her wrist. "It's very light and feminine, isn't it?"

Natasha laughed. "You all sound like perfume experts."

Gabriel's eyes twinkled. "And what do you think of it?"

"Oh, I like it too, but it's a little flowery for me. I think I'd prefer one of those marine fragrances you were talking about yesterday." Natasha grinned at the perfumer, who laughed.

"The scent will change as you wear it. You may find it becomes spicier as the day goes on. Some people describe the rosewood-amber combination like that." He paused. "To properly test fragrances, it's best to live with it for a while. Sleep with it. Then you'll know if it works with your skin."

"Well, I like it," Jamie declared, sniffing her wrist again. "And I'm definitely buying a bottle."

"No, no, no!" Gabriel threw up his hands in horror. "We will be gifting the fragrance to you all, of course. Without you, this perfume would not exist. No, no, Jamie. Your ancestor sailed the seas with the original scent. It will be our honor and privilege to supply you and your friends with this re-creation." He turned to the woman who, having heard his expostulations, had drawn nearer. "Is that not right, Amelie?"

Amelie Lestrade's face was expressionless. "Of course. But remember, the fragrance belongs to me."

Gabriel's expression darkened. "Amelie," he began.

"You understand that, right?" Amelie Lestrade stared intently at Jamie. "Just because you found the bottle under the sea, it doesn't give you any rights to my fragrance!"

Jamie blinked. "Well, of course I understand that." She

gave the perfumer a tentative smile. "It must have been a challenging job to re-create an old perfume."

"And it is a re-creation. It's not just a copy. It may be similar to the one you found, but it's not exactly the same," Amelie repeated.

"Amelie!"

Gabriel Manout was scowling now. He tucked a hand under Amelie's elbow. The Plumeria perfumer tried to remove it, but Gabriel tightened his grip, giving the other women a forced smile.

"Remember, watch how the scent evolves on you over the course of the evening. Then you will know if *Rosa del Mar* is for you. Please excuse us now." He hustled Amelie away from the counter.

The Grand Island perfumer towed Amelie Lestrade into a corner of the room, where he released the woman, took a deep breath, then started talking in a low voice. Holly couldn't hear but she could clearly see that as Amelie tried to interrupt, Gabriel took a step closer, waving his finger in her face. Holly's eyebrows shot up as Amelie turned on her heel and walked away.

Natasha had been watching as well. "Don't seem to get on that well, do they? I wonder how they managed to work together to create the *Rosa del Mar* perfume?"

Holly shrugged. "Amelie's a little intense, that's for sure."

"Intense? She's a nutcase." Jamie was definite. "Why would she even think I'd want to own her perfume? I mean, it obviously belongs to Plumeria."

"No, surely not. It must belong to her. And Gabriel," Holly said. "It's an artistic creation, right? They must own it."

"I don't think so," Jamie began.

Sage laughed, intervening before Jamie could complete

her thought. "It's a bit complicated, actually. A fragrance is characterized by its formula, which is, or should be, the intellectual property of its creator—in this case Gabriel and Amelie. But it's also characterized by its brand name, which, for *Rosa del Mar*, is Plumeria Perfumes. In 2013, the French courts decided that perfumes couldn't be protected by copyright." She paused then clarified, "The formula of a perfume can't be protected. Ownership of the perfume, however, is clear. It belongs to the company that employs the perfumer."

Holly frowned. "But I'm sure Gabriel told us he owned his formulas."

"He owns his own business," Natasha pointed out. "He makes the perfumes he sells. It's kind of a moot point. Besides, if people are able to re-create a centuries old perfume like this one, I'm sure they could re-create modern ones as well. There must be all sorts of copying in this industry. Knockoffs of expensive perfumes and things."

"True." Sage nodded. "But it might not be exactly the same. That's why I prefer to deal with small operations like this. The Wimsey Plantation too. You know what's being used and you can see the way the products are made. It's authentic."

"Well, authentic or not, that Lestrade woman is weird." Jamie sniffed at her wrist again. "But I have to admit she's good at her job. The longer this is on, the more I like it. Are you getting it for The Black Cat, Sage?"

"Definitely." Sage glanced across the room. "In fact, I'm going to go talk to Lily about it now since I'm leaving tomorrow." She paused, then smiled. "In case I don't catch you later, it was lovely seeing you all again, dead bodies notwithstanding. Let me know when you're coming to

Juniper and I'll repay the barbecue." She gave them all a quick hug and hurried to catch Lily O'Connor.

Jamie gave her wrist one more sniff, then glanced around the room before grinning at Holly and Natasha. "Well, now that we've tried the perfume... Ready to do some snooping, you two?"

16

Holly's eyes bulged. "What do you mean, 'snooping'? We can't do that, Jamie!"

"Sure we can."

"What? Right under the nose of Plummet? He'll probably arrest us too!"

Jamie grinned. "By snooping, I really meant ask some questions." She sighed in regret. "I know we can't actually poke around the building."

"What sorts of questions?" Natasha's eyes were bright. "I've never done any detective work before. How do we start?"

Jamie fished in the bag she carried over her shoulder. "Well, I did a summary of everything we know so far." She paused with a grin. "Gosh, I feel like I'm channeling my inner Myrtle, just saying that."

Holly rolled her eyes but couldn't help a small smile. "Which reminds me—we haven't called her yet."

"And we're not going to!" Jamie was adamant. "Becky can fill her in if she wants to. I wonder if she's done any research yet. You should call her, Holly, and ask."

"It's only been a few hours. I know Becky's a genius on the computer, but I think we have to give her a little more time. And besides, she's probably still at work." Holly sighed when her friend frowned. "Fine. I'll call."

Jamie beamed. "Good. Now, Nat, look at this."

~

As Holly made her way out to the patio to find a quiet spot to phone Becky, she wondered where Rob was. The inspector hadn't joined them at all during the presentation. Peering over the balustrade, she saw that all three small cars were still in the parking lot, although some of the local dignitary guests were now leaving.

Lily O'Connor stood on the bottom steps, shaking the hand of the mayor of Azalea Village. As the mayor left, she looked up, catching Holly's eye. She gave the Hibiscus islander a somewhat tired smile before turning to see off the next visitor. Beside her, a dark-haired man laid a consoling hand on her shoulder.

"She doesn't look very happy, does she?" Thomas had approached unnoticed and was peering down at Lily as well.

"No. Who's the man with her? Do you know?"

"Jake O'Connor. Her cousin. I met him inside." Thomas grinned. "For a guy who works in a perfumery, he's got a lousy sense of smell. Gabriel was being all French and throwing up his hands in despair."

Holly giggled at the image. "Where have you been all this time, anyway? I didn't see you while we were waiting to test the perfume."

"I was first in line for the perfumes, then I was talking to Susan Hill for a while, then that incompetent policeman snaffled me again." Thomas rolled his eyes in disgust.

"For what? He doesn't still suspect you, surely?" Holly stared at the journalist in alarm. "Does he?"

Thomas shrugged, sticking his hands into the pockets of his jeans as he leaned against the balustrade. "Who knows? Honestly, he's a disgrace to his profession."

"I hope you didn't tell him that!"

"I managed to restrain myself." Thomas rolled his neck until it cracked. "So, what are you doing out here? You know Plummet's told everyone they have to stay until he finishes all his interviews, right? Everyone who was on site during the suspected time, that is. Sylvie Lestrade is raging. And the staff aren't too happy either that he's called them all in."

"He called in the staff? Why?"

"Well, one *hopes* it's because he's finally deigned to read the medical report," Thomas said. "He's—and I use the word in the loosest sort of way—interviewing Lily O'Connor's niece right now."

"You mean Kat Santorini?" Holly asked. "What questions could Plummet possibly have for *her*? And exactly how many people are we talking about? Since you seem to know everything."

Thomas buffed his fingernails on the front of his red polo shirt in an irritatingly smug manner. "I do seem to have a knack for information, yes." He grinned when Holly rolled her eyes. "Well, from what I have gleaned from yonder young constable, who hasn't yet learned the wily ways of investigative reporters, our plodding policeman has interviewed, or is in the process of interviewing, thirteen people. How he actually managed to create a list of suspects is beyond me. I'm positive the good sergeant was the brains behind it."

"Thirteen? Who are they? And stop all the fancy alliteration! Just spit it out, Thomas."

"Gabriel Manout, Lily and Jake O'Connor, Cressida and Seth Billings, Amelie and Sylvie Lestrade, Kat and Mick Santorini, Susan Hill, Faith and Carleton Sayers, and yours truly."

"Who are those other people? I know all the perfumers and Kat and Mr. Santorini. And you just said that's Jake. Come to think of it, Kat mentioned an Uncle Jake as well, but who's Seth Billings? And Faith and— Who'd you say?"

Thomas shook his head in mock reproof. "And this is why the Hibiscus Island Detective Club needs me. Like the mighty Plummet, I know all."

"Would you stop that?" Holly gave him a withering glance. "It's no wonder Jamie thinks you aren't serious about her if this is how you behave all the time."

Thomas's eyebrows shot up. "Oh ho! Say that again? Jamie White actually told you she thinks I'm not serious about her? And what conversation were you two having to precipitate such a remark? Did she say she would like me to be serious?"

"Yes. I mean, no. I mean—" Holly glared at the journalist. "Don't change the subject, Thomas. Tell me who those people are."

Thomas grinned at her. "Your wish is my command, Miss Gold, but I warn you, I'll be returning to this topic another time. Okay, okay." He held up his hands in defense. "Seth Billings is Cressida's cousin. Their fathers are brothers. Mr. Billings works as a gardener on the estate. I believe he is a qualified arborist. Did I get that right? A tree surgeon, isn't it?"

Holly pursed her lips. "Well, an arborist deals with the management of trees at a biological level, while a tree surgeon focuses on the maintenance work that has to be done to keep a tree healthy. They're both important jobs and require specific qualifications, but if he's an arborist, it means he can do tree inspections and design individual plans for shrubs and trees."

Thomas's mouth twitched. "You mean like healthcare plans?"

"Yes," Holly snapped. "And since the livelihood of this perfumery depends on the flowers that grow on the trees and shrubs, I'd say it's a very good idea to have an arborist on staff!"

"Okay, whoa. I didn't mean to make fun of it. Boy, I'm not doing too well with you today, am I?" Thomas cleared his throat. "Moving on. Faith and Carleton Sayers. Elderly married couple. Carleton works in the gardens as well and Faith helps out in the perfumery. She's like Kat. Does everything. The Sayers have worked here for years. Frankly, I doubt they could move the body anywhere. They must be in their eighties."

"Huh." Still annoyed, Holly processed the information. "So, we have the locals who are here all the time, and then we have the perfumers who flew in for the conference. Do you happen to know when they actually arrived on the island?"

"I asked that very same question. Cressida said Sylvie Lestrade has been here for a week, visiting friends. Susan Hill arrived on Tuesday and, again according to Cressida, was making a nuisance of herself at the perfumery every day. Manout arrived on Monday. They were all here when Dickenson arrived on the island." Thomas eyed Holly with interest. "What are you thinking?"

"Susan Hill said Dickenson had arranged a meeting with her to talk about her mother's work. I'm just wondering if he arranged meetings with any of the other perfumers as well."

"He did tell me he had a story." Thomas pursed his lips. "I think we should do some research about the big four."

"What big four?" Jamie had come out onto the patio. "Why are you two out here discussing the case without me? And what did Becky say, Holls?"

"I haven't called her yet." Holly indicated Thomas. "Our intrepid reporter here was filling me in on all the things he conveniently hasn't shared yet."

Jamie's head swung to Thomas, her eyes narrowing. "Like what?"

The journalist flinched.

HOLLY HAD JUST FINISHED LEAVING a message for Becky—the librarian hadn't answered her call—when she spotted Rob coming out of one of the ground floor entrances, accompanied by Inspector Plummet and Sergeant Frampton. Rob shot her a brief smile before resuming his conversation with an annoyed-looking Plummet.

Holly strained to hear, trying not to peer over the balustrade railing in too obvious a fashion. Had Rob persuaded Plummet to let him help with the case?

"Oh, very well! I think it's a complete waste of time and manpower, but if you insist, let's get it done. You'll organize it, will you?"

Rob murmured something inaudible.

"Right, then. I'll leave you to it."

The Azure Island inspector climbed the stairs to the main entrance of the perfumery, muttering under his breath.

"Commissioner's blue-eyed boy, that one... Ridiculous... Interfering civilians... Money talks..." He entered the main room, calling in a sharp voice, "Constable!"

Rob finished talking to Sergeant Frampton, who immediately called over two policemen, gave them some terse directions, then pulled out his phone to make a call.

"Looks like Rob's been given permission to assist the Plum." Jamie joined Holly, resting a jean-clad hip on the railing, a considering expression on her face as she gazed down at the inspector.

As if he felt their eyes on him, Rob glanced up, then smiled. "I'm irresistibly reminded of Shakespeare right now," he called.

"Huh?" Jamie asked inelegantly.

The inspector's eyes twinkled. "'But soft! What light through yonder window breaks?'"

Jamie frowned. "Is that from a play or something? I didn't really like Shakespeare in school."

Thomas, who had come up beside them, laughed. "Oh, come on, White. You must know that one." He leaned over the balustrade, declaiming loudly, "'Romeo, Romeo, wherefore art thou, Romeo? Deny thy father and refuse thy name, or if thou wilt not, be but sworn my love, and I'll no longer be a Capulet!'" He placed his hand on his heart in dramatic fashion.

Rob, who had started up the stairs as Thomas began, now joined them on the veranda. He grinned. "'Shall I hear more?' Hmmm. No, I think not."

His dry tone made Thomas laugh. "You know your Shakespeare pretty well, Inspector."

"Well, that play anyway. I played Romeo in my final year at school. Some of the speeches have stuck." He winked at Holly. "I was pretty good, if I do say so myself."

"Where've you been all this time?" Jamie asked. "Has the Plum agreed to let you help?"

"I am working on the case, yes." Rob looked around. "Could we move this conversation over there, please?"

He led them to the far end of the veranda where some Adirondack chairs were arranged to overlook the passion-flower fields. Satisfied they were out of earshot of anyone inside the building, Rob gestured to them to take a seat.

"What were you telling Sergeant Frampton? And who's the Commissioner's blue-eyed boy?" Holly asked.

Thomas's eyebrows shot up as he leaned back in his chair, stretching his legs out. "Blue-eyed boy? Who said that?"

"Never mind. It's not relevant." Rob stopped any speculation in an abrupt manner. "Sergeant Frampton is arranging for the perfumery to be properly searched, which means we'll be clearing the building shortly. It also means I'll be held up here for a while." His look at Holly was regretful. "I'm sorry, Holly. I know this was supposed to be a holiday."

She sighed. "It's okay. Is there anything we can do to help, or do you want us to stay out of it altogether?"

"Holly! What are you doing, girl?" Jamie was aghast. "Don't ask him that!"

Rob's grin was wry. "If I thought there was even the slightest chance of you doing that, I would absolutely say yes. But actually..." He paused, hesitating.

"Actually? Actually what? Ooh, are you going to ask us to help? Like, officially?" Well, color me impressed." Jamie eyed Rob with unmitigated approval before continuing, "I mean, we'd be investigating anyway, of course, but it'll be easier if we don't have to sneak around behind your back."

As Rob cast his eyes heavenward, Holly gave Jamie a violent nudge.

"Not that we sneak, of course," Jamie added.

Thomas sniggered. "No. I'd say you're pretty blatant about it."

"Shut up, Miller." Jamie's response was perfunctory. "What do you want us to do, Rob?"

Rob drew in a deep breath, then released it. "This is highly unorthodox, so don't make me regret it," he warned.

"Of course not." Jamie crossed her heart. "We've got your back."

"Right. Well, Lily O'Connor and the other perfumers are going out to dinner tonight. I understand we were all invited as well."

Jamie nodded. "Yep. Seven o'clock. At Azalea Village. Why? Oh, I suppose you can't come now."

"I can't. But I want all of you to still go."

"That's it? That's all you want us to do? Go to dinner?" The disappointment in Jamie's voice made Rob's lips twitch.

"That's it."

"Hmmm." Thomas wore a shrewd look. "And what? You want us to sound them out for you. Quite a few of your suspects will be there, won't they?"

"Well," Holly counted on her fingers, "seven out of the thirteen, anyway."

Rob blinked. "Seven out of thirteen? How do you know — Never mind. Of course you know."

"What about Mr. Santorini, Seth Billings, Jake O'Connor, and the Sayers?" Jamie asked. "They won't be at the dinner."

"I'll be interviewing them." Rob's lips twitched in sudden amusement at the intent expressions on every face. "You're all a bit like ferrets, you know."

Holly grinned but Jamie was frowning.

"But surely Plummet already talked to them. Do you mean you don't think he did it prop—"

Rob held up a hand, cutting her off. "Don't ask questions I can't answer." He sighed as they all exchanged glances of interest. "Just please. Don't ask."

"Gotcha, Inspector." Thomas grinned. "Let me just clarify. At this dinner—and can I just say it will be a pleasure to accommodate you in this way—I take it you'd like us to gently lead the suspects to talk about themselves? Reveal any perfidy among the perfumers, so to speak?"

Jamie and Holly both rolled their eyes.

"I'm more interested in how they met, who's worked with whom in the past, when and where—any little tidbits like that."

"Are you now? Do you think this crime is rooted in past history then, Inspector?" Thomas pulled out his phone as he spoke. He raised an interrogative eyebrow.

"This isn't a press interview, Mr. Miller." Rob was serious as he looked at them all. "Just go to dinner and chat. That's all I want you to do."

17

Holly and Jamie drove back together to the Ocean Science Center, leaving Thomas to take Mr. Graham. Halfway along the main drive of Plumeria Perfumery, Jamie pulled over to the side of the road.

"What are you doing?" Holly asked.

Jamie hopped out of the tiny car to peer over the hydrangea bushes. "I wanted to see this trail Miller said he was on. To see if it goes near where the body was. Would you recognize the spot?"

"Um, I really don't think Rob wants us poking around the crime scene."

Jamie ignored her, pushing her way through the shrubbery to stand on the trail, then beckoned to her. "Come on, Holls. This is one of Plummet's main pieces of evidence against Miller. We need to see if it's even valid."

Holly sighed as she climbed out of the car. "Rob doesn't think Thomas is a suspect at all. And since he's now involved in the case, I expect he'll make that clear. You're just being nosy."

Jamie brushed some tiny hydrangea leaves off her teal

shirt as she shot a grin at her friend. "Naturally. That's why I waited till Miller was out of sight. No need for him to be here too."

The trail was a narrow path that hugged the side of the road, occasionally veering off to wind around trees. Holly glanced up at the frangipani trees as they walked back toward the perfumery, noticing they seemed to be planted according to color. She paused under one tree laden with red-orange flowers that resembled a sunset.

"Oh, now this is a pretty one! I wonder if Mr. Santorini would give Gramps a cutting of it as well."

"What is it?" Jamie peered at the tree. "I mean, it's obviously a frangipani, but what kind?"

"Probably a variety of *Plumeria rubra*. There are tons of them." Holly picked up a flower that had fallen to the ground, bringing it to her face. "Wow. Strong scent." She handed it to Jamie, glancing around at the trees surrounding them. "They're using a white and yellow variety in the perfumery right now. I wonder what it smells like?"

Jamie sniffed the flower. "Don't they all smell the same? I've never noticed a difference." She tucked the frangipani into her hair with a grin. "What do you think? Pretty, right?"

"You could never be a perfumer." Holly rolled her eyes. "No, frangipanis don't all smell the same. At least, our frangipanis at the inn don't. There's a white one that's super strong but we have a pink one that's much milder."

Jamie had stopped listening. Instead, she was frowning at another wider path that branched off from the main trail. This one appeared to lead straight to the perfumery buildings, now visible through the trees.

"I hate to say this, but Plummet might have been on to something when he cross-examined you about these trails.

Anyone could walk along here, go down that path, and get to the perfumery."

"And how does that help us?"

"Maybe Dickenson came this way."

Holly stopped walking. "Why would you think that? Why wouldn't he just have driven up to the building?"

"Where's his car?" Jamie smirked when Holly's mouth opened and then closed. "Exactly. He was staying at the Fire Drake Inn. He must have walked up here, just like Miller did." She frowned. "So, he could have been killed anywhere, really. Not necessarily in the building."

Holly pondered this. "But the body was moved. Why move it from one outside place to another? The perfumery makes more sense as the scene of the crime because you couldn't leave the body there to be found. And we know he was supposed to meet his cousin there. She said so."

"Mmm. True." Jamie made a disgusted noise. "I can't believe Plummet didn't listen to Miranda Shaw. I mean, what sort of policeman is he? If Dickenson was killed in the perfumery, just think of all the people who have been wandering all over it the past couple of days. There's probably no evidence left!"

"Well, to be fair, no one knew a crime had even been committed until Friday. And by that time, we'd all been in every room." A splash of yellow caught Holly's eye as they passed another trail, this one heading towards the passion-flower fields. "Wait." She tugged on Jamie's arm to stop her. "Look. That's police tape over there. It's got to be the *Plumeria pudica* grove."

Jamie sighed. "Honestly, Holls, why does everything have to be technical with you? Why can't you just say frangipani like a normal person?"

"Uh, that would be because we're surrounded by frangipani trees. How else would you know which ones I was talking about?"

"Well, telling me the botanical name of a plant doesn't actually help. All you needed to say was 'police tape.'" Jamie glanced back and forth between the tape visible between the trees on one side, and the perfumery building visible on the other. "Huh. It's doable. The body could have been transported from the building to that grove."

"Maybe. I wonder how though?"

"How? Well, this path is wide enough for a wheelbarrow." As Holly raised a skeptical eyebrow, Jamie added, "Or one of those buggy things we're driving."

Holly couldn't help a grin as her friend immediately began to search the ground. "I think it would be hard to fold a body into one of those little cars. Especially if rigor mortis had set in. Which it might have done. And I don't think you'll find tire marks, if that's what you're looking for. The ground's like rock." She glanced at her watch and gave an exclamation. "And you don't have time to look now anyway! I want to change before we go to dinner. Don't you? Come on. We can tell Rob later about the path."

LILY O'CONNOR HAD GIVEN them directions to a restaurant in Azalea Village about a twenty-minute drive from the science center in the opposite direction of the perfumery. It was still light when the Hibiscus islanders arrived, pulling up in front of the building in the little orange cars.

While Thomas rubbed his hands together at the thought of the Italian cuisine advertised on the sign outside the restaurant, Holly and Mr. Graham exclaimed at the sight of the azalea shrubs spilling out of the gardens that bordered both sides of the main street. In the evening light, they glowed in an array of colors—magenta, hot pink, orange, red, salmon, and white.

"Unbelievable," Holly breathed. "They're just stunning. I wish we could grow these at home!"

"They wouldn't do well." Mr. Graham shook his head in fellow feeling. "But I agree with you, Holly. This is an incredible display. I must say, I like the way they've put these flower beds in. I wonder if we could do something similar in Bridgeport."

"Instead of planters, you mean?" Holly pursed her lips. "It would mean digging up the roads. I'm not sure how people would feel about that."

Standing in the door of the restaurant, Jamie beckoned to them with impatience, pushing her long brown hair over her shoulder. Gold hoops glinted in her ears above a close-fitted black blouse worn with jeans.

"How many clothes did you bring?" Holly had asked when Jamie had pulled the shirt out of her bag.

"It's called being prepared." At Holly's dismayed expression, she'd tossed a silky green shirt at her. "Here, wear this. You can't go to dinner in a t-shirt. At least dress up those jeans a little bit."

With Mr. Graham in trousers and a white button-down and Thomas similarly spruced up in dressy jeans, Holly was glad she'd borrowed the top. At least she looked presentable. And green was her favorite color.

"Come on, you two," Jamie repeated, turning to go inside.

Thomas grinned. "Let the snooping begin."

Lily O'Connor greeted them with a smile as they approached the table next to large plate glass windows that looked out onto the azalea-stuffed streets.

"Ah, you found it. Good. I'm afraid Amelie was unable to join us tonight. She's been unwell this past week, and I'm afraid this death has upset her further."

Sylvie Lestrade nodded. "She is sensitive, my daughter. Most *artistes* are."

As everyone settled themselves around the table, Lily signaled a waiter, who bustled over to take their orders, then frowned.

"Where could Gabriel be? I know I told him the correct time."

Sylvie Lestrade gave a thin smile. "Gabriel is always late. Always."

"You must know him well, Madame Lestrade." Thomas lost no time in starting his cross-examination. "I understand he worked at your perfumery on Azure Isle when it was still operating."

The silver-haired perfumer nodded, the tiny sapphire drops in her ears catching the light as she did. Her blue suit perfectly matched the earrings and the sapphire bracelet she wore on one wrist.

"Gabriel was my protégé," she said.

The loud sniff that came from Susan Hill at this statement had Sylvie Lestrade narrowing her eyes. Before either could speak, however, Lily interrupted, relief in her voice. "Oh good. Here he is. Oh, and Callum Stewart is with him. We'll have to get another chair after all." She looked around for the waiter again.

After a short period of bustle, with everyone moving chairs and reseating themselves around the round table, all to the accompaniment of profuse apologies from Callum

Stewart and "No, no, it's quite all right" from everyone else, they were finally settled.

Holly found herself between Cressida Billings and the director of the Ocean Science Research Center. Across from her, Jamie had Lily O'Connor on one side and Susan Hill on the other. As soon as everyone was seated, Lily beamed and held up her glass. "Well, cheers, everyone. To *Rosa del Mar* and the people who made it possible."

~

"I DIDN'T REALIZE you and Gabriel knew each other." Holly took another sip of soup before glancing at her table companion.

Callum smiled, leaning back in his chair to wipe his bearded mouth. "Oh yes. We've known each other some time now. Believe it or not, we met at a marine science conference. He gave a talk about how marine seaweeds can be used in perfume making." He laughed. "It was one of the highlights of the conference, actually."

"Yes, he told us a little bit about that." Holly grinned. "Seaweed isn't something I've ever associated with perfumes."

"No, I'm sure. We kept in touch after that," Callum continued. "Right now, I'm helping him with some of his chemical research on a particular type of Sargassum seaweed he's experimenting with here. Fascinating stuff. There's a seaweed absolute used by some perfumers which is normally made from bladderwrack. That doesn't grow in our part of the world, so Gabe's been experimenting to see if he can get similar results from Sargassum."

"Really? Interesting. We use Sargassum in our gardens back on Hibiscus. It's great compost material. I haven't seen any on the beaches yet though. Do you go out to sea to collect it?"

"Yes, and luckily for Gabe, the weather's been good this week." Callum's eyes twinkled as he added, "He gets very seasick in rough weather."

"Oh, you've been out on the boat this week?"

"Yes. Every day. Gabe uses the Center's lab when he's here, so he times his visits for when it's not so busy." The director chuckled. "He's absolutely terrible at keeping time —you saw how late we were tonight—so it's best if the lab has a light schedule that won't be messed up if he doesn't arrive when he says he will."

Holly smiled, wondering how she could discreetly ask if they'd been out all day on Thursday. Before she could frame her question, Cressida leaned around her to address the science director, who was buttering a roll.

"Callum, did I hear you say Gabriel is using seaweed? Natural seaweed? I thought he dealt mostly with synthetics."

Callum waved his bread roll in the perfumer's direction. "Gabe! These people are interested in your seaweed project."

The talk around the table quieted.

"Seaweed?" Sylvie Lestrade made a moue of distaste. "You are using seaweed in your perfumes now, Gabriel?"

The Grand Island perfumer grinned. "I'm quite interested in the marine fragrances, yes. I was talking recently with a colleague in India who's experimenting with a species of red algae he thinks might make a good base fragrance. I thought it'd be worth experimenting with our local varieties so I'm running some tests on Sargassum. Callum's been kind enough to let me use his lab when it's not busy."

"Why don't you just do your research on Grand Island?" Jamie asked. "You must get Sargassum there too. It's all over the beaches on Hibiscus at certain times."

"Oh, we do, of course," Gabriel agreed. "But Grand Island is quite a bit larger than the rest of the archipelago and my perfumery is inland. I can come here for a week and get a lot of research done in a short period of time. And I can get fresh Sargassum without having to wait for it to wash up on shore. Callum runs me out in the Center boat, you see. We got quite a lot done this week."

"Gabe's been analyzing the volatile compounds in Sargassum to determine which ones might be responsible for the smell. Fresh sargassum has quite a nice fragrance, I think," Callum added.

"How exactly do you do that?" Thomas asked. He'd fished his phone out of his pocket and was poised to take notes. "Analyze the compounds, that is? I imagine it's the same process whether its seaweed or frangipani, right?"

Gabriel wiggled his hand from side to side. "Sort of. We can use gas chromatography mass spectrometry to determine the chemical analysis of the essential oils of a plant— or seaweed—yes. But the process to obtain those essential oils might be different. It depends on the plant."

"Interesting. So how would you obtain the essential oils from seaweed?" Thomas asked.

"Well, my colleague in India is using an old-fashioned mortar and pestle to grind his red algae. Then he extracts it in methanol and concentrates it through slow evaporation. Then he re-dissolves the concentrate in methanol and runs it through the GC-MS. That gives him a reading of all the compounds in the algae."

Jamie grinned. "Any chance you could repeat that in English?"

The perfumer's eyes twinkled in response, but Sylvie Lestrade gave a disdainful sniff. "Crush the leaves, dissolve the leaves, evaporate, re-dissolve, and run through a machine. It is a simple process."

Holly winced as Jamie's smile vanished and her eyes narrowed.

"But you're saying you might not use that method for, say, a frangipani?" Oblivious to the undercurrents, Thomas continued to tap rapidly on his phone. "Why not?"

"You'd never use a mortar and pestle for frangipani." Sylvie sniffed. "It's too fragile."

Lily jumped into the breach, diverting Sylvie Lestrade's attention as Holly managed to catch Jamie's eye. She made a subtle "calm down" motion with her hands, breathing a sigh of relief at the approach of waiters with the main course. Jamie drew in a deep breath, then leaned back to allow the waiter to slide a plate of salmon in front of her.

18

"Well, that was a waste of time!" Jamie exclaimed in a loud voice as she marched into the cottage, Thomas, Holly, and Mr. Graham trailing behind her. "I learned nothing. Nada. Zilch. Zip!" She flung herself onto the sofa, irritation oozing from every pore. "I barely spoke to Lily since she had to keep soothing the egos at the table. Honestly, that Lestrade woman! Talk about rude. And as for Susan Hill, she's a grunter."

"A what?" Holly blinked at the unexpected word.

"A grunter. One of those people who every time you say something just grunts. A conversation killer. Painful, just painful." Jamie blew out her breath, stretching her legs out in front of her. "Just chat, Rob said! Ha!"

As Holly sank into one of the armchairs next to a small brick fireplace, Jamie directed a questioning look around the room.

"What about you lot? I hope you did better than me. Mr. Graham? You seemed to be getting on pretty well with Madame Prima-donna Lestrade."

The historian blushed but his eyes were bright. "Well,

I've not done much sleuthing before, but I must say, it's quite exciting. I see the appeal it has for Myrtle."

Holly suppressed a smile as Mr. Graham adjusted his position in the upright chair he'd chosen and leaned forward.

"We chatted about a lot of things, but with regards to the specifics, Madame Lestrade told me she went to Plumeria on Thursday around four o'clock to find out why her daughter hadn't met her at the spa as planned."

"The spa? Sylvie Lestrade says she was at a spa? What time?" Jamie's eyes narrowed.

"She said all afternoon. I didn't get exact times. Should I have?" Mr. Graham's forehead creased in worry.

"No, it's fine." Holly's smile was reassuring. "I'm sure Rob will check up on that."

"Well, she said Amelie didn't show up at the spa, and when she got to the perfumery, she wasn't there either. Apparently, she'd gone home sick and the lab was locked. Madame Lestrade was about to leave as well when she saw Cressida in the garden and went to talk to her about the AGM. There appears to have been some problems with paperwork related to their meeting."

"How'd she get to the perfumery?" Thomas, who had been listening from the kitchen, now came into the living room with a cup of coffee. He leaned against the wall. "Did she say? Because I saw her getting in Lily O'Connor's car as I was leaving that day in my taxi."

Mr. Graham frowned. "She didn't mention that, but I would assume a taxi dropped her off. Perhaps she was expecting to get a ride back to her hotel with Amelie."

"Funny that she isn't staying with her daughter, isn't it?" Jamie said. "I wonder why Amelie wasn't there tonight? Did anyone hear? No? Oh well." She sighed, slouching further into the sofa.

"Holly? Did you get anything from Cressida?" Thomas raised an eyebrow.

"Not much. But she was at the perfumery all day on Thursday prepping for the event. She seems to have been everywhere. *Enfleuraging*—is that a verb?—cleaning, taking orders, all sorts of things. Lily wasn't on site all day, so Cressida was in charge. She didn't seem to mind. Sounds like she and Lily have a good partnership running that place." Holly's eyes lit up suddenly. "Cressida did tell me one interesting thing, though. You know why Rob's been asked to help with the case?"

Jamie shook her head. "I thought he asked Plummet."

"No. According to Cressida, Sylvie Lestrade called the commissioner on Grand Island in a fury at the way Plummet treated her. Apparently, she knows him personally." Holly grinned when Jamie began to smirk. "The commissioner assigned Rob to the case because, Cressida said, of his experience with murder cases."

Thomas laughed, putting his empty coffee cup on a nearby table. "So, our inspector is the blue-eyed boy Plummet referred to. Boy, that must stick in Plummet's throat. Well, it's good that Tucker's on the case. He'll get things done properly. And we can pass on everything we've learned to him which I'm sure he'll appreciate."

Holly eyed him with interest. "And what did you learn tonight, may I ask? You certainly seemed to be having a good time."

The journalist held his hands out in a deprecating manner, a grin tugging at his mouth. "What can I say? People like to talk to me."

Jamie scowled. "Gloating is a sign of an inferior intellect, you know. Go on, then, Miller. Make us all feel bad."

Thomas's grin widened. "Oh, well, I lucked out. Gabriel and Callum are both talkers. They kept the conversation going without much work on my part. Callum, obviously, wasn't at the perfumery at all on Thursday—in fact, he was out at sea with some interns, he said."

"And Gabriel?" Jamie asked.

"He said he was here at the Ocean Science Research Center, working in the lab on his marine fragrance project. We can confirm that with Nat, I suppose. Lily picked him up here around four thirty and they drove to Plumeria so she could check that everything was ready, and then they were going out to dinner. He told me Amelie had left early as well. He'd wanted to get something from the lab, but it was locked."

"Surely there must be another key," Holly said.

Thomas shrugged. "Guess not. Or he didn't know where it was. Or he didn't care. He was more interested in telling me about the restaurant he, Lily, and Sylvie ended up at. I did ask him about his career though. You know, how he got started, where he studied, all that sort of thing."

"He worked with Olivia Hill, didn't he? Susan's mother?" Holly slipped her shoes off and curled her feet underneath her. "Susan said he'd left them and gone to Azure to Sylvia Lestrade. And Sylvie said he was her protégé, remember?"

Thomas nodded, sitting down beside Jamie on the sofa, who moved over to make room for him. "Sylvie apprenticed at a perfumery in France. When she moved to Azure way back, she operated a very small, very exclusive perfumery. She headhunted Gabriel. Stole him out from under the Hills' nose. Olivia was livid."

"Understandable." Jamie nodded. "With only a couple of

perfumeries in the islands, the competition must have been intense."

A series of chimes interrupted the conversation.

"Oh, that's my phone." Holly jumped up. "It might be Becky. She said she'd call tonight, remember?"

"Feels like ages ago now. Here, set her up on the coffee table so we can all see." Jamie swept aside some magazines to make a space. "Mr. Graham, come sit here."

The elderly historian smiled. "If you don't mind, I think I'll go to my room. It's been rather a long day, and I'm going on another dive tomorrow. I think I'll turn in." He lifted a hand in response to the chorus of "Good night" that followed him out of the room.

Holly had answered her phone and had Becky on the screen. "Give us two seconds while we get you set up." She glanced around, looking for something to lean the phone against.

"Hang on. I have a phone stand you can use." Thomas left the room, returning moments later with a stand. As Holly placed the phone in it, the journalist leaned forward to wave at Becky on the tiny screen. "Hey, Becks! How's Hibiscus? Still standing?"

"Barely." Becky rolled her eyes. "Drama everywhere. What's going on over there? Where's Rob?"

"He's been seconded to the investigation." Thomas grinned. "Apparently, he's an expert on murder now. The commissioner appointed him."

"Commissioner Johnson?" Becky smiled. "Nice man."

"Oh, you know him?"

"I met him once, when Rob got hired. He told me he was highly impressed with my brother's record of solved cases."

"Rob solved murder cases in England?" Jamie asked, surprise in her voice.

"Well, of course he did. He's a detective inspector. What did you think he did over there?"

Jamie shrugged. "General police stuff. Like Holly's dad."

"Rob worked with the Criminal Investigation Department in his local command in England, not in the uniformed ranks." Holly smiled at Jamie's astonishment. "He's told me a little bit about it, but I didn't know the commissioner thought so much of him."

"Huh. Well, who knew our inspector was such a dark horse? No wonder Plummet's peeved. Probably thinks he'll be shown up." Jamie wriggled to get more comfortable on the sofa, then rubbed her hands together. "Okay, Becks. What've you got for us? Start with the victim, okay? Did you find out anything about Dickenson?"

As Holly squashed herself onto the sofa on Jamie's other side, Becky flipped through a notebook across the sea in her living room on Hibiscus Island.

"Jonathan Dickenson. Cousin to Susan Hill, nephew of Olivia Hill. His mother was Olivia's sister and was also involved in the perfume industry. Their father—Jonathan's grandfather—was an amateur perfumer. He played around with enfleurage in a home setting. It was Olivia who took it a step further and turned it into a proper business. She handled the creative part, while her sister took over the financial side. Interestingly, the cousins took on the opposite roles as their parents."

"What? You mean Dickenson was a perfumer?" Jamie's eyes widened in surprise. "I thought he was a journalist."

"Oh, he is—was, I mean. But he grew up in the perfume business. Summer holiday jobs, that sort of thing. Apparently, he had an amazing nose for fragrances. There was quite a write up in an old paper about how he helped create a signature scent for the business. Olivia is quoted as calling him an 'up-and-coming talent.' He seems to have developed a lot of recipes in his time there."

Holly's brow furrowed as she considered this information. "Why'd he choose journalism, I wonder? And what about Susan Hill? I assumed she was a perfumer, but it doesn't sound like it from what you just said."

"She's not," Becky confirmed. "She's the president of Grand Island Perfumes but she's strictly on the business side of things. She has nothing to do with making the fragrances. She's quoted as saying that although she has no nose for scent, she can sniff out a good business deal anywhere. I have no idea why Dickenson chose journalism instead of perfumes." The librarian paused. "I did, however, find an article about a scandal connected to Grand Island Perfumes and Gabriel Manout."

"A scandal?"

"What sort of scandal?"

Thomas and Jamie spoke together, leaning forward to peer into the phone. Becky laughed at their eager expressions.

"It was a long time ago. Just after Gabriel moved to Azure Isle. Olivia Hill claimed he had stolen the formula to a special fragrance she had created. Gabriel denied it, saying he had created the perfume and therefore the formula was his to do what he wanted with."

Holly frowned. "I don't think that's true, though. Sage was talking about this earlier. She said the formula of a perfume is owned by the business where it was made."

"Yes, and that's what Olivia Hill's lawyer argued when she took Gabriel to court over the matter. Various courts have ruled in different ways over this issue." Becky flipped a few pages in her red notebook. Her eyes were bright as she continued, "It's really quite interesting. I'm familiar with copyright of written materials, but the law is murky when it comes to perfumes. For instance, one court ruled that the smell of a perfume is copyrightable when just three days earlier the French High Court had ruled the opposite. Basically, the first court said if a scent is original, it could be copyrighted. But the originality requirement doesn't mean the scent has to be entirely new. It just means the maker has put some of his own creativity into it."

Thomas leaned back with a whistle, stretching his arms across the sofa. "Well, that sounds like it would be a nightmare to prove either way."

"Exactly." Becky nodded. "It's why people document the creation process so carefully. If you're ever sued for imitation, you need to be able to prove any similarity is coincidental."

"What happened in Gabriel's case?" Jamie's eyes were intent.

"They compromised. Gabriel kept the formula but agreed not to use it to manufacture any fragrance that would compete directly with the Grand Island Perfumes scent."

On the screen, Becky lifted her notebook out of the way to allow a small black cat into her lap, wincing slightly when it began kneading the pink leggings she wore.

Her grin caused Thomas to raise an eyebrow. "You're looking remarkably similar to that cat of yours right now, Becks. Very smug. So, tell us, what's the connection to this murder?"

"Well, Sylvie Lestrade has a daughter who is also a perfumer."

"Amelie Lestrade. Yeah, we've met her. She's an oddball. Sage told us she trained with Olivia Hill when she was a teenager. But that would have been before Gabriel's time, right?"

Becky blinked at the interruption, then regrouped. "Well, Grand Island Perfumes did run summer workshops for quite a few years. I imagine Amelie attended one of those. My point was that when Gabriel Manout went to Lestrade Fragrances, he worked with Amelie."

"Ohhhh." Jamie's eyes lit up. "I get it. Gabriel gave the formula to her, right?"

"He says not. And Sylvie Lestrade denied it emphatically. She threatened a lawsuit of her own against Susan Hill, who backed down." Becky grinned. "But just over three months ago, Amelie Lestrade released a perfume that has created great interest in the perfume world."

"*Frangipani Allure.*" Holly supplied the name, then frowned. "And?"

"And the story of the stolen formula has started floating around again. A few veiled references to it, here and there. Nothing overt." Becky shrugged. "There's no proof that Amelie Lestrade used Gabriel's formula to create the scent, and no one is saying it outright, but—"

"—if Dickenson found proof, then that might be a motive to kill him," Jamie concluded.

19

The following morning, Holly was in the kitchen making herself a cup of tea when Rob entered. He came up behind her, resting his chin on her head and wrapping his arms around her with a sigh.

"Good morning. I'm sorry I missed you last night, but everyone was asleep when I finally got back."

Holly twisted around. "Gosh, you look exhausted! What time did you get in?"

"Late." Rob rubbed his hands up and down Holly's arms before dropping a kiss on her forehead. "Is that tea?"

"Yes. Want a cup? Anything else? Toast? Eggs?"

Rob smiled. "Toast would be great, but I'll make it." He gave her another quick kiss before opening the fridge in search of bread, butter, and jam.

As she refilled the kettle and pulled out another teacup from the white-painted cupboard, Holly eyed Rob with concern. He didn't just look tired, he looked glum, and that wasn't an emotion she associated with him.

"Where are the others?" Rob piled toast onto a plate,

then slid into one of the chairs at the kitchen table. "It's very quiet."

"Well, it's after nine," Holly pointed out, bringing two cups of tea to the table. She sat down opposite him. "Mr. Graham left with Peter Mackenzie for his dive. They're visiting a wreck on the south side of the island, he said. He won't be back until the evening. Thomas and Jamie..." She paused, her eyes dancing.

Rob groaned as he buttered his toast. "Do I want to know?"

"Oh, it's nothing bad. Not really. They've gone off with Natasha to her lab. Thomas expressed a burning desire to understand how gas chromatography and mass spectrometry works, so Nat's giving them a chemistry lesson. Because it's Sunday and the lab isn't being used today. Or not really, she said."

"A chemistry lesson? Why on earth?" Rob's eyes narrowed as he lowered the slice of toast he'd raised to his mouth. "Does this have anything to do with last night's dinner? What happened?"

"Partly. And partly because of what Becky told us."

As Holly filled Rob in on the previous evening's conversations, the inspector continued with his breakfast, a small frown creasing his brow at intervals as he listened.

"A potential stolen formula, huh? Interesting." Rob absently sipped his tea. "What do you think of Mr. Manout, Holly?"

"He's charming, in a debonair sort of way. Enthusiastic about his profession. People seem to like him." Holly started to clear the table. "Why? Is he your prime suspect? How come?"

"I don't have a prime suspect. If there's one thing that's

not lacking in this case, it's suspects." Rob spoke in a wry tone. "There's a plethora of them."

Holly frowned. "You haven't been able to rule out anyone yet? Well, other than Thomas, of course. I thought you were re-interviewing everyone after Plummet made such a hash of it."

Rob raised his eyebrows above his teacup, making Holly blush slightly.

"Well, he did, didn't he?" she protested.

Rob set his cup down. "As a matter of fact, we have ruled out two people. Carleton and Faith Sayers. Mr. Sayers had hip surgery a month ago. He's only able to do very light gardening at the moment, so he works in the slat house on site in the mornings. He was with Mick Santorini all morning and left at lunchtime for a doctor's appointment. He wasn't at the perfumery all afternoon."

"And Mrs. Sayers?"

"Helping to clean in the morning with Kat Santorini and Cressida, then packing perfumes with Kat before taking her husband to his appointment. They went home after that. They're also in their mid-eighties, and only keep working at the perfumery because they're considered family. And they love it." Rob smiled. "Mr. Sayers told me multiple times that he'll be back in the passionflower fields in a couple of weeks."

"Sounds like Gramps," Holly noted. "I doubt he'll ever stop working in his garden. It's nice when people love their work like that though. So, no alibis for anyone else?"

Rob shook his head. "Not as yet. It would help if we could discover where Dickenson was actually killed before his body was taken to the frangipani trees. That might rule out a couple of people."

"No luck yet, huh? I thought your search might have

turned up something by now." Holly began to stack the dishes in the sink. "I guess you'll be going back there today, then."

"Yes. I'm sorry." Rob crossed the kitchen to pull Holly into his arms again. "I know you wanted to go to Twilight Lake today." He glanced at the kitchen clock. "I told Sergeant Frampton I'd be back at Plumeria at one, but I have a little time still. Feel like a walk? I heard there's quite a nice one that goes along the coast from here. It would only take about half an hour, and I'd like to spend some time with you today."

Holly eyed him with suspicion. "It's not a mountain hike, is it? You swear it's flat ground?"

"Promise. Fee up at reception tells me there are some gorgeous views. Well?"

"Give me five minutes to put my sneakers on." Holly grinned, gave him a kiss, and fled to get ready.

THE TRAIL WOUND along by the coast past clumps of black mangrove trees with their silvery green leaves and snorkel-like roots poking up out of the mud. Sally Lightfoot crabs scuttled away into the mud as the pair approached.

"They're called what?" Rob paused to watch the five-centimeter-wide brown crabs disappear into the roots of the mangrove.

"Sally Lightfoot," Holly repeated with a grin. "You must have seen them on Hibiscus Island. They live on the rocks along the coast. Bright red spots? You can find their molted shells sometimes."

"These aren't red," Rob pointed out.

"Probably juveniles. They get brighter as they get older."

Holly pulled on Rob's arm to get him to keep walking, then interlaced her fingers in his. "This is nice."

The inspector smiled, tightening his grip. "Very nice. I wish we could have gone to Twilight Lake as planned, though."

Holly shrugged. "We can always come back another time. Turtle's only a short flight from Hibiscus, after all. And who knows? You may solve the case today and we'll be able to visit the lake tomorrow."

As the trail turned inland, they walked in companionable silence for a while, broken only by the occasional observation. The path took them through a grove of frangipani trees, making Holly laugh.

"We don't seem to be able to get away from these things, do we? But I have to say, they smell fabulous."

Rob picked a white-and-yellow flower from a low-lying branch, then placed it in Holly's hair. He surveyed her with a smile. "Looks nice too. What was it you called them again? Plumeria something."

"*Plumeria rubra*. These white-and-yellow ones are quite common but they're very pretty." Holly's smile faded when she saw the inspector was frowning. "What's the matter?"

"No, that's not what you called them before."

"Uh, yes, I did. Like I said, they're pretty common." Holly mock scowled. "Are you questioning my horticultural knowledge, Inspector?"

Rob didn't grin in response. Instead, he picked up another flower from the ground and stared at it. "Then what did you and Mr. Santorini call the tree we found the body under? It was a Plumeria too, wasn't it?"

"Yes, but it was *Plumeria pudica*. Different species. The flowers grow in tighter clusters, have different leaves, and they're not as fragrant as the—" Holly stopped speaking to frown in earnest. "Okay. Tell me what you've just realized. Because I can tell you've had a lightbulb moment."

Rob brandished the blossom in his hand. "So, this flower is not a *Plumeria pudica*? Are you sure?"

"Yes." Holly was exasperated now. "What's going on?"

"This flower that I'm holding right now," Rob said slowly, "is the same as the one that Dr. Shaw found inside Dickenson's shirt when she examined the body."

"Ohhhh." Holly fell silent for a moment. "But that means—"

"—Dickenson was killed where this type of flower could fall on him." Rob gave a sharp nod. "You'll have to come and identify the one that was on the body, Holly, to confirm it for me. Miranda Shaw took photos and I'll need an expert to look at them. The actual flower, too, since it's been preserved as evidence."

As Rob started back along the trail, Holly scurried to catch up.

SERGEANT FRAMPTON BLINKED in surprise from behind his desk as the inspector, with Holly in tow, interrupted what appeared to be late morning coffee at the police station in Azalea Village.

"I thought we were meeting at the perfumery at one, Inspector. Did I get the time wrong? I've been catching up on paperwork."

"No, no, Sergeant. You're quite right. I just wanted to see the Dickenson file. Specifically, the photos of the flower found in his shirt."

"The flower in his—?" The sergeant blinked again.

"Well, sure, Inspector, I'll just grab it for you. I believe Inspector Plummet has it right now."

The big burly sergeant disappeared down a narrow corridor. A moment later, Plummet's voice could be heard.

"Wants the file? For what reason?... Flowers? What are you talking about, Sergeant?... Who's here? Oh, never mind, send them through."

As an apologetic Sergeant Frampton relayed the message they'd already heard, Rob gave a polite nod, then gestured to Holly to precede him along the corridor.

Inspector Moore's office, now preempted by Inspector Plummet, was a small room with large windows on one side that overlooked the ocean. An L-shaped desk sat in one corner with a desktop computer taking up most of the space, and a small sad-looking African violet plant in the corner. Certificates hung on one pale blue wall while another sported a large framed photograph of police officers in full dress uniform. Behind the desk, Inspector Plummet scowled at them.

"Well, Tucker? What's this about flowers?"

He listened with irritation to Rob's explanation, then looked Holly up and down. She gritted her teeth, forcing herself not to react to the contempt in his gaze.

"You say Miss Gold is an expert?"

"I do. And I would like her opinion on the photographs Dr. Shaw took. Could I have the file please, Inspector Plummet?" Rob held out a firm hand.

"Pfft. Do as you wish." Plummet pushed a folder towards him.

Rob flipped through the hard copies of reports, pulling out some photos. "These are close-ups, Holly. There's no need for you to see the body again. Here. What do you think? Can you identify those flowers?"

Holly glanced at the photo of a white-and-yellow flower with five petals set in a whorl. "That's a *Plumeria rubra* variety. You can tell by the shape of the petals and the color of the centers. The yellow spreads up the petals more than it does in *Plumeria pudica*, which is pure white with a tiny yellow center." She looked at Rob. "This flower definitely didn't come from the tree we found the body under."

"Thank you." Rob handed the file back to a now-frowning Inspector Plummet. "Well, Inspector, I think this means our theory that the body was moved is correct. Now we need to find out where Dickenson could have acquired these flowers."

"There are frangipani trees all over that property." Inspector Plummet's scowl deepened.

"Yes, but I don't think we need to hunt too far."

"Huh?"

"The perfumery is currently using this type of flower in its *enfleurage* process," Rob explained to the confused inspector. "I suggest, Inspector Plummet, that we have Sergeant Frampton and some constables do a search of the working part of the perfumery for any evidence that Dickenson may have been killed there."

"Oh, of course," Holly breathed.

"The working part of the perfumery?" Plummet was silent for a moment. "Huh. You know the Lestrade woman will have an absolute fit if we invade her daughter's laboratory, don't you? I hope you're prepared for another call from the commissioner, Tucker." He added in a huffy tone, "But do as you wish."

"I'll tell the sergeant, then." Rob produced another polite smile before ushering Holly out of the room.

Holly stayed silent until Rob had spoken to Sergeant Frampton, arranging to meet him and the constables at the perfumery. Once they were outside the building, she released her breath in a loud whoosh.

"Well, he's not a happy inspector, is he?"

Rob smiled. "No comment. I'll run you back to the science center, Holly, but then I'm afraid I'll have to get back to work. I really am sorry about all this. It's not what I thought I'd be doing on holiday."

"Oh, don't be sorry. Really, it's a good thing you were here, Rob. I don't think any progress would have been made on this case if you weren't." Holly held up her hands. "Okay, okay. I won't say anything more. I'll find Jamie and Thomas and see what they're up to."

Rob frowned as he opened the door to the little orange car. "You said they were doing something with mass spectrometry in Natasha's lab, didn't you? Do you know what exactly?"

"Nope. They rushed off in great excitement before I had a chance to ask any questions. But I'll find out. And if it's relevant in any way, I'll let you know."

20

J amie and Thomas weren't at the cottage when Holly was dropped off, so she headed to the reception area to get directions to Natasha's lab. Fee, the helpful and kind woman in charge, pointed out a tiny path that wound between the two main buildings of the center.

"Go down there, along the water's edge, and you'll see the lab at the far end. It's a low building on its own."

Holly ambled along the path, observing with interest the outdoor tanks that housed marine specimens. She paused to peer into one of the concrete enclosures.

"It's empty right now." Natasha spoke behind her. "But one of my interns will be using it shortly, I hope. What do you think of our setup here, Holly?"

"Well, I don't really know what it all is, but it looks impressive." Holly smiled at the marine scientist, who waved an expansive hand around.

"This is the outdoor area for experiments, specimen holding, research, anything really. We have three wet benches and several seawater hookups, plus tanks, heaters, and any other accessories. There are some larger tanks for the bigger specimens around the front of the lab too. And this is on top of the indoor labs. It's a great place. I love working here." Natasha beamed, rocking back on her heels. "You here to see the dynamic duo?"

Holly grinned. "I am. Do you know where they are?"

"In my lab. Come on. I'll show you."

"You didn't leave them in there alone, did you?"

"Good grief, no." Natasha laughed. "I want my lab to still be standing at the end of the day, thank you very much. No, I left one of my interns in charge." She held a door open for Holly. "In here."

The lab was a long room lined with black counters covered in stands of test tubes, balances, bottles of all shapes and sizes, microscopes, and more machines that Holly didn't know the name of. Above them, mounted on white-tiled walls, glass fronted wooden cupboards were equally crowded with an assortment of different items. One wall of counters had windows over them looking out across the sea, while at the far end of the room, sat two desks with computers. Whiteboards covered in charts and graphs filled any empty spaces on walls. Down the center of the room were several multi-drawered workstations with black countertops and standing shelves above them.

It was professional and casual looking at the same time, organized in some chaotic fashion that obviously made sense to the scientists. A young woman in cut-off jean shorts and a tank top glanced up as they passed, giving Holly a quick smile before returning her attention to whatever she was doing with beakers, test tubes, and a calculator.

Holly followed Natasha through the room to a door at the far end. As Nat opened the door, Thomas's laugh floated out.

"That's fantastic. Why did we never do this sort of thing in school? Hit it again, Jamie."

There was the sound of a hammer hitting something followed by more laughter.

Natasha grinned as she and Holly entered the room. "Ah, the old banana in liquid nitrogen experiment, huh, Rachel?"

The young woman who'd been watching Jamie wield the hammer turned around with a laugh. "Oh well, we were just waiting for the GC-MS to finish up and this is always fun. The samples should be done by now, though, so we can have a look at the graphs whenever you're ready."

Jamie had turned around at the sound of Natasha's voice. Safety goggles perched on her nose, a hammer was in her hand, and her face was alight with laughter. "Holls, come and see this. Rachel put a banana in liquid nitrogen. Look what happened to it." She gestured to the pile of frozen chunks of banana scattered on the counter.

Wearing his own safety goggles, Thomas grinned. "It's great. It freezes like rock."

Natasha laughed. "Yeah, the high school kids love this when they visit."

"I'll bet they do." Jamie removed her goggles, handing them back to the intern. "Thanks, Rachel. Did you say the samples were done?"

The young blonde nodded. She led the way to a computer in the corner of the room, then sat down and started clicking around on the screen.

"What did you test?" Holly asked.

Jamie grinned and fished in her pockets, pulling out two tiny bottles. "These two perfumes from Plumeria. I bought them yesterday. Rachel only needed a drop of each to analyze."

"I'm still not sure exactly why you wanted to do this." Holly raised an eyebrow at Thomas.

"It was what Becky said about the perfume scandal, coupled with Gabriel's explanation of how they analyzed the perfume we found on the shipwreck," the journalist explained. "We think Dickenson might have had proof that *Frangipani Allure* was stolen, right? Well, I'm wondering if he analyzed the two perfumes somehow and found they were similar."

Holly frowned. "Is one of those bottles the frangipani one?"

"Yeah."

"But you don't have Gabriel's perfume, so how—?"

"Well, no, but maybe Rob could get hold of it if he needed to," Jamie said.

"We really just wanted to see how this process worked," Thomas added. "I like to understand what I'm planning to write about."

As a printer whirred behind them, Natasha collected the papers that emerged from it. She spread them out on the desk. Thomas and Jamie bent over them, heads almost touching as they peered at the graphs.

"What do these mean?" Jamie asked, tracing the jagged peaks that bore a vague similarity to an ECG scan.

"Each peak represents an aroma compound," Natasha said. "Either synthetic or natural."

"So, it's like a formula?" Holly asked.

"No. It just lets you see the general structure—and the main components—of a perfume. Think of it like an x-ray," Natasha explained.

Thomas frowned. "But if you ran an analysis of two different perfumes and the peaks matched, that would constitute proof they were the same?"

"It might. Sample differences can cause differences in the graph, but if they were virtually identical, then yes, it might be accepted as evidence." Natasha shrugged. "I'm not in the fragrance business so you'd have to consult an expert for more details. I'm sure there's a whole pile of legal stuff related to this."

"Hmmm. Tricky to prove anything, I imagine." Thomas gazed down at the graphs, then smiled at Rachel. "Well, thank you very much for this."

The intern grinned. "No problem. I've never been part of a detective investigation before. Usually I'm doing pigment analysis of seawater. This was kind of fun."

After thanking Rachel again, Jamie and Thomas followed Natasha and Holly from the lab. The marine scientist paused outside.

"What are your plans for the rest of the day? I'm afraid I'm going to be stuck here till evening now."

"I'm on my own," Holly said.

Jamie raised an eyebrow in surprise. "Why? What's Rob doing?"

"Oh. I haven't told you yet, have I? Rob's had a breakthrough. He's searching the working part of the perfumery right now. He thinks Dickenson may have been killed there."

"What?" Jamie and Thomas spoke in unison.

"I'll fill you in," Holly promised, "but what are your plans for the rest of the day? Are you doing anything special? Can I tag along?"

Thomas and Jamie exchanged glances.

"I don't have to," Holly added in a hurried voice. "If you wanted to do your own thing, that's perfectly okay. I can amuse myself."

"Don't be ridiculous." Jamie dismissed her concerns

with a wave of her hand. "We're going to have lunch in Silver Landing. And of course you can come along."

Thomas grinned. "You can tell us all about Rob's breakthrough on the way back to the cottage to get the cars. Thanks for the use of the lab, Nat. Very helpful. I'll send you a copy of the article I write."

"No problem. I'll see you later." With a quick wave, Natasha vanished back into her lab.

Jamie linked arms with Holly. "Okay, Holls. Now. What's happened?"

IN THE PASSENGER seat of the little orange car, Holly flinched as Jamie zipped around another corner on the narrow winding road.

"Could you slow down just a little?" she pleaded, clutching her seat with both hands.

"I'm only doing thirty miles an hour," Jamie protested. "These things don't go that fast."

"It feels like it though!"

Jamie laughed. "It's a lot more rugged here than Hibiscus, isn't it? I just love these mountains too. I was reading some of the brochures in Fee's office before we went to the lab and realized they have absolutely tons of hiking trails here. There's one that follows an old aqueduct around a mountain and ends up at a lake where you can see an enormous colony of seagulls at this time of year. They nest right on the ground around the lake. Pretty neat. And then there was another one that starts in a little valley before going straight up the mountain and on to the rim of a crater lake. I've decided I have to come back here someday for a proper holiday."

Holly smiled at the enthusiasm in her friend's voice. "I'd like to come back again too. So would Rob. He hasn't had much of a holiday this time around, poor thing."

"Mmm." Jamie pursed her lips as she drove. "I've got to say that thing with the flowers was pretty good, Holls. Do you think Rob's right? That the flowers on Dickenson were the same ones that they were making perfume with?"

"I don't know. They looked very similar, but I didn't see the ones in the *enfleurage* room up close. I expect Mr. Santorini or that arborist they have at the perfumery will be able to tell him." Holly pointed at a sign up ahead. "Silver Landing. Turn left, Jamie."

Behind them, Thomas, in the second little car, also turned down the two-lane narrow road that led to the main town on Turtle Island. The road sloped down toward the sea, leveling off as it reached the coast. Red-roofed houses lined both sides of the street, their tiny lawns enclosed behind white walls or railings sporting the occasional palm tree, vegetable plot, or ornamental flower bed. Red or magenta bougainvillea draped across many a veranda; neat round topiary-like shrubs of blue plumbago stood like sentinels in front of others; and every house had hydrangea shrubs.

"This must be just. stunning in the summer!" Holly exclaimed. "If we come again, it has to be when the hydrangeas are in bloom. Where are we going for lunch?"

Jamie slowed as she came to an intersection. "There's a restaurant right on the water beside the square. By a church apparently. Fee said we can't miss it."

"That's a square up ahead. Oh, and there's the church! Gosh, it's beautiful." Holly pulled out her phone to take a photo of the brick-edged white building with its elaborate carved front door and square-turreted belltower.

Jamie turned into a nearby parking lot and switched off the engine, then waited until Thomas had finished parking beside her before opening the door. Holly hopped out, gazing around in delight.

The church sat in the center of the cobbled square with steps leading up to it from all sides. Surrounding it were small red-roofed shops, cafes, and restaurants, which over-flowed onto either side of a narrow road that ended at a long pier edging the ocean. Fishing boats were drawn up to the dock and what looked like a small fish market was set up nearby.

People bustled in and out of the shops or sat on benches in a small garden at the edge of the square, shaded by cassia trees. Big planters, overflowing with red salvia and pink petunias, added vibrant color at intervals.

"Pretty place." Jamie's voice held approval as she and Thomas joined Holly. "We should look around. I still need to get a thank-you gift for Maggie for looking after Teddy."

"After lunch." Thomas gestured toward a small restaurant at the corner of the square. "That's our place, and I see Gabriel—oh, and Callum too, it looks like—waiting for us."

21

_____

Holly glared at Jamie as they walked towards the restaurant. "You didn't tell me you were meeting them."

"It was spur of the moment," her friend responded with a smirk.

"It was not! Rob doesn't know about this, does he?"

"Shh." Jamie grinned. "It'll be fine, Holls."

Callum Stewart greeted them with a smile. "I hope you don't mind but Gabriel and I had just got back from a seaweed trip when he mentioned he was meeting you. I ran him over by boat, and he suggested I join you."

"Absolutely fine," Thomas responded, holding the door for everyone to enter. "Gorgeous weather for boating today, that's for sure."

Once seated at their table, Jamie smiled at the science center director. "We visited Nat's lab today, you know. It's pretty cool."

Callum laughed. "I think so too. What did she show you?"

"Oh, we were seeing how the gas chromatography thingy

worked. Nat's intern Rachel put some perfume samples through it for us. And she also froze a banana in liquid nitrogen. Now that was fun."

"You were analyzing perfumes?" Gabriel's voice held surprise. "Why would you do that? Which perfumes?"

Thomas put down the menu he'd been studying. "Just two samples from Plumeria Perfumes. I'm writing about the release of *Rosa del Mar* for the paper and wanted to see how the process of analysis worked. It's quite fascinating, actually. Gave me a new appreciation for your work, Gabriel."

"Ah, I see." Gabriel smiled. "Well, the analysis was just the beginning. Amelie and I still had a lot of nose work to do after that. Some tweaking of ingredients, adjustments to amounts, that sort of thing. But yes, it is a fascinating job. You said you had questions for me, Mr. Miller, when you invited me to lunch. What would you like to know?"

"Well, actually," Thomas leaned forward slightly as he spoke, "I was wondering if I could get your take on Susan Hill's claim that you took a formula belonging to her mother, Olivia Hill?"

Holly's mouth dropped open in shock. Seriously? She shot an accusatory look at Jamie. Oblivious, her friend continued to regard the perfumer with an interested expression.

To Holly's surprise, Gabriel laughed. "That old story again? I suppose you heard it from Susan. She can't let it die." He rolled his eyes. "I took nothing from Olivia Hill that I wasn't entitled to. I had a contract with Grand Island Perfumes that said what I created belonged to me. When I left, I took what I'd created."

"What about the court decision that says a business owns any perfume made by people who work for it?" Jamie asked.

"Doesn't apply here." Gabriel shrugged. "We're not bound by any court decisions except those on Grand Island. And when Olivia Hill was misguided enough to take me to court, they ruled that the formula belonged to me." He wagged a finger at Thomas as the journalist opened his mouth. "However, as you've no doubt discovered from your research, in the interests of goodwill, I agreed not to use my recipe for my own business, or give it to anyone else, since the perfume we had made from it was already considered a signature scent of Grand Island Perfumes. And I've honored that agreement. The formula—the recipe—belongs to me. I own it. But it is used by Grand Island Perfumes to make their fragrance for as long as they wish. If they cease production, I will, should I wish, be able to create the fragrance once again under my own name, at my own perfumery—Manout Perfumes."

There was a slight pause, during which a young waiter approached to take their orders. As soon as the man had left, Thomas returned to the discussion.

"You haven't shared the formula with anyone? Only Grand Island Perfumes has access to it?"

"Correct." Gabriel's eyebrows rose. "Why?"

"I wondered if someone could copy it."

The perfumer gave a very Gallic shrug of his shoulders. "As you no doubt realized today, Mr. Miller, with your analysis of perfumes, it's possible for people to discover the separate aroma compounds within a fragrance and reproduce it to the best of their ability. Will it be identical? Unlikely. A nose is still required, and most people do not possess one fine enough to make the tiny necessary tweaks. But could it be similar? Certainly."

Thomas had been taking frantic notes as Gabriel spoke. "Is it possible that your perfume—the one from Grand

Island Perfumes—was copied and tweaked? You worked with Amelie Lestrade when you were on Azure Isle, didn't you?"

Gabriel frowned. "I did. What are you implying, Mr. Miller? That Amelie Lestrade took my formula? Why would she do that? She is a competent perfumer herself."

"Is *Frangipani Allure* similar to the perfume you made for Grand Island Perfumes?" Thomas cut straight to the chase, pausing to watch Gabriel's reaction.

"*Frangipani Allure*? Not at all. It is significantly different from the Grand Island Perfumes scent I created, I assure you. It has entirely different base notes, for one. It is a beautiful perfume, however. Amelie's finest creation to date, in fact, and one that will make her name in the industry."

"She hasn't had a name until now?" Jamie asked.

"Frankly, no. She is good but not a master. Her nose is not as sensitive as some." Gabriel's shrug was matter-of-fact.

Jamie studied the perfumer thoughtfully. "How long were you on Azure Isle, Gabriel? Sylvie Lestrade told us you were her protégé. I've heard she's quite a well-renowned perfumer in her own right."

The perfumer raised an eyebrow. "Protégé? I wouldn't say that, but I certainly enjoyed my time there, and I learned a lot. Sylvie was born into the perfume world. She apprenticed at a fine perfume house in France and worked there for many years before 'retiring' to Azure Isle."

His air quotes made Holly smile. "I take it she didn't really retire."

Gabriel laughed. "Not at all. While in operation, Lestrade Fragrances was a highly exclusive perfumery. Sylvie only produced a few scents, but they were wonderful ones."

"But Amelie's aren't as good?" Holly was curious. "Why

not? We heard she was brought up in the business since practically birth."

"As I said, Amelie is a competent perfumer, yes, but she is not her mother. Sylvie... Ah, Sylvie had a nose *incroyable*." Gabriel kissed his fingers flamboyantly, suddenly becoming very French, before he sighed. "That is one reason Amelie accepted a job at Plumeria Perfumes. It is... hmmm... difficult... to grow up in the shadow of greatness. And it has been good for her. She is thriving there."

Before anyone could respond, Callum interrupted, a shade of relief in his voice. He rubbed his hands together. "Ah. I see our salads coming. Excellent. I'm starving."

HOLLY STOOD on the dock at Silver Landing as Callum started the boat engine. Gabriel gave her a cheerful wave before sitting down next to him. As the boat pulled away, she turned to see where Thomas and Jamie had gone.

After the initial interrogation of Gabriel, Callum had steered the conversation into more general waters. He had regaled them with descriptions of dive sites around Turtle Island, before beginning a spirited discussion about the need for invasive species control in island waters. This had instantly diverted Thomas and Jamie, both keen divers and environmentalists, and the rest of lunch had passed without incident.

Spotting Jamie emerging from a small shop, paper bag in hand, Holly started to cross the square, only to pause when her phone buzzed. Rob's name appeared on the screen.

"Hello?" She waved to get Jamie's attention as she listened to Rob on the other end. "Oh. Well, yes, I can, but we're in Silver Landing right now so it'll take a while to get to you... Jamie and Thomas are here too... Yeah, we had lunch with Callum and Gabriel..." Holly winced at the silence that followed this statement. "I didn't actually know until I got here, Rob... Yes... Yes... Okay. I'll be there as soon as possible... Yep, me too. Bye."

"Was that Rob? What did he want?" Jamie had crossed the square in time to hear Holly's last words. "Is it to do with the case? Has he found out anything? We kind of bombed out with the stolen formula idea, didn't we?"

"Yeah. And Rob's a bit annoyed that we had lunch with Gabriel, by the way. I didn't mean to tell him," Holly protested when her friend groaned. "It just slipped out."

"Oh well." Jamie shrugged. "So, what did he want?"

"He wants me to go identify flowers again." Holly frowned. "I don't know why Mr. Santorini couldn't do it. Or the other gardener. Cressida Billing's cousin, I think it is."

Jamie shook her head instantly. "They're suspects. Weren't they on site when the murder happened? That probably means Rob can't ask them to be experts."

"Oh, I hadn't thought of that. Yeah, you're probably right. Well, I told him I'd go straight to Plumeria. Is it okay if I take the car and you go back with Thomas?"

"Go back?" Jamie was astounded. "Don't be silly, Holls. We'll come with you, of course. Where's Miller got to? He wandered away while I was buying this stuff. Oh, there he is." She waved with enthusiasm, catching the journalist's attention.

"What'd you get?" Holly eyed the gold-embossed paper bag with curiosity as they waited for Thomas to reach them.

"A thank-you gift for Maggie. For looking after Teddy. What do you think?" Jamie rummaged in the bag, pulling out a tiny gift box. Opening it, she showed Holly the small gold earrings in the shape of turtles. "Will she like them?"

"She'll love them." Holly smiled as she examined the detail on the jewelry studs. The tiny gold turtles were perfect. "And she'll say you didn't need to do this. You know that, right?"

Jamie returned the box to the bag. "Doesn't matter what she says. I'll bet Teddy's been spoiled rotten the whole time I've been away." She glanced up as Thomas approached. "Holly's been called in as an expert on the case! We've got to get to the perfumery ASAP."

"Really?" The anticipation in the journalist's grey eyes matched the expression on Jamie's face. "Well then, let's rock and roll, people!"

ROB WAS WAITING in the parking lot of Plumeria Perfumes when they arrived. Beyond a slight sigh as they all emerged from the tiny cars, he didn't comment on Thomas and Jamie's presence, instead focusing on Holly.

Gesturing to the two men beside him, he introduced them. "You know Mr. Santorini, of course, Holly, but I don't think you've met Mr. Billings. He's the arborist here at the perfumery. Holly's a qualified horticulturist, Mr. Billings."

A lean, rugged man with dark brown hair and brown eyes, Seth Billings looked nothing like his blonde cousin. With a rueful grimace, he shook Holly's hand, then Thomas's and Jamie's.

"Good thing you're here, Holly. Since we're suspects, our identification of the frangipani flowers in question is apparently invalid."

A slightly smug look crossed Jamie's face at this confirmation of her theory.

"Oh... Well..." Holly was flustered.

Rob sighed. "Now, Mr. Billings, we've been over this."

"Yeah, yeah, I get it." Seth sighed too. "At least you've been polite about it, Inspector. Unlike others I could name."

Rob cleared his throat in warning as Jamie opened her mouth, making her close it again. "I'll need Holly to come with me to the *enfleurage* room, and then, after she's seen the flowers, I'd like for her to see the trees the flowers have been harvested from. We'll be right back so if you'd just wait here, Mr. Billings, Mr. Santorini."

Both men nodded, Mr. Santorini's face creased in concern while Seth Billings merely looked glum.

"We'll stay here too." Thomas pulled out his phone as he spoke. "I'd like to pick your brains about the horticultural side of the perfume business anyway, if you don't mind, Mr. Santorini. For my article about *Rosa del Mar*."

The elderly head gardener blinked in surprise. "Well, I don't know..."

"Just stick to horticulture, Miller." Rob smiled at Mr. Santorini. "Be kind. He doesn't know a rose from an onion."

A bark of laughter escaped Seth while Mr. Santorini relaxed perceptibly.

"That was nice of you," Holly said as Rob escorted her around the building to one of the doors that led into the lower level and the working part of the perfumery.

Rob shrugged. "I don't really think either of them committed the crime. Mick Santorini was with Mr. Sayers in the slat house all morning, had lunch with his granddaughter, then was in the garden all afternoon planting annuals of some kind..."

"Alyssum and blue salvia," Holly supplied.

Rob laughed. "Yes. Those. Besides, I was there when he found the body, and he wasn't faking that illness."

"And Seth Billings?" Holly asked.

"Started work at ten, was in the passionflower fields doing some sort of horticultural magic with Jake O'Connor until one thirty. Had lunch off site with a reputable witness, and then was working again with Jake all afternoon." Rob grinned at Holly's raised eyebrow. "Said reputable witness being our very own police surgeon, Dr. Shaw. But Billings is right that any identification by either him or Mr. Santorini wouldn't cut it in court. So, it's just as well my own personal expert is available." He held the door open for Holly. "Suit up."

"Suit up?" Holly eyed the coveralls and gloves with surprise. "Are you serious?"

"It's probably a case of locking the door after the horse has bolted," Rob admitted, pulling a pair of coveralls on over his own clothes, "but we're following procedure as much as possible now."

"You mean because if Dickenson was killed in the *enfleurage* room, there were people in here the whole next day, right?" Holly struggled into the lightweight suit as she spoke.

"Unfortunately, yes."

"Have you found any evidence that he was killed here?" Holly paused. "Never mind. Forget I asked that."

Rob grinned and held out paper booties. "Put these on too."

22

As Holly shuffled into the *enfleurage* room, feeling very conspicuous in her crime scene outfit, a similarly attired Sergeant Frampton and Dr. Shaw glanced up with smiles.

"Ah, it's our flower specialist. Hi, Holly." Miranda gave her a little wave. "I've got the original flower here for you, and the photos, and a microscope in case you need it." She gestured toward the instrument resting on plastic on the counter.

"I don't think I'll need it, but thanks." Holly gazed at the piles of frangipani flowers still resting on the white fat in the glass trays with some dismay. Many of the flowers had turned brown around the edges. "Oh dear. This is going to really mess up the pomade, isn't it?"

"Yes. So we've been told multiple times." Miranda made a face. "And we'll be even more vilified when we tell them we've found nothing to indicate Dickenson was killed here."

Rob sighed. "Are you sure?"

"Positive." Miranda started to unzip her coverall. "Technicians have been over this room with a fine-tooth comb.

And I've personally checked every smooth surface and object in the room. Nada. Ditto the separating room and the packing room." She grinned at Holly's surprise. "Double duty here on Turtle sometimes. I'm a pretty good forensics person, though I do say so myself."

Sergeant Frampton nodded. "It's only the lab to do now, Inspector, but you'll need to speak to Ms. Lestrade. She's refused to let us in."

"Refused?" Rob's eyebrows drew together. "I spoke to Lily O'Connor yesterday. She said the lab would be made available. You mean you haven't examined it yet?"

Miranda snorted as the sergeant shook his head. "Amelie Lestrade won't give us access."

"Hmm. Well, surely there's another key?"

"Apparently it's missing."

"Missing? Since when?" Rob frowned.

Miranda waggled her eyebrows. "No one seems to know. It wasn't noticed until we asked for it. It leads one to suspect, though, doesn't it?"

"It does." Rob was grim. "Well, I'll have a chat with Ms. Lestrade. I assume she's on site?"

The police surgeon grinned. "Oh yes. She's with Lily. In her office. Expressing her opinion about police in her perfumery. Very loudly."

"We have a locksmith on call, Inspector." Sergeant Frampton's voice was bland. "Should you need one."

"A locksmith?" Rob paused. "Is this a normal occurrence on your island, Sergeant? People refusing to comply with police directives?"

"Well sir, things are a little different—" The sergeant stopped speaking, his lips twitching in amusement at Rob's heartfelt groan.

"Don't tell me. It's an island thing." The inspector

pinched the bridge of his nose, ignoring Holly's giggle. "If I had a dollar for the number of times I've heard that since I moved to this part of the world— Well, never mind. No, Sergeant, I do not require a locksmith. Miss Amelie Lestrade will be opening her lab forthwith."

As Rob strode from the room, unzipping his coverall in one fluid and irritated motion, a clearly entertained Miranda chortled.

"Good man, that." The sergeant's voice held approval. "I'm thinking your dad would have liked him, Miss Gold."

"It's Holly. And I think so too." Holly fingered her coverall. "Can I take these things off then?"

"Better leave them on till you go. You ready to look at these flowers?" Miranda picked one off a tray. "I've got to say they look just like the one on the body to me. And Seth Billings says it's just the common variety. Nothing special about it."

"That's what I thought too," Holly admitted, taking the flower. "But if Dickenson wasn't killed in here, I don't see how this identification is even relevant now."

"Best follow the inspector's instructions anyway, Holly," Sergeant Frampton said.

"Okay. Where's the photo again? And the original flower?"

Holly laid the two specimens, one admittedly a little the worse for wear, and the photo side by side on the counter, peering closely from one to the other. She frowned. "Hmm."

"What? Aren't they the same?" Miranda came up alongside her.

"There's a slight difference. See here?" Holly pointed to the flowers.

"Uh... No. I mean the color's a bit different, but this one's practically dead now."

"The petals are shorter in this one. And they're closer together and overlap more distinctly. See? You can see a clear spiral effect in this one."

Sergeant Frampton had approached. "That's the flower that was on Dickenson, right?" He picked up the flower that had come from the tray with the pomade to look at it more closely, then peered again at the photo and the wilted flower. "It's a very slight difference. Could it just be a normal variation? I don't expect every flower on a tree looks exactly the same."

"No, but if you look at all of these on the trays," Holly swept her hand around the room, "the petals are all separated and they're all the same length, more or less. They don't spiral like the one that was on the body. You can see it's a clear whorl in this photo."

"A whorl?" Miranda raised an eyebrow. "That's what you call it?"

"That's the pattern," Holly explained. "The flower itself is a variety of frangipani. I think it might be Celadine, but I'm not exactly sure. I'm not an expert on frangipani varieties—there are a lot of them. But it definitely isn't the common yellow-and-white variety like the ones in the trays." She paused. "Mr. Santorini would be able to confirm if it's Celadine. Or my Gramps."

The sergeant frowned. "Mick Santorini isn't really a suspect any longer, but still, we shouldn't use him as an expert. Can you get hold of your grandfather? Maybe send a photo?"

Holly made a face. "He's not keen on cellphones, but my mom might be able to track him down. I'll call her."

Maggie answered the call after just a couple of rings. "Holly? What's wrong? Is this something to do with that murder? How on earth do you all manage to keep finding dead bodies?"

"Hi, Mama." Holly ignored Miranda's snort of laughter. Maggie's voice had been clearly audible through the phone. "Yeah, it's sort of to do with it. I wondered if Gramps could confirm a flower ID for me. Do you think you could find him and ask?"

"As it happens, he's right here having tea with me." Maggie paused. "Identify a flower?" She paused again. "Yes, dad. She said a flower. No, I don't know what flower. Here, talk to her yourself."

"Hello, Holly girl." Gramps's voice rumbled through the phone. "Got yourself caught up in another investigation, eh? What's this about a flower?"

"It's a frangipani, Gramps. I'm pretty sure we have one of them at the inn, but I need you to confirm my identity of it. It's not the common yellow-and-white one, though. Similar, but with shorter petals and a tighter whorl... What? Its scent? Well, I don't know, Gramps. The only one I have is practically dead and I don't know where the tree is. I haven't smelled one properly... Oh. Yeah, hang on. Give the phone back to Mama and she can switch to video."

"You've found lots of dead bodies, have you?" Miranda leaned against the counter, eyes dancing as she listened to the voices coming from Holly's phone as her mother and grandfather sorted themselves out.

"Not by choice, I assure you." Holly refocused on her phone as her mother's face appeared briefly, then disappeared as her grandfather claimed the phone peering closely at it.

"Where's this flower, Holly girl?"

Holly switched views so she could hold the phone above

the half dead flower found in Jonathan Dickenson's shirt. "It's this one."

"Humph. Well, that's a pitiful specimen, isn't it?"

A chuckle escaped Sergeant Frampton as he pushed the photo towards Holly. "Try this. It was fresher when we took it."

"Ah. Hmmm." There was silence on the other end of the phone for a moment. "Hmm. Looks like Celadine to me."

"Show him the other flowers too," Miranda urged.

Holly carried the phone over to the chassis trays. "What about these, Gramps?"

"Common yellow-and-white," was the instant response. "Not the same as that other one." There was a pause. "What's that they're sitting on? Lard?"

"Yeah, they're being used to make perfume." Holly grinned at the snort that emanated from the phone, then flicked the camera view again. Her grandfather's face filled the screen. "Celadine, you said, Gramps? That's what I thought too. We have one at the inn, don't we?"

"No. But Myrtle has one."

"Oh, that's where I've seen it. That's right." Holly nodded. "Small tree, right?"

"Yes. Grows about fifteen feet, I'd say. She hasn't yet deigned to give me a cutting." Gramps snorted again. "Bit selfish, really. Very strong scent, Celadine. Like I said, nice plant." He paused. "Is Mick Santorini still in charge at that place, Holly?"

Holly nodded. "Yes. Gramps, I have—"

A crafty expression crossed Gramps's face. "If he has a Celadine, Holly, ask him for a cutting for me. Maybe two, if he can spare them. Tell him it's Stuart Mackintosh asking. He'll know who I am. Oh, and Holly, I believe he's got some

Bridal Bouquet frangipani he's been promising me for years. *Plumeria pudica*. You know it, don't you?"

Sergeant Frampton and Miranda were openly grinning now as Holly sighed.

"Yes, I know it. And yes, Mr. Santorini still works here. And yes, I'll ask him for cuttings." She smiled at her grandfather. "Thanks a lot, Gramps. I'll go let Rob know what he said."

"Happy to be of help. And don't forget my cuttings, Holly girl. Right. Bye." He hung up abruptly.

"Well, he sounds like a real character." Miranda straightened up from the counter. "So, now all we have to do is find this Celadine tree, right, Sergeant?"

The sergeant raised an eyebrow. "We don't need to keep you from your work, Dr. Shaw."

Miranda waved an airy hand. "No, no, I'm happy to help. I think you're going to need to get Seth Billings or Mr. Santorini involved, though. Unless you plan to have poor Holly here hike all over the property in search of a frangipani tree."

Sergeant Frampton pondered for a moment. "I think I'll check with Inspector Tucker first. Why don't you wait outside, Holly, and I'll come and find you when I'm ready."

"I'll go with her." Miranda grinned as she slithered out of her coveralls. "Take those things off, Holly, and let's go find your friends."

Mr. Santorini wasn't outside when Holly and Miranda emerged, but Jamie and Thomas were laughing with Seth Billings as they perched on the low wall that surrounded the parking lot.

The arborist's smiled widened when he saw Miranda. "Well, hello there, Dr. Shaw. How's the medico business?"

"Good." Miranda grinned, sitting down beside him. "So, Holly found out something interesting."

Holly sighed as all heads spun her way. So much for waiting to see what Rob said. She frowned at the doctor, who gave an impenitent shrug.

"Within two minutes, the whole island will know anyway, Holly, so what's the difference? I know it's got to be the same on Hibiscus."

Jamie grinned. "It is. What did Holly find out? Let me guess. The flower found on the body isn't the same as the ones being used to make perfume, right?"

"That's obvious. It couldn't be."

Everyone looked at Seth Billings in surprise.

"And how would you know that?" Miranda asked.

The arborist shrugged. "Well, the body was found under Bridal Bouquet and we're using the common *Plumeria rubra* for *enfleurage* right now. They're not the same." Jamie and Thomas both frowned in confusion.

"What's Bridal Bouquet? That's not what Holly called it," Jamie said. "She said it was pud... pud... something."

Seth grinned. "*Plumeria pudica*. Same thing. Bridal Bouquet is its common name."

The sound of footsteps on gravel signaled the approach of a still-frowning Rob.

"Did you get the room unlocked?" Miranda asked, whistling in surprise when he nodded. "Well, I'm impressed! Good job, Inspector. I take it I'm needed, then."

"If you don't mind, Dr. Shaw. I think Sergeant Frampton would appreciate the help. Ms. Lestrade is leaving now." At Miranda's raised eyebrow, he shrugged. "She's been ill for the past week, apparently. Sergeant Frampton has her address if we need to get hold of her. And frankly, I'd as soon not have her in the room while you search it. She's quite unhappy about it."

Miranda nodded. "I'll get started then."

Rob zeroed in on Holly. "The sergeant tells me the flower was identified as Celadine. Is that correct?"

"Celadine?" Seth Billings asked. "That's the flower that was on the body?"

Rob's eyebrows drew together. "Do you know it?"

"Yeah, of course. We have a few Celadine trees on the property." Seth frowned. "I'm not sure why Dickenson would be out there, though. They're at the far end of the jasmine fields. Mick got the trees about, oh, five to seven years ago. We couldn't fit them into the big frangipani groves, so we started a second collection." He pointed out beyond the passionflower fields and oleander hedges that surrounded them. "They're over there. Do you want to go see?"

The inspector sighed. "Yes please, Mr. Billings."

23

Rob glanced around. "Where's Mr. Santorini?'

"Just coming. He went to get some water." Jamie nodded towards the steps of the perfumery where the head gardener could be seen carefully descending.

Mr. Santorini listened to what the inspector had to say, then nodded. "It's a bit of a trek across the fields, but yes, we can take you to see the trees. I can't imagine why anyone other than us would be out there. If you like, we can take the truck the long way round. There's a rough road that circles the property. We generally use it when we're harvesting the oleanders. Or we can walk. It'll take about the same amount of time either way."

"Walking it is."

Holly fell into step between Rob and Mr. Santorini as the older man led the way to a small path that cut through the rows of passionflower fencing.

"My grandfather sends his regards, Mr. Santorini."

The man gave a small laugh. "Does he? And how many cuttings does he want?"

Holly grinned in response. "He'd like some Bridal Bouquet and some Celadine, please. If you can spare two of each, he'll take them."

"Not a problem."

Behind them, Holly could hear Thomas talking to Seth Billings.

"So, I thought you picked the flowers for *enfleurage* in the mornings. But I'm sure I saw you on Thursday with a tub of flowers. How come you were picking them so late?"

The arborist grinned. "We usually do collect flowers in the morning, except for the frangipani."

"And the night-blooming jasmine." Mr. Santorini glanced sideways at Rob. "Some flowers are more heavily scented at night, Inspector, so we pick the blossoms in the late afternoon instead of morning. Frangipani is one of those."

The arborist nodded. "Jake and I were picking the things from about two thirty onwards."

"Do you actually hand pick the flowers?" Jamie asked, surprised.

"Yeah. They're fragile and we don't want them bruised if we can help it." Seth made a face. "It's a bit tedious, but you do get faster with practice. We drive the truck under the trees—I've pruned them to make sure we can reach the flowers—we pick them, pop the flowers into tubs, then deliver them to the perfumery. Kat and Faith, or whoever else is on duty, spread them on the *corps*."

"So, you were delivering the flowers to the *enfleurage* room from what time to what time?" Jamie asked.

"Oh, I think we brought the truck in around four, I guess. We park it round the back and then hoof the tubs round to the enfleurage room. Normally we'd have been done in half an hour or so, but Cressida grabbed us to help with setting up chairs for the lecture."

"So, Kat had the flowers in the *enfleurage* room?" Jamie clarified.

Seth nodded. "Big job. I gave her a hand finishing up after the chairs. Around five."

"Just you? I saw someone leaving on a motorbike when I walked up the road," Thomas said.

"Yeah, that would've been Jake. Came to me in a big panic and said he'd forgotten his mom's birthday, and they were having a family thing." Seth rolled his eyes. "Typical Jake. Anyway, it was no biggie. I wasn't doing anything that evening."

Rob stopped walking. "Where exactly are these trees that you were harvesting?"

"There's a grove of them near the main driveway. There's just room to drive the truck between them. We use ladders for some of the other trees, if Amelie wants the flowers from them, but for the common yellow-and-whites we use the truck."

"And you were picking flowers from two thirty onwards you say? Could you see the main driveway from where you were?"

Seth shook his head. "No. Sorry, Inspector. I know what you're getting at, but we wouldn't have seen that Dickenson guy if he walked up the road. He'd have had to come quite far out of his way along the small trails for us to have noticed him. And we didn't."

Rob nodded as he resumed walking alongside Mr. Santorini.

"Mind you," Seth added, "I wouldn't know if I saw him or not, would I?"

"What do you mean?" Rob stopped again. "You saw a photo. Surely you'd know if you'd seen the man or not. It was a very recent photograph. Easily recognizable."

"Never saw a photo."

Rob's mouth opened, then closed again. He pinched the bridge of his nose. "You didn't see a photo of Dickenson? Did you, Mr. Santorini?"

The head gardener shook his head. "Should I have?"

"Yes, you should," Rob snapped before drawing in a deep breath and forcing a short smile. "It must have been an oversight. We'll get it fixed. Now, where are these trees?" He marched on, his shoulders stiff with irritation.

Holly fell back to walk alongside a grinning Thomas and Jamie.

"Oooh, Rob's mad!" Jamie whispered. "What do you want to bet Plummet was supposed to show that photo around and didn't bother?"

"Plummet's absolutely useless." Seth Billings rolled his eyes. "Inspector Moore, on the other hand, is like your inspector. Good bloke. It's too bad he's—"

"—hiking in the Alps," Holly and Jamie chorused together. "We know."

THE CELADINE FRANGIPANI trees were part of a small group of trees, some in full flower, others only showing buds. A ladder lying on the ground beside one tree made Mr. Santorini frown.

"What's that ladder doing here? It should have been taken back to the equipment building, Seth."

"It wasn't me." Seth's brow creased as he too stared at the ladder.

"Maybe it was Jonathan Dickenson," Jamie interjected. "That could be how he got the flowers on him. Is that the Cela... Cela..."

"Celadine," Holly prompted.

"Yes. Celadine." Jamie shot a grin Holly's way.

"How would this Dickenson person get one of our ladders? Can't have been him." The head gardener dismissed the suggestion. "Maybe it was Jake? I'll have to ask. Not like him to forget equipment, though."

Seth snorted. "He forgets things all the time, Mick. He's always running back to the maintenance shed for stuff. Drives me crazy."

Mr. Santorini frowned again as Rob crouched briefly beside the ladder. "Anyway, there's your Celadine frangipani tree, Inspector. As you can see, we have four of them. Strong scent but not often used in our perfumes."

"Why not?" Thomas picked a flower from a low-lying branch, bringing it to his nose, before raising his eyebrows in approval. "It's really strong. Nice fragrance too."

"Not enough blooms. It'll only make a small amount of pomade," Seth said. "It's used. Just not often."

Jamie had been prowling around the trees. "Is that the road you mentioned, Mr. Santorini? The one you can take from the perfumery?"

A beaten red earth track lay just beyond the grove of trees, stretching away in two directions.

The head gardener nodded. "It circles the whole property. We have over thirty acres of land here, but we try to avoid using the truck among the low flowers like passionflowers. Don't want dust on them, if we can avoid it."

"There're tire tracks here, Rob." Jamie pointed to shallow ruts in the grass that edged the road. "Looks like someone drove out here recently. I'll just take a photo, shall I?"

Holly suppressed a smile as Jamie pulled out her phone, circling the marks to take photos. Beside her, Rob uttered a faint sigh.

"Thank you, Jamie, but I'm sure vehicles drive along here frequently."

"Nope." Seth's voice was casual.

"What do you mean 'nope'?" Rob's eyes narrowed.

"Property road only. No access to the main roads from it. There are boundary walls around the whole place. See?" Seth pointed to a low drystone wall in the distance. "That separates us from the farm fields next door. The only way for vehicles to get on this property is by coming up the main drive and then onto the tracks."

Mr. Santorini nodded in agreement. "Seth's right. Only perfumery vehicles use this road."

"How many vehicles do you have?" Thomas asked over his shoulder as he crossed to where Jamie was still taking photos.

"One pickup truck and a few small golf buggies. Turf utility vehicles they call them. Ours have six-foot-long cargo beds at the back. They're useful for getting around when the truck's being used. And we can fit several flower tubs in them. They're great for oleander and jasmine harvesting."

"Do you use those on the trails through the woods near the road as well?" Jamie asked. "They looked wide enough."

The arborist nodded. "Yes, but not very often. We mostly use the carts for the low-lying flowers, and to move any branches and so on from when we clean up. We have a woodchipper we take around sometimes, or we move debris to the compost pile. And we do a lot of walking around here too."

Rob joined Thomas who had crouched down to look at the tracks more closely.

"Could be a golfcart. I'm not sure what tires they have." Thomas grinned. "You may need Jamie's photos after all, Inspector. Unless you'd like to take your own."

Ignoring him, Rob pulled out his phone, punching a few buttons. "Sergeant Frampton? Do you have a police photographer you can get hold of?... Yes. I'll need some official pictures taken, please... What? Really? Good work, Sergeant... Yes. Okay... What's that?... No, don't do that. We'll walk back. And we'll need to check all perfumery vehicles... Yes... Okay. Good. I'll be back shortly, Sergeant. Oh, and Sergeant, it seems Mr. Billings and Mr. Santorini weren't shown photographs of the victim. I'd like them to see one, please... No, I quite understand, but perhaps you could get hold of one... Thanks."

Everyone had fallen silent as Rob spoke. Holly and Jamie exchanged speculative glances as he hung up, but it was Thomas who broke the silence.

"Sounds like the good sergeant found something?"

His interrogative tone produced nothing but a slight smile from the inspector. "Sergeant Frampton is sending a police constable out here to take photographs. Holly, will you and Jamie wait here and show him these tracks?" Without waiting for an answer, he continued, "And I'll ask you gentlemen to accompany me back to the perfumery, if you will. I'd like you to look at a photograph of the victim."

"Miller already knows what Dickenson looked like. He sat beside him for an hour." Jamie's voice was suspicious. "Why do you want him to look at a photo?"

"He doesn't." Thomas grinned. "This is the inspector's subtle way of making sure a suspect isn't left near vital evidence."

"What?" Jamie's mouth dropped open. "No, it's not. You don't really suspect Thomas still, do you, Rob? You can't!"

The journalist's eyebrows shot up before his smile widened. He placed a hand on his heart. "Did my ears deceive me, Miss White? Did you just refer to me as 'Thomas'? I am touched beyond measure."

"I didn't—" Jamie scowled, taking a step back as Thomas approached. "What are you doing?"

"Fear not, gentle maiden, I shall return anon. In the meantime, accept this tribute, I beg." Thomas held out a frangipani blossom.

Holly pressed her lips tightly together as Jamie glared at the journalist, speechless. When she didn't take the flower, Thomas made a move to place it in her hair, only to have Jamie step back.

"Stop that," she hissed. "I mean it, Thomas. Quit it."

Thomas laughed and let the flower fall to the ground. In a flamboyant gesture, he kissed his hand to Jamie, then turned to Rob. "Shall we, Inspector?"

"The constable should be here any minute. And I promise you, I won't arrest Miller just yet." Rob's eyes twinkled at the sight of Jamie's flushed face.

Mr. Santorini and Seth, who had started walking back to the perfumery, glanced back, puzzled by the laughter.

"I don't care if you do!" Jamie snapped. "Just go, won't you?" As Rob and Thomas walked away, the latter still chortling, Jamie's eyes snapped towards Holly. "And don't you say a single word."

"I wouldn't dream of it." Holly bent down to pick up the flower, offering it to her friend with a knowing grin. "Go on, take it. You know you want to."

Jamie stared at the flower. "It was just a joke. A silly one too."

"Mmm. I'd call it flirting, myself." Holly smirked,

holding out the flower again. "He doesn't expect you to wear it, you know. Call his bluff and see what happens."

Jamie pursed her lips, thinking. A tiny smile flickered at the corner of her mouth before she turned around. "Put it in my braid, then."

Holly's grin widened.

24

Holly was lounging on the grass near the frangipani trees as Jamie prowled around in search of clues when she heard an approaching golfcart. Seth, accompanied by a police constable in uniform, drove along the narrow property road.

The cart was a sturdy utilitarian vehicle with, as Seth had said, a long metal cargo bed at the back. As the arborist pulled up near them on the road, being careful to avoid the tracks in the grass, Holly noticed a number of tools in the floor of the bed.

"The inspector let me bring the cart so I can take the ladder back." Seth swung out of the vehicle with a grin. "There's room for you two as well, if you don't want to walk back."

"Sounds good to me." Jamie bent down to peer at the tires on the cart. "Huh. Do all the carts have this same type of tire?"

Seth had picked up the ladder and now slung it into the back of the vehicle. "Yep. At least, I expect so. They're from the same company." He shrugged, leaning against the cart as the constable took photos. "As I said, they're the only vehicles on the property other than the truck, and that hasn't been out here for a couple of weeks. Or not that I know of, anyway."

"Who else might come out here to pick flowers?" Holly asked. "I mean, I assume that's the only reason people would come to these trees, right?"

"Most likely," Seth agreed. "Anyone at the perfumery, really. Apart from me, Santorini, and Jake, who concentrate on the gardens, everyone else switches jobs as needed."

"Yeah, Kat told us that too." Holly sighed. "I suppose the ladder could have been here for ages."

"Nope."

At the arborist's laconic response, both women looked at him.

"How do you know that? You said you hadn't been out here." Jamie raised an eyebrow.

"I said the truck hasn't been out here. I was out here on Wednesday checking the trees for Amelie. No ladder here on Wednesday, so someone brought it out after that."

Jamie pursed her lips in thought. "You were checking the trees for Amelie Lestrade? Why?"

"She wanted to know if there were any flowers. Nothing unusual in that. She's always asking me to check flowers. Usually frangipani or passionflowers, since the different varieties bloom at different times. Sometimes she checks herself but on Wednesday she asked me." Seth shrugged. "And there was no ladder here then. It could have been brought out on Friday or Saturday, though."

"During the symposium? Who would have done that? Everyone was working at it, weren't they?" Holly asked.

"That's true. We were pretty busy on Friday with all those people," Seth admitted. "I don't think anyone had time to go flower-picking, although we still had things to do in the garden. And come to think of it, Jake was washing all the carts on Friday, and I had the truck all weekend. Thursday and Friday too, actually. I was helping a friend move and Mick said I could take it."

"So that means the ladder was probably brought out here on Thursday. The day of the murder! And since Dickenson had one of these flowers on him, there could definitely be a connection between this and his death." Jamie looked at the offending ladder in the back of the cart. "He couldn't have hit his head on it, could he? Maybe we should check for blood!"

"Rob did that already. I saw him looking at it," Holly said. "And why would someone take the body away from here but not move the ladder? Especially if it had blood on it?"

Jamie deflated. "True."

The police constable, who had finished taking his photos and had been listening to the conversation, now grinned and held up his camera. "I've got the photos the inspector wanted, so perhaps we could be getting back now, Seth, if you don't mind."

"Sure." Seth gestured to the cart. "Climb in, ladies."

As Holly clambered into the back seat, a thought struck her. "Seth, did you see the photos of Jonathan Dickenson yet?"

The constable opened his mouth, then thought better of it. He stared out over the fields, feigning deep interest in them.

Seth nodded as he started the engine. "Plummet had just arrived with a file folder when we got back with the inspector. He showed me one. And yeah, I've seen the guy." He paused. "Kat said she recognized him too."

"You saw him?"

"Kat Santorini, you mean?"

Jamie and Holly spoke together.

The constable made a move as if to speak, then shrugged and leaned back in his seat. Holly eyed him uncertainly.

"Maybe we shouldn't be talking about this."

Seth laughed. "Brian doesn't mind, do you, Bri? I should have introduced you guys. Constable Brian Hawkins. We were at school together, but he was a few years beneath me."

"What he means is, he was a prefect when I was in sixth grade." Constable Hawkins grinned. "And talk all you want. Just don't ask me any questions because I can't answer."

"We won't," Holly assured him with a smile. "And since Seth didn't introduce us, I'm Holly and this is Jamie."

Jamie gave a friendly nod before zeroing in on Seth. "You said you saw Dickenson? When?"

"Lunchtime Thursday. At the Fire Drake Inn. I was having lunch there with Miranda." Seth slowed for a pothole in the road.

"You saw the victim?" Jamie repeated. "Exactly what time was this?"

"It was just before two. I'd left the table to go to the restroom and saw the guy leaving through the foyer. Didn't know who he was at the time, of course, but your inspector was right. He was easily recognizable in the photo."

"Did he have a bruise on his face?"

"A bruise? Not that I noticed." Seth grinned. "Your inspector asked me that too. I hear you guys help him out with cases sometimes. That true?"

"You said Kat recognized him too. When did she see him?" Holly intervened before Jamie could get sidetracked.

"A few months ago."

"A few months ago?" Jamie repeated with incredulity. "You mean he came to the perfumery to visit? Or he had a meeting, or what?"

Seth shrugged. "No idea. She just said she recognized him from when he was here before. You can ask her if you want. She hasn't left yet. Your inspector and Plummet are still asking questions."

~

SETH DROPPED HOLLY, Jamie, and Constable Hawkins near the perfumery, then zipped away to return the cart to the maintenance shed. At the top of the stairs, Holly and Jamie paused at the sight of Rob and Inspector Plummet sitting near one of the windows. Lily O'Connor and Cressida Billings sat across from them on the other side of a small table, looking both anxious and furious at the same time.

Holly hesitated. Should they go in? Rob wouldn't want them to interrupt official police business, she knew.

"Psst. Over here." Thomas beckoned to them from the veranda, putting a finger to his lips.

As Holly and Jamie crossed towards him, Rob glanced out the window. He gave no sign of noticing them but returned his attention to Plummet.

"And I say," the Azure Isle inspector raised his voice in irritation, "that only someone with access to a key could have done it!"

Holly's eyebrows shot up. Thomas yanked her down onto the Adirondack chair beside him.

"Sit still. I've been taking notes," he muttered. "I'll fill you in on what you missed later." A small pencil and notebook were on his lap, the paper covered in shorthand.

"Impressive." Jamie's whisper was approving. She sat

down on his other side just as Lily drew in an outraged breath.

"And I say, Inspector Plummet, that you're wrong! Amelie Lestrade and I are the only ones with a key and neither of us is a murderer! And nor is Cressida!"

Holly and Jamie exchanged incredulous glances.

Keeping his tone mild, Rob intervened. "No one is accusing you, Ms. O'Connor. But we have found evidence that suggests Dickenson was killed in the laboratory, so we do need to ask some questions."

"I understand that, Inspector Tucker, but that's not what he—"

"Ms. O'Connor, if I could just check a few things?" Rob interrupted, his voice pleasant but firm. "It won't take long. Now, you've told us there are two keys to the lab, isn't that so?"

Lily nodded. "Yes, but—"

Rob cut her off gently. "I'm not accusing anyone. I'm just trying to get the facts. Okay?"

Lily took a deep breath, then nodded. "Okay."

"Right." Rob smiled at her. "So, there are two keys. Ms. Lestrade has one and you have one. Where do you keep your key?"

"In my office."

"And who has access to your office?" Rob asked.

Lily paused. "Well, it's not locked during the day. Usually, it's just me and Cressida who are in there, but..."

"But?" Rob prompted as her voice trailed away.

Cressida intervened. "Well, this last week, we were getting ready for the symposium. So, of course, people were in and out more than usual."

"What people?" Plummet snapped.

Rob closed his eyes briefly, making Jamie wince in sympathy.

"Poor Rob," she whispered.

Lily and Cressida directed joint glares at the Azure Isle inspector.

"Everyone!" Lily snapped. "It was a lot of work to organize this event! I'd say every single person who works here came in at some time or another."

Rob intervened before Plummet could speak again. "Did you notice when the key went missing?"

"No. I'd only have noticed if I needed to get into the lab if Amelie wasn't there. But I didn't. And I wasn't here on Thursday, Inspector Tucker. Or at least, I wasn't here from ten onwards. I had an appointment in Silver Landing, and then a meeting to attend. I didn't get back here until around five. I had a quick word with Cressida, made sure everything was ready for the next day, and then took Sylvie Lestrade and Gabriel out to dinner as we'd planned. I certainly didn't unlock the lab, lure Mr. Dickenson inside, and kill him! I didn't even see the man! And I was with someone every minute I was here!" She shot another glare at Plummet.

"Yes, we've double-checked your whereabouts, Ms. O'Connor." Rob's sympathetic smile took any offense out of his statement and produced a tiny answering one in Lily. "Where exactly do you keep the key to the lab?"

Lily relaxed slightly at Rob's gentle handling. "On a key rack behind my desk. Along with the keys to the maintenance shed, the downstairs doors, the conservatory doors, and the *enfleurage* room. I don't know when it went missing, Inspector, because I wasn't looking for it."

"Me neither," Cressida added. "I didn't even know it was missing until today, when you asked for it."

Rob nodded. "I understand." He ignored Plummet's

snort. "It was something we needed to check up on, though. Now, can I just confirm once again who was in the building on Thursday? I believe, Ms. Billings, that you were here with Kat Santorini and Faith Sayers setting up displays in the morning. Is that right?"

"Yes. We wanted to make sure all our samples were filled and that the Frangipani Room was spotless," Cressida replied readily. "And after we'd done that, Kat and Aunt Faith were working in the packing room, just tidying up and making sure everything was ready for the staff who would be in on Friday. We have quite a few hourly paid workers."

Lily produced a small smile. "Seniors, mostly, who just want something to do—a chance to socialize, meet visitors to the island, and earn a little money."

Rob nodded as he consulted his notebook. "We know Mr. and Mrs. Sayers left during the lunch hour. What did Miss Santorini do then, Miss Billings?"

"Well, we had lunch from one thirty until about two thirty," Cressida said. "I ate in the office, but Kat went and had lunch with her grandfather. Probably in the slat house. That's their usual place. Then, after lunch, we were in the *enfleurage* room."

"All afternoon?"

Cressida nodded. "We had to remove all the flowers from the *corps* on Thursday, ready to receive the fresh batch. It takes a bit of time. There are always a few bits that stick, and we have to go over them with tweezers."

"Hmmm. You can't see the laboratory from there, can you?" Rob frowned.

"No. It's at the other end of the corridor, around the corner. You probably remember it from your tour, Inspector."

"I do. The catacombs, I believe you call them." Rob gave

a slight smile. "So you cleaned the *corps*, the two of you. Did either of you leave at any time?"

"I did," Cressida admitted. "The company bringing the chairs arrived around three thirty, so I went out to tell them where to unload. Then, just as they finished, Seth and Jake arrived with tubs of fresh flowers around four, I guess. I needed them to help set up chairs in the lecture room, so I took them up there. At about the same time, Sylvie Lestrade arrived in a taxi. Lily was picking her up here for dinner, but Sylvie came early to see Amelie. I told her Amelie had already left for the day because she wasn't feeling well. Then Sylvie started harassing me about stuff for the AGM, so I was still outside when Lily drove up with Gabriel."

Lily nodded. "I took them both inside with me. Susan Hill was already in my office, fuming about a meeting she was supposed to have had at four."

Cressida nodded. "Oh, that's right. I forgot about her. Yeah, she drove up at the same time as the truck with the chairs. Said she had a meeting and could she use the office." The woman rolled her eyes. "I had no idea what she was talking about and no time to deal with it, so I just said yes."

Lily chimed back in. "Of course, when I arrived, she'd been there for nearly two hours. I didn't know her meeting was supposed to be with her cousin, or that the cousin was Jonathan Dickenson, or that he was dead, so I told her she'd made a mistake. She snarled at all of us, Gabriel snarled back—those two have never got on—and it was at that point that your friend Thomas walked in."

25

_____

On the veranda, Thomas smirked even as his pencil traveled rapidly across the paper.

"Which means Kat Santorini was alone downstairs for a long time." Inspector Plummet sounded smug.

"So?" Lily eyed the inspector with distaste.

"So, Kat Santorini admits to knowing Jonathan Dickenson. As Mr. John Smith, a visitor who was here three months ago asking questions about Plumeria and its perfumes! What do you have to say about that? Eh?"

A snort of amusement escaped Thomas. Seeing Rob's head instantly turn to glare at them through the window, Holly gave the journalist a hard nudge. His grin was unrepentant.

"The man's a fool," he muttered. "What on earth does he think that has to do with anything?"

Lily O'Connor clearly felt the same way. She stared at Inspector Plummet as if he were a particularly revolting bug. "I fail to see your point, Inspector. Are you trying to say that Kat killed Jonathan Dickenson? Because she recognized a photo of him? That makes no sense whatsoever! If that was her reason, why would she tell you she'd recognized him?"

"And how do you even know the man was in the lab at that time? In fact, it seems to me that no one actually saw this Jonathan Dickenson in the building at all, let alone in the lab!" Cressida was indignant.

"That's true, you know," Holly murmured. "No one has said they saw Dickenson. Apart from Seth, that is, who saw him at the Fire Drake Inn. He's like a phantom. If the police really did find evidence that he was killed in the lab, how did he get there without anyone noticing?"

"Yeah, we need to create a timeline." Jamie kept her voice equally low. "When we get back to the cottage tonight, let's make a chart and see where everyone was at all hours of the day. For instance, was Susan Hill really in that office all afternoon? Doing what?"

"Wait a minute. She told me about that." Holly pursed her lips, thinking. "It was when she first thought the body might be her cousin, remember? I'm sure you were there..." She snapped her fingers. "Yes. She said she was on a video call while she was waiting for Dickenson to show up. She was annoyed because people kept interrupting her. I wonder if Rob knows that. She must have told him when he questioned her, wouldn't you think?"

"Yeah, unless Plummet antagonized her like he's doing with everyone else," Jamie replied.

"Shh." Thomas frowned at them.

"I think we'll leave it there for now," Rob was saying. "I'm afraid I may have some more questions tomorrow, though."

Lily nodded. "Of course, Inspector Tucker. We quite understand. I assume you want us to remain closed tomorrow again?"

"Please." Rob's smile was rueful. "And the people who

were here on Thursday will have to be available for questioning as well." He paused. "How is Ms. Lestrade, do you know?"

"She said she was still feeling ill today when I called her," Cressida offered. "She came down with a bug of some kind a week or so ago, and I think it got exacerbated with all the stress around the release of *Rosa del Mar*. Amelie doesn't do well with stress."

"Mmm. I'll need her address, then. I know it's late, but I really do have to ask her some questions today."

"I'll write it down." Lily paused. "Would you like me to go with you, Inspector? Amelie can be... high-strung."

Plummet produced another loud snort, but Rob smiled at the perfumery owner. "That's very kind of you, but no. I'll arrange something."

"Sorry Inspector." Sergeant Frampton spread his hands apart in apology. "But we only have one female constable and she's on holiday."

Rob sighed. "Never mind. I'll take you with me, but I do need a woman as well. It'll have to be Holly."

"Or me," Jamie piped up. "You could take me."

Rob and Sergeant Frampton had cleared the premises by allowing everyone to go home, ensured the building was secure, given final instructions to the policemen who would be watching the place, listened with stoicism to Inspector Plummet's grumblings, and were about to leave to interview Amelie Lestrade when the sergeant had dropped his bombshell.

Well, it wasn't really a bombshell, Holly admitted. *More like a hiccup.*

Jamie's face fell when Rob shook his head. "No. I actually have another job for you and Miller, if you don't mind. It will require Nat as well. That is, if the package I requested has arrived, Sergeant?"

"Oh right. Yes, it did." Sergeant Frampton crossed to his police car, rummaged inside, then came back with a small box. "Beautifully packed too, I must say. And I got the other sample from Lily O'Connor as you requested, Inspector."

"What sample? And what's in the box?" Jamie was agog. "What do you want us to do?"

Thomas's eyebrows had arched skywards. "I imagine he wants us to get Nat to run some perfume samples through her machine. Is that the Grand Island Perfumes scent in the box, Inspector."

"There are perfumes in there, yes." Rob nodded to the sergeant, who handed the sealed box to Jamie, then, with a grin, produced another small bottle.

She held it up in front of her. "*Frangipani Allure*? But we've already tested this."

"And I'd appreciate it if you'd ask Nat to run another test. A couple, if she can manage it. And some on the samples in the box." After a brief hesitation, Rob beckoned a constable over. "Constable...?"

"Hawkins, sir."

Rob smiled. "Constable Hawkins, will you accompany Mr. Miller and Miss White? I'll need you to act as a witness, if you don't mind. And perhaps you should take charge of the samples."

"Yes sir. This way, Mr. Miller, Miss White."

"What about our cars?" Jamie asked.

"I'll call Roger Aguiar. He owns the rental business. He'll bring his truck and deliver them back to the center." Sergeant Frampton pulled out his phone. "Don't worry. He's used to it. People are always driving up into the mountains without a full charge. I'll be right with you and Miss Gold, Inspector."

～

HOLLY CLIMBED into the back seat of the police car, waving out the window to Jamie, as the other woman's police car, driven by Brian Hawkins, pulled out of the parking lot. Rob closed the door behind her, then hopped into the front passenger seat.

"Are you okay with this, Holly? I'm sorry to involve you, but I really do need a woman present if I'm going to interview Ms. Lestrade at her home. Someone neutral."

"Yeah, sure." Holly hesitated. "Rob, do you think Amelie did it? I mean, it was her lab, after all."

"It's possible. The missing key bothers me. As does a motive. I think I have an idea about that, but..." Rob's brow furrowed as his voice trailed away.

"But surely that would be the perfume." Holly was puzzled by Rob's uncertainty. "If her perfume was copied from the Grand Island Perfumes scent, she wouldn't want people to know that, would she? And if Jonathan Dickenson had proof that she copied it, it would damage her reputation."

Rob rested his elbow on the open window, idly tapping his fingers on the car. A small smile played over his mouth. "But that formula, recipe, call it what you will, never belonged to Grand Island Perfumes, or to Olivia Hill. It belonged to Gabriel Manout. And a court already dismissed Susan Hill's claim. Besides, I believe Gabriel Manout told you that the scent he created was radically different from *Frangipani Allure*, didn't he?"

Holly frowned. She leaned forward between the front seats, regarding Rob with suspicion. "But didn't you just get samples from Grand Island Perfumes? What are you not telling me?"

"As I say, I have an idea. With no more information than you have, I might add." Rob grinned as Holly scowled, then straightened up when Sergeant Frampton slid into the driver's seat. "All set, Sergeant?"

"Yes sir." Sergeant Frampton started the car. "Constable Perkins has taken those items into evidence as you requested."

Holly's ears pricked up. *What items?*

"Heavy too. I can't believe people still use those old things," Sergeant Frampton continued, reversing out of the parking bay. "I remember my grandma using one, a small version, of course, to crush spices."

"Wow. You mean you confiscated a mortar and pestle from Amelie's lab?" The words were out before Holly could stop them. "Was that the weapon used to kill Dickenson? Ugh. That's kind of horrible."

"Oh, I forgot you were there." Sergeant Frampton frowned into his rear-view mirror. "You just forget I said anything, missy. I know your daddy taught you better than to repeat police business."

Holly grinned involuntarily at the sergeant's fatherly tone. "He did," she agreed. "Don't worry, Sergeant Frampton, my lips are sealed. But... Was a mortar and pestle the weapon?"

Rob cast his eyes up, but grinned and nodded when Sergeant Frampton shot him an inquiring look. "Oh, go ahead and tell her, Sergeant. She and her little pals have been buzzing around the case the entire time." He waited a beat. "And they've actually been quite useful."

Holly's brow creased again. What did Rob know that she didn't? "I'm sure Jamie will be thrilled to hear that." Her sarcastic tone made both men chuckle. "So, you really think the murder weapon was a pestle? We saw some at the tea plantation, remember, Rob? Kind of small to hit someone with, though. They could only have been about six inches long."

"This one was bigger," Rob said. "Apparently Amelie Lestrade collects them."

Holly considered that fact. "Unusual. Although Gabriel told us he has a friend who's using a mortar and pestle to grind red algae to make perfume out of."

"Looks like Ms. Lestrade was making frangipani perfume in this one." Sergeant Frampton slowed down as he approached a roundabout, waiting for two cars to pass before he pulled out.

Holly frowned. "Frangipani? That can't be right." She shook her head, drawing puzzled looks from both policemen.

"There were frangipani flowers in the mortar," Rob said. "Celadine flowers, in fact. That's what drew our attention to it. Why do you say Amelie couldn't have been using it for perfume purposes?"

"Frangipanis are fragile. Sylvie Lestrade told us you'd never grind them to get their oils. That's why Plumeria uses *enfleurage*," Holly explained.

"Interesting." Rob pondered Holly's words. "Well, Sergeant, this may help us, don't you think?"

"Yes indeed, sir. Yes indeed." Sergeant Frampton's voice was approving as he winked at Holly in the rearview mirror.

"Sergeant Frampton, would you happen to have the address of Mr. and Mrs. Sayers on you?" Rob asked suddenly. "I believe they live in Azalea Village as well, don't they? Do you think it's too late to visit them?"

"Too late?" Sergeant Frampton scoffed. "It's not even five o'clock, Inspector. Carleton Sayers will be in his garden if I'm not much mistaken. He's very proud of his vegetables. Works hard on them too. And Ms. Faith has a fine hand with gingersnap biscuits, sir. She's sure to offer us some with tea." His sidelong glance at Rob was curious. "Any particular reason, sir?"

"I was re-reading their statements earlier and noticed something. I'd just like a little clarification before we go see Ms. Lestrade."

"Ah. Well, Ms. Faith will be thrilled to be questioned again, I'm quite sure, Inspector. And as I said, she makes a tasty ginger biscuit."

As Holly giggled at the anticipatory gleam in the sergeant's eye, a grin tugged at the corner of Rob's mouth.

"Very well, Sergeant, let's go see the Sayers."

26

Carleton Sayers was in his garden, but he wasn't working as Sergeant Frampton had suggested he might be. Instead, he was sitting in a chair, a lugubrious expression on his face. Faith Sayers, compact, plump, and in high dudgeon, stood in front of him, shaking her finger in his face.

"And what did the doctor tell you, Carleton Sayers? What did he say? I'll tell you what he said! He said you have to rest that leg. You can do light work, he said. Light work, Carleton. Does this look like light work to you? I don't think so!"

Grinning, Sergeant Frampton leaned over the wall that surrounded the pretty little white cottage. "Good evening, Ms. Faith. What's your old man been doing this time? Disobeying doctor's orders, eh?"

As Faith Carleton turned around in surprise, her husband heaved a sigh of relief at the interruption.

"Harry Frampton. Come in, mate, come in. Who's that with you? Oh, Inspector Tucker. Nice to see you, sir. Come in. Come in."

A pleased expression on his round pink face, Carleton lurched to his feet, staggering slightly and prompting another round of exclamations from his wife.

"Carleton! What did I just say? Sit yourself down again at once."

"Now, Faithy, just relax. Why don't you go put the kettle on. You'll have a cup of tea, Harry, won't you? And you, Inspector? And who's this lovely young lady?"

Carleton beamed at Holly, who smiled back, charmed by the old man's lilting voice and cherub-like smile.

"I'm Holly. Holly Gold."

Faith Sayers bustled over to Holly, her brown face creased in a welcoming smile. Dark eyes surveyed her from head to toe. "Holly Gold, you say? What a pretty name. Are you a detective too, my dear?"

"No, no. Holly's a horticulturist." Sergeant Frampton grinned at Carleton. "She's Stuart Mackintosh's granddaughter. You know him, don't you?"

"Stuart Mackintosh? Well, I should say so!" Faith's smile grew even broader. "You're his granddaughter, you say? Hmm, yes, I see a slight resemblance. Well, you tell your Gramps that Faith Sayers said hello, you hear? Mr. Sayers and I used to stay at your inn when we went on holiday to Hibiscus. Lovely place. That was back when your grandma was in charge, of course."

Holly smiled. "My Mama runs the inn now. Do you remember her too, Mrs. Sayers? Maggie Gold?"

"You call me Aunt Faith, child. And yes, I remember Maggie and her sister, Laura. Young hellions they were back then." Faith's eyes twinkled as Holly laughed. "Now, I'll go put the kettle on, shall I? And I have some ginger biscuits. I know Harry there likes them. You sit yourselves down with Carleton and I'll be right back. No, no, Holly, I can manage.

You sit down. You too, Inspector." She trotted off towards the house.

Old Mr. Sayers gestured to a seat beside him on the little patio. "Sit down, Inspector. Sit down. How's the case going? Suppose you can't say much about it, can you? You know, Inspector, I have to say I don't think much of your colleague." He tutted, his mouth turning down in disapproval. "A rude man, that Plummet. Disrespectful. When I was his age, I wouldn't have dreamed of speaking to my elders that way."

Sergeant Frampton cleared his throat. "Now, Carleton, you're putting Inspector Tucker and me in an awkward position. You know we can't comment about a fellow police officer."

Mr. Sayers harumphed. "True, true. Still, it's too bad Inspector Moore is away. Now, he's a fine man, Inspector Tucker. You'd get on well with him. I imagine working with that Plummet fellow is very trying at times."

Holly pressed her lips tightly together, trying not to laugh at the look on Rob's face. Sergeant Frampton had no such compunction. A loud chuckle escaped him.

"You're embarrassing the inspector, Carleton," he chided, his eyes twinkling. "How's that leg doing? I heard Ms. Faith ringing a peal over you when we arrived. Trying to do too much, are you?"

The old man's face reddened. "I am not. Got to exercise to get better, you know. Faith's just— Ah, here you are, my dear. Are those ginger biscuits I see?"

"Humph. Don't think I don't know what you were about to say, Carleton! Oh, thank you, Inspector." Faith beamed as Rob jumped up to take the tray from her hands, setting it on a small table. "How do you take your tea, everyone?"

Holly helped Mrs. Sayers serve tea to the men in tiny

porcelain teacups, biting her lip in amusement at the sight of Rob and Sergeant Frampton trying to hold the small handles. Mr. Sayers was obviously used to it, handling the cup with ease while at the same time waving a ginger biscuit in the air.

"So, tell me, Inspector, why are you here? I'm sure it's not just for our company, enthralling as that is."

Rob's eyes were full of laughter as they met Holly's for a brief moment before he replaced the delicate teacup on the table. His smile at the older couple, however, was sincere.

"I really do wish it was, Mr. and Mrs. Sayers, but I'm afraid I need to clarify one part of your statement to Inspector Plummet, if that's alright?"

"Certainly, certainly."

"And I know exactly what you're going to ask, Inspector." Faith Sayers sat upright, her eyes sparkling with excitement. "That Plummet person didn't pay any attention whatsoever and I knew it was important. Well, obviously I didn't know it was important at the time, but afterwards, when we heard about the body, it was obvious to me that we'd seen the victim. I pointed him out to Carleton at the time. I told him, 'Carleton,' I said, 'there's someone climbing over the wall.' And you remember what you said, Carleton, don't you?"

Carleton sighed. "Yes, dear."

"You said," Faith continued, barely drawing breath, "that it was no business of ours and to keep my eyes on the road. That's what you said. As if I was just being nosy!"

Holly looked down at the ground hastily. *Don't laugh. Don't laugh.*

Rob cleared his throat. "That is actually what I wanted to ask about." His voice wavered slightly, then steadied. "I assume this person was a man?"

"Well, of course it was, Inspector. Didn't I just say we saw the victim?"

"Yes, but you didn't know he was the victim until the following day." Rob smiled at the indignant elderly lady. "Did you happen to see what this man was wearing, by any chance? Or was he too far away?"

"I have exceptional eyesight, Inspector," Faith assured him. "He had on a blue-checked shirt and dark trousers. Brown hair. I couldn't see his eyes because his back was to us. Quite athletic because he hopped over that wall like a goat."

"Yes. I see." Rob cleared his throat again. "And what time was this, Ms. Faith? That you saw him hop over the wall, I mean?"

"It was exactly three minutes past two." Mr. Sayers rushed to answer before his wife could open her mouth. "I know because I was keeping an eye on the time. My appointment was at two thirty, and I didn't want to be late."

"And we weren't late," Faith pointed out with some asperity. "There was absolutely no need for you to give me a minute-by-minute update on the time. I know exactly how long it takes to get from the perfumery to the clinic now."

"Could you tell where this man might have been going?" Rob asked quickly.

"Well, I can't say what he did once he was out of sight," Mr. Sayers said, "but after he bounced over the wall, he set off along the property road. It circles the estate, you know, so he'd eventually have got to the perfumery itself. Probably have taken him, oh, twenty, thirty minutes or so."

"And would this route have taken him past the grove of trees that includes the Celadine frangipanis?" Rob asked.

Mr. Sayers considered for a moment. "The Celadine

trees? Yes. That road leads there. But he wasn't found there, Inspector. He was found under the Bridal Bouquet."

"Yes, I know." Rob smiled. "How long would it have taken this man to reach the Celadine trees, though?"

"If he walked fast? About ten minutes. Maybe less since he certainly didn't have a gimpy leg like me! Very agile, as Faith said." Mr. Sayers eyed Rob with deep interest. "Have we helped, Inspector?"

"You have, Mr. Sayers. You have indeed." Rob stood up, smiling at the elderly couple. "Thank you very much, both of you. And for the tea and biscuits, Mrs. Sayers."

"It was our pleasure, Inspector. If you have time to visit again, you're more than welcome." Faith Sayers beamed at Rob, then Holly. "And you remember to tell your Gramps that Faith and Carleton said hello, you hear, Holly?"

Holly grinned. "I'll remember."

HOLLY WAS STILL SMILING as the police car pulled away from the curb. "They remind me of Uncle Stanley and Aunt Elma. Don't you think so, Rob?"

"Apart from Mr. Sayers's Welsh accent, yes." Rob smiled. "Is Ms. Faith from Turtle Island, Sergeant?"

"Born and raised," the sergeant replied. "And that's the original family home they're living in. Renovated a bit over the years, of course. You should hear Ms. Faith's stories of the olden days living here. They're fascinating. It was very rural when she was a child. She sometimes goes into the primary schools and tells the children about it. Takes in old toys, that sort of thing. The kids love it."

"Well, she's a very observant old lady," Rob noted. "That

was definitely Dickenson they saw on Thursday afternoon. You'll recall he had on a blue-checked shirt, Sergeant."

"Yes sir, I do. You think he went along the road to those frangipani trees, do you?"

Rob nodded. "It seems probable, yes."

"But what for?" Holly asked, leaning forward to rest her arms on the backs of the front seats. "Was he going there specially, or do you think he was just taking that route to the perfumery? He was supposed to be meeting Susan Hill, his cousin, at four, and didn't show up. Oh..." She paused. "Does that mean he was dead before four? That would get Thomas off the hook completely, wouldn't it?"

"It's definitely looking more likely that Dickenson was killed between two thirty and four in the afternoon."

"Hmmm." Holly pondered, oblivious to the grins both policemen exchanged. "And you said you confiscated a mortar and pestle from the lab... And Amelie Lestrade supposedly left the perfumery for the day— When did she leave exactly? Do you know?"

"No," Rob replied. "She was gone by four, but I don't know exactly what time she left."

"Cressida said she wasn't feeling well," Holly offered. "And she didn't meet her mother at the spa like she was supposed to that afternoon. At least, that's what Mr. Graham said Sylvie Lestrade said. And if nobody saw Amelie leave, then she must have gone between two thirty and three thirty." She frowned. "But it's strange that Mr. Santorini didn't see her, because he was outside planting annuals at the front of the building." A thought occurred to her. "Unless... Where do the staff park? Maybe Amelie left through a different door? Goodness knows there's enough of them in that labyrinth they have downstairs. The question is... Did she leave before or after Jonathan Dickenson was killed in her lab?"

A hearty guffaw escaped Sergeant Frampton. "She's her father's daughter alright, Inspector. You thought about recruiting her and her friends to the police service?"

Holly blushed, shooting a sidelong glance at Rob. He was grinning.

"The thing is, Sergeant, right now they all work for free. If they joined the police, we'd have to pay them. And, I'm sorry to say, they don't take orders that well." Rob's eyes twinkled as he looked at Holly. "But that was a good summary, and exactly the same questions we've been asking ourselves. Ah, is this the place, Sergeant?"

The police car had turned up a small hilly driveway, at the top of which stood a yellow house with a closely mowed lawn surrounding it. A small white car was parked outside. Sergeant Frampton turned off the car engine, and in the sudden quiet, Holly could hear a dog barking and a woman's voice telling it to be quiet. The voice was familiar.

"I think Sylvie Lestrade is here too," Holly noted as she climbed out of the car. She looked at the two policemen. "Do you still need me to come in? I could wait in the car, if you'd rather."

"No. Come in with us, Holly." Rob straightened the collar of his shirt. "Right then, Sergeant, lead the way, won't you?"

27

As Sergeant Frampton sounded the knocker on the white-painted front door, Holly stood two steps behind, eyeing Amelie Lestrade's garden with curiosity. It was surprisingly bare. In fact, Holly thought, it was the most boring garden she'd seen yet on Turtle Island.

A neatly trimmed green grass lawn was bisected by a paved path that led from the graveled parking area to the front door. A white fence surrounded the lawn, with two bottle palm trees standing sentinel on either side of the gate.

There were no shrubs, no flowers. Not even the ubiquitous Turtle Island hydrangea encroached on the spartan environment.

"I'd have thought a perfumer would want flowers in her garden," Holly whispered to Rob. "It's so... so sterile."

He shrugged. "Maybe it would overwhelm her nose. After all, she works with scents every day."

"Yes, but she told that story about swinging through wild freesias, remember? She must have grown up with flowers around her." Holly paused. "Oh right, you weren't there for her speech, were you?"

Rob shook his head. "No, I only met her very briefly before I was officially seconded to the investigation. And I haven't been able to question her formally yet because she's been ill. Holly, when we're inside, you need to leave the questions to the sergeant and me, okay?"

"Of course." Holly's tone was affronted. "I wouldn't dream of interfering."

A smile flashed across Rob's face. "Of course not." He straightened up as footsteps were heard approaching the front door.

AMELIE LESTRADE DID LOOK ILL, Holly thought, taking stock of the perfumer from the armchair Rob had nudged her towards when they entered the living room. Her face was paler than it had been on Saturday and her eyes were heavily shadowed. Dressed in grey sweats, she clutched the cup of tea her mother had just handed her.

"How do you take your tea, Inspector?" Sylvie Lestrade asked, her hand hovering near the sugar bowl. "Milk and sugar?"

"Just milk please, Madame Lestrade." Rob nodded his thanks as Sylvie handed him a cup and saucer. He smiled at Amelie. "How are you feeling now, Miss Lestrade? Any better?"

Amelie stared at him over her cup, then nodded silently.

"I'm sorry to bother you at home," Rob continued, "but I do need to ask you some questions, if that's alright."

"It's perfectly fine, Inspector," Sylvie said. "Amelie is very high-strung, and the stress of releasing a new perfume— Well, it always takes a toll on her. Isn't that right, Amelie?" Without waiting for an answer, Sylvie continued, "It's completely unnecessary, of course. One knows when a fragrance is a success. If it's good, then there should be no stress attached to its release. If it's bad, well..." She gave an elaborate shrug. "Then it shouldn't be released at all. *Rosa del Mar* is a good perfume. Naturally. Amelie had Gabriel Manout to help her, and he has a magnificent nose."

Amelie's hands tightened on her cup. "Maman."

"When Gabriel first came to Lestrade Fragrances, I was astonished by his creativity, his passion, his... flair. Yes, his flair for fragrance." Sylvie Lestrade sighed as she took a sip of tea, then smiled at her daughter. "It was a good decision to ask him to help with this perfume, Amelie."

"I didn't ask him, Maman. You did." Amelie's eyes flashed as she set her teacup down on the table with a decisive clink. "And I am perfectly capable of creating fragrances by myself. No matter how inferior you may think they are."

Before Sylvie could respond, Rob put his own teacup down. "Miss Lestrade, perhaps we could get these questions out of the way before it gets even later."

Still scowling, Amelie nodded.

"Did you know Jonathan Dickenson? Have you met him before? At any time in your life?"

Amelie hesitated, glanced at her mother, then gave a curt nod. Holly's jaw dropped, but Rob didn't look surprised.

"And when was that?"

Sergeant Frampton had pulled out a notebook and pencil. Sitting beside Holly, he began writing as Amelie answered, her voice expressionless.

"I met him when I was on Grand Island one summer. I was apprenticed to Olivia Hill. My mother thought it would help develop my nose."

"How old were you at the time?"

"Fifteen. There were several of us there that summer. I

was the youngest. Olivia Hill ran summer programs for a few years. There was tough competition to get into them." A touch of malice entered Amelie's voice. "Olivia Hill was very well-renowned. A master perfumer, in fact. It was an honor to be taught by her."

Sylvie Lestrade sipped her tea. Only the slight narrowing of her eyes indicated that she had heard.

"So, Dickenson was an apprentice as well?" Rob asked.

"No. He lived there. Olivia was his aunt." Amelie picked up her cup again. "Jonathan could have been a master perfumer if he'd wanted."

"But he *didn't* want it, did he?" Rob's voice was matter-of-fact. "Even though his aunt told people he was an up-and-coming talent. I'm told Dickenson created some scents that were quite remarkable. Did he make any the summer you were there?"

Holly's eyes widened in remembrance. Becky had told them about that.

Sylvie Lestrade stiffened. "Inspector, I don't see what this has to do with—"

"If you don't mind, Madame Lestrade, I'd prefer it if you don't interrupt." Although Rob's voice was pleasant, the steely look he leveled at Sylvie silenced her immediately.

Glancing sideways at the sergeant, Holly saw his lips twitch, whether in amusement or approval, she couldn't quite tell. She returned her attention to Rob, impressed beyond measure at his interrogation technique.

Amelie had paled at Rob's question. "A... a scent? What do you mean?"

Holly studied her with interest. That question had hit home. Perhaps there was something to their perfume formula theory after all.

"I think you know what one, Miss Lestrade," Rob

replied. "Did you help him with it? He used frangipani flowers, didn't he?"

Amelie froze. "How do you know?" she asked through stiff lips.

Holly's mind was whirling as she thought back over all the information they'd amassed. Facts flashed rapidly through her brain.

Amelie had been on Grand Island at the same time as Jonathan Dickenson; Dickenson had created an amazing fragrance while she was there; Becky said rumors had started spreading about *Frangipani Allure*, newly created by Amelie that year; Jonathan Dickenson had been seen at Plumeria Perfumery, incognito, three months earlier, just after *Frangipani Allure* had been released; Kat had said that Amelie used a specific frangipani flower to make the perfume; Celadine frangipani flowers were in the lab; Jonathan Dickenson had been seen heading towards the Celadine trees...

Ohhh. Holly's eyes widened. So did Sylvie Lestrade's.

"What is he talking about, Amelie? You helped Jonathan Dickenson make a perfume for Grand Island Perfumes? I didn't know that."

"I didn't help him because he didn't need help. Jonathan was brilliant. Everyone said it. They kept saying it!" Amelie's lip jutted out. "I hated that summer. Everyone there was passionate about the work. Excited about it. They were creative and inspired and innovative—all the things I wasn't!"

"But... but you were only fifteen," Sylvie protested. "It takes time and study to become a perfumer. One is not born with a nose. It is developed through training and practice."

"Oh, I know that." Amelie was bitter. "And I trained and trained. I practiced and practiced. But it made no difference.

Apparently, what I didn't have—don't have—is the imagination and... and *artistry* that this job demands. I was constantly compared to you, Maman! Behind my back *and* in my hearing. 'Oh, Amelie is a good perfumer but she's not her mother. Sylvie Lestrade was a genius.'"

Remembering that Gabriel had said something very like this when talking about Amelie, Holly gazed at her with sympathy. It must be dreadful to feel that you could never measure up to expectations.

"But, Amelie, your last perfume was wonderful. *Frangipani Allure* is an amazing scent and—"

Amelie looked away, scowling. A flush crept over her face. The subsequent look Sylvie turned on her was appalled. "Amelie! Tell me you didn't—"

"Didn't what, Maman?" Amelie challenged. "Didn't use one of Jonathan's formulas? Yes, I did, actually. And according to copyright law, it's perfectly fine because I made creative changes to the original recipe."

Rob intervened before a gobsmacked Sylvie could speak. "Let me just clarify, Ms. Lestrade. You're telling us that you acquired one of Jonathan Dickenson's perfume formulas and tweaked it to produce *Frangipani Allure*. Is that correct?"

"Yes, but I changed it. So, it's a re-creation," Amelie repeated stubbornly.

Rob nodded. "I understand that. Did Jonathan Dickenson feel the same way about it?"

Sylvie gasped, her eyes wide as she turned to Rob. "Inspector! Surely you don't suspect my daughter of... of..."

"Ms. Lestrade?" Rob repeated. "Did Jonathan Dickenson know you had tweaked his formula to create your own perfume?"

Amelie scowled. "Yes."

"Did he contact you about it?"

"Yes. He said he'd heard about it and had visited Plumeria." Amelie's scowl deepened. "And then he emailed me to say he wanted to talk. I told him I'd changed it and he said..." Her voice trailed away.

"He said?" Rob prompted, his voice gentle.

"He said it was virtually identical and he could prove it!" Amelie burst out. "He said he'd come to Plumeria to see it and he could tell I'd used his formula. He said *Frangipani Allure* belonged to Grand Island Perfumes and that he was going to write an exposé. But it's not the same! I changed it!"

Sylvie's face had whitened. "Amelie... Did you... What did you do?"

"Did you meet Mr. Dickenson on Thursday, Amelie?" Rob ignored Sylvie, focusing on Amelie. At her mutinous stare, he sighed. "I think you did. And I think it was by the Celadine frangipani trees. Am I right? Did you take a golf cart out there at lunchtime?"

A moan escaped Sylvie. "Amelie..."

Amelie glared at her. "Stop mooing like that, Maman!" She transferred her scowl to Rob. "And yes, Inspector, you're right. I did take a golf cart out at lunchtime, and I did meet Jonathan at the trees. I thought maybe if I showed him the formula, he'd see that I'd changed it. And besides, I needed Celadine flowers for my pomade and he'd told me he was at the Fire Drake Inn. I'd have met him there," she added, "but I heard Seth saying he was having lunch with Miranda. And it was easy enough for Jonathan just to walk across the fields."

Holly kept her face blank with an effort. Amelie's single-minded focus on her perfume was a little unnerving. A thought occurred to her. Susan Hill was supposed to have had a meeting with Jonathan that day too. She opened her mouth, then snapped it shut again at the sergeant's warning glance.

Rob's thoughts had obviously paralleled hers, however.

"Ms. Lestrade, did you know that Mr. Dickenson had a meeting scheduled with Susan Hill at four o'clock at Plumeria?"

"Well, not then." Amelie was sullen. "Jonathan told me about it when we were at the trees. He was being a complete pain about the formula, so I told him he could come back to the perfumery with me and I'd show him the changes I'd made and then he could go meet Susan." She eyed them all with bitterness. "He doesn't even make perfumes anymore! Why would he care so much? It meant nothing to him and all the world to me! It wasn't fair!"

Sylvie Lestrade closed her eyes, sagging back against the sofa with another soft moan.

28

The inspector wore a considering look as he gazed at Amelie Lestrade. "Tell me what happened when you got back to the perfumery, Ms. Lestrade. You took Mr. Dickenson through to your lab. No one saw you, so I'm assuming you went a back way."

Amelie nodded. "There's a door that leads directly into my small *enfleurage* room, so we went that way. I had a tray of Celadine flowers that I'd picked and I needed to put them somewhere safe. And everyone was still at lunch when we got back."

"So, you put your flowers down and then what?" Rob asked.

"And then I showed Jonathan my notes and my formula for *Frangipani Allure*, of course. I wanted him to see that I'd made it mine. And according to copyright law—which, let me tell you, doesn't even apply here—if I make a creative change, it's considered original!" Amelie's voice held a desperate note now.

"And what was your creative change?" Rob sounded interested.

"I use Celadine frangipani in my perfume."

"Ah. Did Mr. Dickenson use a different flower, then?"

Amelie flinched. "No. He used frangipani, too, but a different variety. It's a change," she insisted when they all stared at her. "And that's all that matters."

Sylvie's eyes had popped open. She sat upright, frowning at her daughter. "Are you saying you used the exact same recipe? You used the same amounts, and all the other ingredients were identical? You just swapped one frangipani for another?" Her voice rose in disbelief. "Amelie, that is not a creative change! You can't possibly believe your perfume is original if you did that!"

"Yes, it is! And Jonathan yelled at me just like you're doing!" Amelie's voice went up an octave.

Rob interrupted abruptly. "Ms. Lestrade, did you hit Jonathan Dickenson when he was yelling at you?"

"No, I didn't!" Amelie's voice went higher still. "It wasn't me. It was Jake!"

The room went silent. Amelie's face whitened as she stared at them all in sudden horror. Holly's eyes shot to Rob's face.

"Jake O'Connor?" Rob's sober voice broke the quiet. "Was he with you?"

Amelie's mood had changed radically with her admission. She blinked a few times, then, with a gulp, cleared her throat. "Not... Not at first. H...he wasn't at the trees with me."

"But he came to the lab?"

"Y...yes." Amelie's voice wobbled.

"And he saw you and Jonathan Dickenson fighting."

A sudden tear rolled down Amelie's cheek. "Y...yes. Jonathan was yelling and angry and... and I was angry too and... and then J...Jake came in and he... he grabbed

Jonathan and..." Drawing in a shuddering breath, she stopped talking.

"And hit him on the jaw." Rob sighed as Amelie's eyes flew to his face. "He had a bruise. Did Mr. Dickenson fall, Amelie?"

She nodded. "He hit his head on the way down."

"On the mortar and pestle?" Rob waited for her nod. "I see." He eyed her for a moment. "Do you think you can tell me what happened after that?"

Amelie gave a tremulous nod and started to speak.

HOLLY WAS WAITING outside the police station in Silver Landing when Jamie and Natasha arrived in the Ocean Science Research Center van. Jamie leaned out the passenger window, waving a sheaf of paper.

"We have those analysis things for Rob, and Sergeant Frampton said you needed a ride. Oh, here you are, Sergeant." Jamie handed the pile to the older man, who had just come up alongside Holly.

"Thank you, Miss White. I'm sure the Inspector will appreciate any extra confirmation." Sergeant Frampton took the papers with a smile before bending to look through the passenger window at Natasha. "And thank you, too, Nat."

Jamie was agog. "What do you mean 'extra' confirmation? What confirmation has Rob already got?" Her eyes widened in sudden comprehension. "Oh no. Don't tell me he's already solved the case? Not again!"

At Holly's rueful nod, Jamie slumped back against the van seat. "Seriously? This is the second time he's done this!"

Sergeant Frampton guffawed. "Ha. The inspector was right, I see. He said you'd react like this." Amused at Jamie's despondency, he continued, "Inspector Tucker also said to tell you that, as usual, you've all been very helpful, and he couldn't have solved it without you."

Jamie rolled her eyes, but a tiny smile tugged at the corner of her mouth. "You don't have to try and appease me, Sergeant. Believe me, I'm well acquainted with our Inspector Tucker and his sneaky way of solving cases behind our backs!" She turned her attention to Holly. "Get in, Holls. We left all the guys barbecuing. You can fill us in on the way back. At least we can get all the details before them!"

Thomas's expression rivaled Jamie's for chagrin when he heard the news. "Someone confessed? Who? I figure it has to be either Amelie or Sylvie Lestrade." He stared hard at Holly. "Which was it? I'm inclined to think Amelie because I figured she was the one picking those flowers. And Kat Santorini told me that Jonathan Dickenson had been very interested in the *Frangipani Allure* when he was snooping around incognito a few months ago. There had to be something suspicious about it."

Jamie nodded in agreement as she crossed over to the barbecue to peer at the steaks sizzling on the coals. "Yeah, me too. I was sure it had something to do with Gabriel's perfume and the scandal on Grand Island. But then when he said the perfumes were nothing alike, I thought we were on the wrong track."

"We weren't. Or not really," Holly amended, collapsing into one of the Adirondack chairs beside the fire pit. She stretched her legs out with a sigh of relief. "It was related to theft of a perfume formula, just not the one we thought."

"Rob probably had more clues than us," Jamie groused, slouching over to sit beside Holly. Her disgruntled expression made Natasha laugh.

"I hadn't realized it was a competition." The marine scientist's eyes danced in amusement at Jamie's pout before going inside the adjoining cottage.

"It shouldn't be," Holly agreed. "And I don't think Rob had much more information than we did. He's just very good at his job."

Jamie grinned, albeit reluctantly, at the pride in Holly's voice. She leaned back and kicked her shoes off. "When's he going to get back here? I have questions. Unless you can answer them, Holls. After all, you were there for the finale. Come to think of it, you've been there for the arrest every time!"

Peter Mackenzie, who had been lounging near the barbecue, wielding tongs to flip the steaks, sniggered at this. "Every time? It's like I said. Hibiscus is a lethal little island. Unless, of course, it's you lot. Maybe you're murder magnets or something!"

Coming out of the cottage with an enormous bowl of potato salad, Natasha paused in astonishment. "Murder magnets? What are you talking about, Mackenzie? And why are you talking about it anyway? I told you to wait until we were all sitting down. Jeff and Callum should be back by now. I left a message for them to join us." The sound of barking had her frowning. "And I specifically told Callum not to bring those dogs!"

Jamie laughed as the boxers rounded the corner of the cottage at full speed, their bodies wiggling madly as they hurled themselves on the nearest humans. Slightly more prepared than in her previous encounter, Holly fended one of them off with vigor.

"Down, girl. Down. Which one are you? Charlie? Down, Charlie."

"That's Bailey." Mackenzie pointed with his tongs to the other dog who was furiously licking a laughing Jamie. "Charlie's that one. She's fatter." He gave a stentorian bellow. "Dogs! Sit!"

Both boxers jumped, then plopped their rumps on the ground, looking over their shoulders.

"Such an alpha, Mackenzie." Natasha laughed before raising an eyebrow at Callum Stewart as he appeared at a breathless run. "And what part of 'no dogs' didn't you understand, Callum?"

Holly grinned as she watched him blush under Nat's stern gaze. Callum might be the boss of the center in name, but it was clear that Natasha ruled the roost here.

"They're sneaky," Callum protested. "There were lying in wait in the kitchen, and the minute I opened the door they were out and running. I'm sure they smelled the steaks. Which do smell wonderful, I admit. We worked up an appetite out there today, didn't we, Jeff?"

Jeff Graham nodded. "You should all have come with us. It was a very exciting dive."

"Well, we've all had a pretty exciting day too." Jamie's grin was complacent. "We—or rather Rob—solved the murder case today!"

"Really?"

"Did he indeed?"

Callum and Jeff spoke together, both looking at Jamie with undisguised interest. The Center director hesitated. "Are we allowed to ask who did it? Or would that be considered ghoulish? I'm not well-versed in proper murder etiquette."

Peter Mackenzie's crack of laughter drowned out

Thomas's chuckle. "We were just waiting for you, Callum. Collect your steak, sit down, and Holly will tell us all."

Jamie pursed her lips. "It's usually Myrtle's job to give the denouement at the end of a case, you know. It feels a little weird not to hear her summarizing all the evidence."

"Well, I'll give it my best shot, shall I?" Holly asked in a dry tone.

Jamie grinned and sat back with an attentive expression. "Go for it, Holls."

CALLUM STEWART PAUSED with his fork halfway to his mouth. His eyebrows shot up in surprise as he repeated, "An accident? But... but... Are you sure?"

"Yes." Holly took a sip of her wine. "Amelie was really upset, and Rob's convinced she was telling the truth. It's kind of sad."

"Tell them what Amelie said," Jamie prompted. "About Jake."

"Jake?" Mr. Graham frowned. "I don't think I met a Jake."

"He's one of the gardeners," Holly explained. "Lily O'Connor's cousin. He works with Mr. Santorini and Seth Billings. Kat told Rob and me on our tour that he and Amelie were a couple. Well," she clarified, "Kat said Amelie might be joining the family soon if her Uncle Jake had his way."

Mr. Graham nodded. "I see. And Jake was the one who killed that unfortunate man? But how? You said an accident. What happened?"

Holly filled the two older men in on everything she'd already told the others, with Jamie and Thomas chipping in at odd times.

Jamie summed it all up. "So, basically, Amelie did steal a perfume formula, but it belonged to Jonathan Dickenson, not Gabriel. She held on to it for years, then used it to create *Frangipani Allure*. Jonathan found out about it when it created a buzz in the industry. Something must have triggered him to investigate..." Jamie paused. "What was that, anyway? Did Amelie say?"

"He had family in the perfume industry," Thomas interjected. "He told me that on the plane. Susan Hill must have said something to him. Or maybe it was someone else. He was a journalist. Probably smelled a story."

"Mmm. That makes sense. So, he came down to check it out, and because he has a brilliant nose, realized it was made from his formula. I expect he took a sample and ran tests to make sure, then came back here to tackle Amelie and tell his cousin." Jamie idly stroked one of the boxer's ears as she continued. "He met Amelie, told her he knew all, and they started yelling."

"Meanwhile, Jake O'Connor had, yet again, forgotten something and come back to the perfumery. He passed Amelie's little private testing lab, heard voices through the open door, and stopped to check." Thomas took over the summary. "He saw Jonathan threatening Amelie, pulled him around, and socked him on the jaw. Jonathan fell, hitting his head on the large mortar and pestle that Amelie had in the room."

Mr. Graham tutted sadly. "And that killed him?"

"He hit his head just above the ear," Holly explained. "Miranda said it's the worst place to get hit. That's where the skull is the thinnest and there's an artery there too."

"Plus, he apparently had a super thin skull anyway," Jamie agreed. "He might only have knocked himself out otherwise."

Callum wore a puzzled expression. "But why didn't they just call for help? It was an accident, after all."

"They panicked." Thomas was succinct.

"And they thought if no one associated the body with the lab, then no one would find out about Amelie's stolen formula," Jamie added. "I'm not sure why they took the body to those particular frangipani trees, though. Do you know, Holls? You didn't say."

"Yes. Amelie told Rob that Jake said no one would be going there on the tours. Everyone was supposed to stay in the passionflower fields, maybe see the jasmine and the frangipani closest to the building. Plus, Amelie has a tiny car —and anyway, Jake told her to say she was sick, lock the lab, and leave early—Jake has a motorbike, and Seth was taking the truck home that night. There was no other way to move the body except on one of the golf cart utility vehicles unless they left it in the lab, and they didn't want to do that."

Jamie snapped her fingers in recollection. "And didn't Seth tell us Jake was washing those on Friday? Probably to get rid of any evidence."

"Yes. He took Jonathan's body along the trail—you were right about that, Jamie—to the frangipani grove and left it there." Holly sighed, spreading out her hands. "And then we arrived on Friday and went to the trees."

29

———

"Yes but..." Mr. Graham frowned. "When did they move the body? I thought Thomas saw Jake leaving on his motorbike?"

Thomas grinned. "I did. He came back later. Holly says Rob found out that there was no family event. That was just a ruse so everyone would see him leaving. He came back later—"

"He'd already gone and taken the extra key to the lab so. no one could get in and see the body. Susan Hill told us people walked in and out of Lily's office the whole time she was on her video call. I expect Rob will confirm Jake was one of those people." Jamie stopped talking. "Sorry, did I interrupt? Carry on, Thomas. Carry on."

Thomas who had rolled his eyes with vigor at the interruption, grinned. "He came back later, loaded the body into one of the carts, drove out to the trees and dumped it. Then he went back and cleaned up as much as he could."

Holly nodded. "He missed a little blood on the mortar, which Miranda found when she examined the place. And he didn't take the Celadine flowers out of the mortar either.

That was a mistake. They fell off the counter when he grappled with Jonathan, and no one would put frangipani flowers in a mortar."

"Because they're fragile. And no one would crush frangipani flowers."

Jamie's slightly sour addition made Holly suppress a smile. Her friend obviously hadn't gotten over Sylvie Lestrade's disdainful comments at dinner.

"Plus," Holly added, "Jake O'Connor has no nose for flowers. He works in the garden, but he has no interest in the perfumes made from them. He wouldn't have given any thought to the flowers in the mortar."

"Celadine frangipani flowers?" Mr. Graham's eyes lit up. "Does the perfumery have a Celadine tree? I've been wanting one of those for ages..." His voice trailed away as everyone stared at him. "Oh my! I'm so sorry! That was very inappropriate, wasn't it?"

Holly met Jamie's eyes, which were brimming with suppressed laughter. "N...no, it's... it's okay, Mr. Graham." She took a breath, controlling the urge to break into hysterical giggles.

Thomas's grin was unfazed. "Well, Jeff, you should ask Mick Santorini for a cutting. Holly's getting some, aren't you, Holls? And a Bridal Bouquet as well, I believe."

Mr. Graham, who had flushed violently, relaxed a little as the journalist stretched out in his chair before adding, "Anyway, that's the gist of the story. Our Inspector Tucker has saved the day again, aided and abetted by the Hibiscus Island Detective Club and its associates." He gave a little bow in Nat's direction. "Thank you for the use of the lab, Natasha."

"The lab?" Callum stared at Nat in surprise. "What did

you— Oh, never mind. I remember. You ran an analysis of the perfumes."

Nat grinned. "Yep. And the samples Rob gave us were practically identical to *Frangipani Allure*. I don't think there's as big a difference between the Celadine variety and the one Jonathan originally used as Amelie claimed there was." She shrugged. "To be honest, I don't think they'll need those printouts since Amelie and Jake have confessed, but it was interesting to be involved in a crime investigation, I must say."

"I'm just glad it's over," Holly said with emphasis. "We still have a whole day left of our holiday, you know. Maybe, once Rob's finished all the paperwork, we can still do something fun."

"I vote for Twilight Lake!" Jamie raised her hand. "Who's with me?"

"Oh, if you're going to Twilight Lake," Callum interposed, "you must visit the hot springs. There's a natural pool with a waterfall, slightly off the beaten path so there won't be as many visitors. It's a fantastic place. I'll give you the directions since it isn't signposted."

Jamie's eyes lit up. "Think Rob'll be up for that, Holls?"

"I think he'll love it." Holly was definite.

THOMAS STARTED the applause when Rob walked into the cottage kitchen the following morning, with a grinning Jamie joining in.

"Great work, Inspector," Thomas said with approval. He toasted Rob with his coffee cup. "You were pretty late last night. Any problems with Plummet? I can't imagine he's pleased to have his thunder stolen."

Rob cast his eyes upward, then accepted a cup of tea from Holly with a grateful smile. "I'm not—"

"—going to talk about a fellow officer," Thomas and Jamie chorused in unison.

"I'll bet he was mad, though," Jamie added. "Did you get everything done? Are you officially on holiday again?"

"If you're asking if I completed all the necessary paperwork, then yes, I did." Rob sipped his tea, closing his eyes with pleasure as he swallowed the first mouthful. "Sylvie Lestrade has called a lawyer, of course, but the case is now in the hands of the courts, not us."

"What do you think will happen, Rob?" Holly was sober as she slid into the chair across from him. "It was an accident, after all."

"They'll still be charged. Possibly with a misdemeanor if the courts agree it was an accident and all they did was try to conceal the evidence. Possibly manslaughter if they rule that the blow on the jaw caused the death. I don't know how the lawyers will argue."

"And it's not your problem anymore," Jamie said with emphasis. "You're now on holiday, and we still have a day. We all voted for Twilight Lake. You up for that?"

Rob grinned, stretching his arms behind his head. "Definitely."

TWILIGHT LAKE WAS AS PRETTY AS ADVERTISED, with blue water and hiking trails that meandered around the lake and up into the surrounding mountains. Even with Callum's directions, it had taken them some time to find the hot springs at the far end of the valley in a tiny hollow where Australian tree ferns grew in abundance.

"It's like the land that time forgot," Holly had said as they walked along the narrow path toward the pool.

Azaleas and rhododendron, gaudy in their magenta, hot pink, red, orange, and white blossoms, sprawled around the pool while ginger lilies clothed the slopes of the hills behind it. Ferns of all kinds hugged the rocks around the water, interspersed with huge slabs that invited sunbathing. A small cascade of water emerged out of the fern-clad hill to splash into the pool which, apart from some rocky steps leading into it, was virtually untouched by man.

"And look! We have it all to ourselves," Jamie had gloated when she'd seen the grotto. "What an absolutely stunning place."

Rob had been the first one to leave the water, and now Holly followed him, wading to the edge of the shallow pool to haul herself out.

She took the towel Rob handed her, sinking down beside him on the sun-warmed rock slab with a happy sigh. "It's gorgeous, isn't it?"

Leaning back on his elbows, Rob smiled in agreement. "Remarkable really. I checked the thermometer some bright person thought to put over there, and the water is thirty-eight degrees!"

Holly grinned. "I know. It's like a bath. Although it's a little cooler by the waterfall, I noticed. Are you going to go back in?"

"Maybe later." Rob tugged her towards him. "Right now, I'd like to just lie here and relax. With you. On our holiday."

"Sounds good."

Holly rested her head on his shoulder and dreamily contemplated the mountain slopes. Apart from the sound of splashing water and the occasional laugh from Jamie and

Thomas, who were still soaking in the pool, there was nothing to disturb the peace. Holly's eyes drifted shut.

A splash and a shout made her raise herself to her elbows again. She grinned as she watched Thomas advance towards Jamie with intent, while her friend backed away laughing, hands raised to fend him off.

"Well, that looks like serious flirting to me," she murmured. "Ooh, maybe they've both finally come to their senses. Rob, look."

"What?"

"Jamie and Thomas. Over there. Look." Holly nudged Rob.

He groaned. "I don't want to." His eyes opened briefly as he directed a quelling stare Holly's way. "And I don't understand this incessant need of yours and Becky's to pair those two up. Leave them alone. Just relax. Enjoy the sunshine."

Holly wasn't listening. Instead, her smile widened as she watched Thomas lunge at Jamie, tugging her down under the water. Jamie bobbed up immediately, waited till Thomas surfaced, then pushed him down under the water again.

"And ten! I win!" She was still laughing as she waded across the pool toward Holly.

Behind her, Thomas shook the water from his fair hair, grinning as he watched her sashay away from him. "I'm still ahead in lionfish," he called.

Jamie waved an airy hand. "For now. Enjoy it while you can, Miller. Next weekend I'll crush you."

She climbed out of the pool to sit beside Holly, water dripping from her red one-piece swimsuit as she stretched her long brown legs out in front of her and leaned back on her elbows. Tilting her head to the sun, Jamie sighed with pleasure. "Now, this is a holiday!"

Holly grinned, waggling her eyebrows at her friend.

"Well, you were certainly having fun out there, weren't you?" She ignored Rob's tiny groan, instead looking more closely at Jamie. "Ooh, are you actually blushing?"

"I never blush," Jamie asserted, tapping her fingers on her thigh as she eyed Thomas, who was just emerging from the water. A smile crossed her face. "But you know what? I think you're right, Holls. It's time to take charge of some elements of my life."

"Oh yeah? Like what?"

"Like this one." As her friend jumped to her feet to advance on an unsuspecting Thomas, Holly's grin widened.

TWO DAYS LATER, back on Hibiscus Island, a dumbfounded Becky stared at Holly across the café table. "She did what?"

"Tackled him, knocked him back into the pool, then kissed him." Holly giggled, remembering the shocked looks on both Thomas's and Rob's face, and the smug expression on Jamie's as she'd sauntered out of the pool again. "It was epic. Thomas didn't know what to do. Just stood there gaping like a stranded salmon when she'd finished. And if the water hadn't already been heated, it sure would have been with that kiss! Talk about steamy!" Holly fanned her face with her hand.

"She kissed him," Becky repeated. "And then what?"

Holly giggled. "She came back out of the pool like nothing had happened. And started talking about where we could go for dinner. Thomas kept staring at her with this astonished look on his face. Like he didn't know what had hit him."

Becky blinked, then burst out laughing. "Well, honestly, it's about time, isn't it? They've been dancing around each other for months." She paused. "Does she call him 'Thomas' now?"

"Not often. I think they'll keep up the Miller and White thing. They seem to like it."

Becky glanced across the café towards the counter, where Jamie was serving a customer. "Well, I'm glad they sorted themselves out, no matter what. Now we can all focus on more important things."

"Like?" Raising an eyebrow, Holly sipped her tea.

"Like setting up a book club schedule," Becky replied, glancing up as Jamie came over to sit with them. "We need to practice."

"Practice what?" Jamie asked, leaning back in her chair to smile at Becky. "And how's the bump doing?" She gestured to the librarian's belly.

"The *baby*," Becky said with emphasis, "is fine. And, wonder of wonders, the nausea is finally easing. And thank you for asking, but don't derail the conversation. I was saying we needed to practice our mystery skills. Specifically, golden age mysteries."

"Oh, for the event on Azure?" Jamie eyed Becky in surprise. "Are you actually going? Won't the bump—I mean, baby—be very small?"

"Six weeks, maybe two months, depending on when he or she makes an appearance. Perfectly portable. And yes, I'm going. I am absolutely going!"

Holly and Jamie exchanged glances.

"What's got you all riled up, Becks?" Jamie asked.

"The Book Ends and HISS." Becky's eyes narrowed. "If they think they can out-read a librarian, they have another think coming. We will be winning that treasure hunt, ladies!" She paused, then lifted a warning finger. "And it will be just a treasure hunt. There will be no murders, no dead bodies, no drama of any kind. It's a murder mystery treasure hunt, that's all! Understand?"

Holly grinned. "Yes ma'am! No murders on Azure Isle."

"Except the literary kind," Jamie added.

They both grinned.

ALSO BY LUCY NORMAN

Buried in Bougainvillea

Remains Among the Roses

Obituary for an Oleander

Frangipani can be Fatal

Death by Daylily - available in September 2023

Also available by subscription to my newsletter:

Haunted by Hibiscus

The Poinsettia Puzzle

Visit lucynorman.net

ACKNOWLEDGMENTS

As always, a huge thank you to my family and friends for their support and encouragement; to Lida, my wonderful editor, who fixes all those pesky commas; and to Donna, the talented artist who brings Hibiscus Island to life in her wonderful cover art.

ABOUT THE AUTHOR

Lucy Norman is the author of the Hibiscus Island Mystery series - lighthearted cozy mystery books inspired by the small Atlantic island home where she was born and still resides.

Lucy has a degree in horticulture, loves to read (mystery is her genre of choice but she also likes science fiction and fantasy), occasionally quilts, and collects old children's school stories. She shares her home with an adorable cavapoo, enjoys walking on the island's railway trails, and her favorite place in the world is Scotland, in particular the Cairngorms.

To find out about new releases, please visit lucynorman.net

Made in United States
North Haven, CT
19 June 2023

37971064R10168